A VERY TERRIBLE TEXT

A GOLDEN RETRIEVER BLACK CAT ROMANTIC COMEDY

CIDER COVE SWEET SOUTHERN ROMCOMS
BOOK 1

ELANA JOHNSON

feel-good fiction

ELANA JOHNSON

ISBN-13: 978-1-63876-258-4

CHAPTER ONE

HILLARY

COMING HOME AFTER A LONG WEEK OF GETTING nothing done to a party isn't my idea of a great Friday night. Maybe it's better than coming home alone, grabbing some potato chips, and sneaking up to my dark bedroom.

But...is it?

I've also completely forgotten about whatever we're celebrating tonight, and I don't even want to know.

Grumpy, I know. Maybe I just need a bag of potato chips and then I'll be fine. They usually do the trick, and if they're the salt and vinegar kind, my whole mood can do an about-face.

The thing is, I don't have anything to celebrate—unless complete silence from the woman I'm desperate to interview counts.

I don't think it does, and I don't think potato chips will make someone agree to talk to me.

"Come on, Hillary," I say to myself as I inch past the house, with its bright lights spilling out of the windows and cars filling the driveway and both sides of the lane.

I live with five of my college roommates, though I graduated six years ago. I still don't have the documentary credits I want, but I push that aside as my phone rings.

After easing off the road so I can answer the call from my boss, I chirp, "Hey, Michelle."

"Are you sitting down?" she asks.

"I'm in my car," I say. "Not even home yet." And not in a party mood. Thankfully, my room is on the third floor, and hopefully I can make a quick escape.

"Kevin called, and Cat has agreed to meet with you next week."

My heart pounds into my throat, making it impossible for me to respond.

"Hillary?" Michelle asks. "Are you still there?"

I clear my throat, but my words have failed me. So much for that degree in film with a minor in journalism. Shouldn't I always have the exact right thing to say?

"Anyway," Michelle forges on. "I told him you'd clear your schedule, and he's going to email when you can see her."

"Great," I manage to say, my eyes only taking in the darkness in front of me. We do have a neighbor here, but the farmhouse sits back on the five-acre plot of land, surrounded by an orchard and a beautiful lawn that's well-taken care of.

"Great," Michelle parrots back to me, and she says, "See you Monday. I want to go over your questions and topics."

"Yes, ma'am," I say. I've been organizing and fine-tuning my questions and topics for Catarina Morgan, the only woman willing to speak about a controversial merger that happened in the eighties.

She's seventy-seven now, and she lives in an elderly care facility that has some serious security. She, of course, has a lot of money, and no one talks to her without the approval of her manager and son, Kevin.

The call ends, and a smile finally touches my face. I still don't want to party, but I don't want to sit in my car either. The house has parking on the other side, which only those of us who live there know about. Hopefully.

I have to drive back down the lane and around the big block of five-acre estates to get to it, but there is a parking space there. Tahlia Tomlinson owns this house after inheriting it from her aunt, and she was my roommate the year I was a freshman and she a senior.

Inside the house, I find several people hanging out in the kitchen, and I keep my purse shouldered as I open the fridge and grab my container of potato salad and a cup of olives. Maybe not the best dinner, but I don't think a meal is a meal without potatoes.

"Hillary," Claudia says, and I turn toward her and toe the fridge door closed.

"Hey." I lean in and hug her. She lives on the third

floor too, and we share the bathroom up there. Tahlia has the master suite on this floor, and three other women live on the second level.

"What's going on tonight?" I ask, glancing over to five people I don't know.

"Oh, one of Tahlia's former students got into Yale. So Tahlia threw her a party."

No wonder I don't know any of the people here, and no wonder most of them look a decade younger than me. They are.

"Amazing," I say, smiling. "I'll be sure to congratulate her."

"You just gonna head upstairs?"

I nod and turn back to the fridge, praying there will be ice for my water bottle. "I have some French lessons to do." I have news too—I got my interview!—but I can save it for another time, when there's actually people I know and love surrounding me.

I fill my water bottle and escape upstairs. My room is a safe haven for me, and I sigh as I close the door behind me, all evidence of the party raging below suddenly gone. Good. If I can contain it inside my own room, then our neighbors won't be calling the cops.

I start my self-guided French lessons and pull the notebook I take everywhere with me from my purse. As I stand at the desk and leaf through it, a smile comes to my face.

"You got the interview," I tell myself as if I don't know.

And I get to sleep in tomorrow, and suddenly life is all potatoey goodness.

———

WHAT'S NOT potatoey goodness is the sound of a lawn mower pulling me from my dreams the next morning. Yes, light pours in through my closed blinds, but it can't be very late in the day.

"Stupid Liam," I mutter. Yes, he takes good care of his property—and Tahlia even hires him to come help over here sometimes too.

He's got all the tools required, and plenty of toys, like bikes and motorcycles and cars, though he claims those are broken down and he's learning how to fix them.

I press my eyes closed as my irritation rises, hoping he'll finish up so I can go back to sleep. If anything, the growling sound of the lawn mower intensifies, and it feels like he's cutting grass in my very bedroom.

Frustrated, I throw my blanket off and stomp over to the window. I yank the blinds up, and sure enough, there's my next-door neighbor mowing his lawn right along the edge of our property.

He sometimes uses a riding mower, but today, he's pushing the machine, and I stare as he walks right by my window and continues along the line of grass that's already done. He's wearing a pair of tan shorts that only go halfway down his muscular thighs, a pair of work boots, and a baseball hat that shades his face.

Nothing else.

His bare shoulders span a magnificent width and taper down a trim back to his waist—and that's when I yank my gaze away.

My first thought is to text the other women, because while Liam has an acidic tongue and a surly personality, he's a pretty sight to see.

He reaches the top of the line and turns back, giving me a clear sight line to his chest. Oh, mashed potatoes and gravy. I have to do something besides stare, and my default is irritation.

I pull open the window and lean out of it. "Hey!" I wave my hand, remembering why I got up before seven-thirty a.m.—and it wasn't by choice. "Hey! Up here!"

Liam looks over, and he lifts one hand in a wave too, albeit hesitantly. I'll admit, we're not the best of friends. Or even friends. Or even acquaintances.

"No!" I yell. "Stop mowing! It's too early!" I make a slashing motion across my throat, hoping he gets that that means to cut the blasted mower already.

He does, his step slowing to a stop. He reaches up and pulls something out of his ears, maybe earbuds or maybe earplugs.

"Hey," he calls. "Good morning."

"No," I yell back. "It's *not* a good morning. Do you *know* what time it is?"

His dark hair and dark eyes only seem to get darker as he frowns. "Time to mow the lawn," he says, starting up the mower once more.

"Liam!" I yell, but he shoves his earbuds back in and starts strutting in front of me again.

"Unbelievable," I say, spinning from the window. "This is so not happening. Not today." I slide my feet into a pair of flip flops, and I leave my bedroom, ready to give Liam Graff a piece of my mind for his Saturday morning wake-up mows once and for all.

CHAPTER TWO

LIAM

It's hot in Cider Cove already this morning, and my task list today is out of control. So I really don't need the angry redheaded storm coming toward me, though Hillary Mays is my definition of gorgeous.

I've known her for a couple of years, since she moved into the Big House next door with Tahlia and their other roommates. *Known* is also a relative term, as Hillary has always been on the aloof side. Cordial, sure. Maybe even nice a time or two in passing. But I don't really *know* her.

As she marches across the long grass that Tahlia's asked me to tame, I find I'd really like to tick all of Hillary's boxes and see what comes out the other side.

Don't be ridiculous, I tell myself as she gets closer and closer. She's wearing a tiny pair of pajamas—a tank top and a slip of shorts in pale pink.

They almost blend into her skin, and dearie me, my

momma would be horrified at the thoughts running through my head.

Why am I smiling?

She's here to yell at me, and I take my hands off the bar that keeps the engine running. It cuts out, and I remove the earplugs from my ears as Hillary says, "This is the *one day* I have to sleep in, Liam, and you always ruin it."

She crowds right into my personal space and swats my chest. "Why can't you wait until nine to mow?"

I flinch away from her, though she can't hurt me. At least not physically. I'm afraid this woman could tear my heart out and leave it flop-pounding on the ground. I've had that happen before, and the stack of unrealized dreams I have could fill a whole cupboard.

"It gets too hot," I say. "And I have a lot of acreage to do today."

She glares, those hazel-green eyes as mesmerizing as they are piercing. "You work all day in the heat. One hour won't make a difference."

"It does in how much I can get done," I say.

"Start somewhere else," she says.

"Then I waste time in travel." Two can play her game, and I can see I'm pushing those buttons. Oh, boy, she's even prettier with that flush climbing into her cheeks.

"You're impossible."

"You're a princess," I shoot back. "I'm here doing *your*

lawn. Do you want to do this?" I give the mower a little push, but it doesn't go very far.

She folds her arms, and her lips barely move as she growls, "I am *not* a princess. I've had a long week at work, and I wanted to sleep in. It's not a crime."

"Neither is doing a job I was hired to do."

"Liam," she says with such disappointment.

"I didn't complain about your party last night."

"It was not *my* party."

"It was here at your house. I was up half the night, listening to laughter and music."

"All the more reason for us to both be sleeping." She throws her hands up into the air. "Just one day." She shouts those words into the sky. Hey, at least it wasn't at me. "Do I need to get a hotel so I can sleep in?" She strides away from me, her legs a distraction I'm going to be thinking about all dang day.

I watch her flip-flop her way across the lawn and up the steps to the porch of the house. She throws me a glare, and I salute her. Probably cheeky and rude, but she's the one who yelled at me from a third-story window and then took the time to come all the way down here to chew me out for doing something literally millions of people across the country are doing right now. In her pj's.

I keep mowing the lawn, and no one else comes out to yell at me, which means I'm free to think about Hillary the whole time.

———

BY THE TIME I finish with the lawns and landscaping jobs, I'm beat. I just want to shower, put on my cowboy garb, and hit the sports bar where they'll be showing reruns of rodeos. Once upon a time, I thought I might be a cowboy. Like a legit cowboy, who worked a farm or a ranch—my own, of course.

Then, I'd finished high school, and the cowboy scene really only appealed to me in terms of wearing the hat and boots.

I love hats with my whole soul. I own at least a hundred of them, and every time I think about my financial situation, I consider selling some of them.

I never do, though, and somehow another job or another contract comes my way. Enough for me to keep this house that I bought when it was condemned and boarded up. I lived in a trailer on the property for a year while I fixed it all, rebuilding from the foundation sometimes, and the studs others.

Then, I got to wear my hardhat. I wear that one the most, as I own my own company, Blue Ladder Builders, and I have a general contractor's license.

Now, though, I don my deepest, darkest cowboy hat, straighten the buckle at my waist, and head for the door. I need to get Hillary Mays out of my head, and my hormonal attraction to her this morning told me perhaps I'm ready to get back into the dating pool.

"Nothing too serious," I say as I pick up my keys and get behind the wheel of my truck. Maybe a kiddie pool, where there isn't a deep end, and I can't drown too easily.

As I rumbled past the Big House, I first admire their lawn. I do good work, if I do say so myself. Then, I see the women on the front porch. Tahlia, a blonde woman with a warm personality, waves, and I lift my hand in acknowledgement. I am Southern, after all.

A couple of the others smile and wave too, but not Hillary. She sits with her lips pursed and her eyes tracking me and my truck for every inch it takes for me to go past her, the house, and the rest of the property.

Even when I get to the sports bar, I feel her eyes on me.

I manage to shake them when I see Aaron Stansfield, my best friend. He laughs and says, "There he is. What took you so long? You missed the bronc riding."

"Yeah?" I pound him on the back in a healthy man-hug, glad he's got his cowboy hat on too. "Who won? Byers? Or was this the one with McCaw?"

"McCaw," he says, motioning for someone to bring me a menu and a drink. A pretty brunette appears and hands me a menu.

"What'll you be drinkin', cowboy?" she asks, her T-shirt really tight across her chest. She smiles, her lips pink and her teeth white.

I can't help wondering what Hillary would look like

on a date. What would she wear? Would she smear something red or pink or mauve all over her mouth?

"Diet Coke with raspberry," I say. I've never had too much of a problem getting a date, but I haven't asked anyone out in a while either. I glance over to Aaron, sure I can't just blurt out a request for this waitress's number. Or to know if she has a boyfriend.

You're not dating a waitress in a place where you come all the time, I tell myself as she walks away.

So I pick up the menu as if I need to look at it, then put it down and meet Aaron's eye. "Does she have a boyfriend?"

Aaron's blue eyes widen. He never just blurts out random questions he already knows the answer to. So when he asks, "For whom? You? *You* want to go out with Suzie?" it sounds like an attack.

"Sure," I say, glancing away. "I'm—I want to go out with *someone.*"

"Not Suzie," Aaron says, and I catch him shaking his head out of the corner of my eye.

I pick up the glass of water she brought with the menu. "Why not?"

"She's high maintenance," he says. "Don't you remember when Josh took her to a concert? She called him four times before ten a.m. the next day."

I smile, because I do remember that now. "She liked him is all."

Aaron shakes his head, a smile twitching against his lips. "She's too eager for your first foray back into dating."

"Foray?" I laughed and look over to the TV mounted to the wall.

"What's prompting this?" he asks. "Or rather, who? Who did you meet?"

"No one," I say instantly, which is a dead giveaway that there's definitely someone. But that's why cowboy hats are the best, because I duck my head and bam. I can hide behind the brim while my face burns, only looking up when Suzie returns with my drink and the question, "What'll you be eatin' tonight, cowboy?"

She cocks her hip and grins, and if she doesn't have a boyfriend, she can get one easily.

But Aaron is right. It's not going to be me.

When I get home, I sigh. "Great Saturday," I tell myself, and while Hillary still plagues me, most women I've thought about in the past few years disappear pretty quickly. She won't be any different.

Still, as I fall asleep, it sure is nice to be thinking of a woman instead of where my next paycheck is coming from.

CHAPTER THREE

HILLARY

"I have to do what?" I look up from my phone, where Tahlia has just sent a message about our "Spring Honey-Do Projects Around the Big House."

This isn't my first year here, and we do a big Spring clean-up every year. I came close to moving to New York for a documentary once, but it didn't pan out. Nothing has for me, and I tell myself that I'm happy working for a small research production company in Charleston.

And I am. I'm doing all the things I love—except actually producing the documentaries. I want to be there for filming, for the sale of it to a studio, for the release, the hype of it all.

"I can get Luke to come help with the wood pile," Claudia says, referencing her brother.

I'm never going to get another Saturday to sleep in, as

we all have full-time jobs, and the only time for projects like what Tahlia has texted out is a weekend.

"You want me to find someone to fix the roof." I don't phrase it like a question as I look up at Tahlia.

"I made hash browns," she says, sliding a perfectly crispy browned load of them onto my plate.

"You can't make me do this by feeding me potatoes," I say.

She only laughs and turns back to the stove. "Your eggs are coming right up, Emma."

"Fine," she said. "I'll figure out how to get those rocks off the back fence."

At least I'm not the only one who got an impossible job. When Tahlia returns to the table with Emma's perfectly cooked over-easy eggs, she glances at me.

"You know, we live next door to a general contractor."

Surprise punches me right in the lungs. "Liam?"

"Yep." Tahlia smiles like she knows something I don't. But I actually do know Liam Graff is a general contractor.

I also know there is no way I'm calling him to come look at our roof.

"The leak is right above your room," Tahlia adds. "And needs to be fixed sooner rather than later."

"Okay, *Mom*," I say, because my mother said "sooner rather than later" plenty of times, mostly when I needed to clean my room.

She moves on to something else, and I tuck into my

potatoes and orange juice. So my roommate *can* buy me with potatoes, but that doesn't mean I have to call Liam.

There are probably hundreds of people who could come fix the roof, and the easiest option isn't always the best one. Another thing my mama has said a million times.

I spend the morning reviewing my notes about Cat, and then finalizing my questions and topics to go over with my boss in the morning.

When I go back downstairs, I find Emma and Lizzie crowded around Claudia as she swipes and taps on her phone.

"What's going on?" I ask as I flop onto the end of the love seat.

"Claudia joined Matchmakers, and her profile is *lit up.*" Emma seems overjoyed at this, and, not for the first time, I consider joining the singles dating app too. It's been all the rage around Cider Cove, the other suburbs of Charleston, and the city itself for a while now. I guess the developer is a Charleston native, and it's a regional app for those who live right here. It's got restaurant and activity suggestions too, to plan the perfect date should a couple decide to take their relationship off the app and into real life.

I haven't joined, because I'm not sure I'm ready to be with someone again. I feel like I've spent my whole life being part of a group or a couple, and I just need time to figure out who I am as a whole before I become half of something else.

"Oh, his name is Ethan," Emma says, leaning closer. "That's a no, Claudia."

"He's cute," Claudia says.

"No." Emma straightens and shakes her head. "No Ethans."

They continue to quip back and forth over the men coming up on Claudia's feed, and I toy with the idea of texting Liam. The problem is, I don't know what to say. It's not like our last interaction ended on a good note, and he's just nasty enough to make me apologize before he'll even let me ask him about his roof-fixing rates.

It's always okay to apologize, runs through my head, in my mama's voice. I've been thinking about her a lot today, and maybe I need to call her too.

I tell myself my mama can wait, because if the interview goes well, I'll want to talk to her then. She's been watching my career with some degree of...leeriness, and I want to prove to her and Daddy that I'm good enough to be an investigative journalist who makes documentaries.

So I'll text her tonight that I might have something to tell her soon.

Right now, I have a much bigger problem at hand: the roof. I've never been into gossip much, though I do love listening to my roommates talk about This Man at Work, or That Man in the Office.

I smile at Claudia as she says, "Guys, look at *him*. He's The One." Her fingers move faster than ever, and she grins and grins as she obviously types something flirty and fresh to The One.

A twinge of longing pulls through me. I do like having someone special to text, laugh with, share my life with. Maybe I *am* ready to start looking for a boyfriend.

Not a fiancé, automatically comes into my mind.

"Then what's the point of dating?" I huff to myself, and then I get to my feet. "Any ideas on how to ask Liam Graff to fix the roof?"

That gets all three of the women in the room to look at me. Claudia actually sets her phone aside. "Liam?"

I nod, because I do think he'll be the easiest person to contact about the roof. I hate trying to decide who's reputable and trustworthy—and not just out to take my money for a roof repair because I'm female and so is everyone else in the house.

She looks at Lizzie, who probably is the most diplomatic of us all. "Good luck?" she guesses, and that doesn't instill any confidence in me at all.

"Want to switch tasks?" I ask.

Emma actually snorts. "No way," she says. "Especially not if your task involves talking to Liam."

"He's talkable," I say with a shrug, not sure why I'm defending him. "I mean, he's not hard to look at."

Claudia grins in a way that I've seen before and positively do not like. "Maybe if you lead with how hot he is, he'll be more agreeable."

I'm the one who snorts now. "Please."

"Liam is always really nice about the treats we take him at Christmas," Lizzie says.

Just then, the scent of something baked and sugary meets my nose. I turn toward the kitchen at the same time the other ladies look that way too. "Is Tahlia baking?" I ask. Of course she is. Tahlia often spends her Sunday afternoons in the kitchen, and we all love her for it.

I head that way without waiting for anyone to confirm, and in the kitchen, I catch Tahlia bent over, pulling something out of the oven. "What are you making?" I ask, hopefully in a sweet, casual voice that doesn't alert her to my need for whatever she just took out.

She slides the sheet pan holding four mini-loaves of bread onto the stovetop and turns to face me. "Don't worry. One of these is for you."

I smile as she reaches for the bowl of icing. "I can help," I say easing into her side. I'm sure the other girls have followed me, but I don't want the world to overhear me. "I'm going to ask Liam about the roof," I mutter-say. "Do you think this will sweeten him up a little?"

Tahlia doesn't react in an overdramatic way. She barely looks at me as she says, "I think *you're* the one who needs to be sweetened up before you talk to Liam." She gives me the raised eyebrows then, and I have no response for them. Or her.

"Sweet potato fries," I mutter-swear, and I look at the freshly baked loaves of bread.

"You can have one for yourself," Tahlia says as she

pours the glaze over the first loaf. It pools in sugary good-ness along the edge of the loaf pan, and my mouth waters for a lemon zucchini bread lunch. "And one for Liam."

"Thank you, Tahlia," I say. "You're the best."

She grins at me and finishes with the glazing. She bumps me with her hip and then leans her head against my shoulder. "I know I am."

"I'm going to go gather my spuds," I say, and she knows that means I'm going to put together the perfect argument for why Liam should fix our roof for almost nothing. And that I'm going to get perfectly rested so I can be nice to Liam when I show up on his doorstep in a couple of hours, desperate for his help.

I climb the two flights to my room and close the door behind me. Only then do I manage to take a full breath, and I swear it's full of the scent of Liam's cologne, the sweat of his skin from when he mows lawns, and the stench of pure desperate hope.

———

HOURS LATER—ALMOST twilight—I finally make it to the front porch of the farmhouse where Liam lives. This place is absolutely stunning, and while I've seen the house before, it holds a certain charm I'm certain it didn't last time I'd been here. Of course, it's been years, so it's not like I have many reference points.

Soft yellow lights line the porch, and he has a wreath—

an actual *wreath*—made out of a bicycle tire and then various car parts. The metal glints back the light, and I have to admit, it's beautiful against his heavy wooden door.

I reach up and knock, my knuckles barely making any sound against the wood. Maybe he won't answer, and then I'll be able to say, *I tried. Didn't come to the door. Oh, well.*

Then I'm back to the problem of researching roofers, a task I have no time or patience for right now. So I stand my ground and look at his doorbell camera. If he has an app on his phone, it's already alerted him that I'm here. Even if he hasn't checked it, he can at any time. He'll know I was here, holding a peace offering of lemon zucchini bread and wearing a slightly crazed look, I'm sure.

My mind races through options. I have the man's phone number, because Tahlia has it pinned to the bulletin board in the kitchen. He's listed under "Emergency Contacts," and I could've texted before making the trek across his five acres to this spot on the porch.

I didn't, because I'm too much of a chicken. I figured a face-to-face conversation would be better, and now I can't even alert him to my presence on his porch.

"Come on, Hill." I say the words before I remember he'll be able to hear them on that blasted camera. I lunge toward it and press the middle button, sending a peal-shriek through his house.

That's *loud*, and I wonder how big his place is to need a doorbell like that. Tahlia says he has a shop for the vehicles and toys he works on, and maybe the doorbell rings clear out there. Wherever "there" is.

I wait for what feels like a very long time, and just when I'm about to take my bread and leave, Liam opens the door. "There is someone here," he says.

"Hey." That's my great journalism major coming out. Why does this man tongue-tie me so? I practically throw the bread at him before I realize what he's wearing.

He looks like he could be competing in the Tour de France tomorrow morning, what with the skin-tight Spandex from shoulder to thigh. It's dark blue and somehow, I can see the ripples in his muscles beneath the fabric.

Of course you can! my brain shouts at me. *That body-suit is a second skin!*

Liam, in all his glory, leans against the doorframe. "Hey," he repeats back to me. He nods to the loaf of bread in my hands I've completely forgotten about. "Is that for me?"

CHAPTER FOUR

LIAM

I'm not sure if Miss Hillary has dressed up just for me, or if Aaron somehow told her that pretty sundresses with big flowers and a tight waist are my favorite, or if she's just perfect for me. What I do know is she looks as delicious as the bread in her hands. I'm sure Tahlia made that, but I don't care. Hillary's here on my front step to hand it to me.

"Yes." She thrusts the bread toward me, and I take my time taking it from her. I look at it, and then lift my eyes to hers, wishing I was wearing a hat. A few minutes ago, I *was* wearing a biking helmet, which only reminds me that my hair must be mashed to my scalp.

I casually reach up and run my fingers through it in an attempt to look less stupid, but then I remember what I'm wearing. I feel naked in front of her, but there's literally nothing I can do about it. "What's this for?" I ask, sensing something deeper happening here.

"You're a general contractor, right?" she asks, shifting her weight from right to left and pushing that hip out. She knows how to make a man look twice, that's for dang sure.

"Yep," I say, needing this conversation to be done in the next thirty seconds for my own sanity.

"The roof on the Big House is leaking," she says. "I was wondering if you could come check it out, give me a bid—a quote—whatever, and...yeah."

My eyebrows go higher and higher with every word she says. "You want to hire me?"

"Yes. I mean, maybe."

"To work on your property?"

Hillary's jaw jumps, which means she's not here because she wants to be. Oh, that lights me up, and I find I want her to change her mind about me.

"Yes," she says. "We do have a budget, of course. Maybe you'll be too expensive for us."

"I'm starting a big project this week," I tell her. "I'd have to fit you in around my regular schedule with the Summerwoods." I don't tell her I'll fit her anywhere she wants to go. I can barely believe I'm thinking it.

"Might be some early mornings." I raise my eyebrows again. "On the weekends."

A pretty blush colors her cheeks, but she keeps her chin high as she says, "I see."

She's got some real fire behind those eyes, and I want

to be burned by it so badly. "And," I add, my tongue moving faster than my brain can keep up. "You have to apologize for yelling at me yesterday."

A scoff comes out of Hillary's mouth before she can stop it. I cock one eyebrow in challenge, and she snaps her lips shut. She's wearing makeup, and I wonder if she wore that dress to church this morning or if she put it on just to come over here. There's no shade of red on her lips, but they're full and nude and begging me to taste them.

I pull my thoughts tightly and tie them off. When she doesn't immediately shout out an "I'm sorry, Liam," I give her a smile and lift the loaf an inch or two. "Thank you for this, Hillary. Can I send you my schedule and we can find a time for me to come do an estimate?"

"Yes," she said with miles of diplomacy in her voice. "Do you have my number?"

"No, ma'am," I say, employing my Southern manners and hoping they earn me a couple of points the way my momma always told me they would.

I don't actually have my phone with me, because I'd chucked it on the counter along with my helmet when I heard the doorbell. She whips hers out of a pocket in her dress and says, "Ready?"

"Can I just give you mine?" I gesture to my ridiculous biking outfit. "I don't really have a pocket for a phone."

Her gaze moves down my body, and her face flames red as she meets my eyes again. Oh-okay. There might be more here than I thought.

"Why do people who go biking have to act like they're competing for the next Nike sponsorship?" she asks.

I blink at her, sure she doesn't want a real answer. I pinch an inch of Spandex away from my body. "It's wind resistant."

"But you're not in a race."

"But we like to *feel* like we are." I grin at her. "Like we might win something."

"It's silly."

"You're right."

She opens her mouth to say something else, then falters.

"It also helps not to have layers blowing behind you," I say. "Getting all caught up in the spokes and stuff. Do you bike?"

More blinking, which only alerts me to her long lashes. "I mean, I can ride a bike."

I hook my thumb over my shoulder, as if she can see the shed behind the house where I keep my bikes. "I went mountain biking on some trails outside Columbia. It's gorgeous right now." I stop myself short of inviting her along the next time I go. I scan her down her to pink-painted toenails. "A real sight to see."

"That's...great, Liam." She doesn't sneer my name, and I'm going to take that as my win for tonight. I don't have her number yet, but I've got this bread too. Two wins. And while Hillary hasn't apologized, she also hasn't yelled at me, so that might be a third quasi-win.

"I could take you sometime," I say, really doubling down in a way I haven't with a woman in a while. "When you're not busy."

Shock enters those pretty hazel eyes, and she quickly focuses on her phone, which is still in her hands. "I have your number," she mumbles. "Tahlia has you as one of our emergency contacts."

"Perfect," I drawl. "Text me, and then I'll have your number, and we can set something up."

"For the Big House," she says, narrowing her eyes.

"Yeah," I agree, though it's not exactly the type of date I'd like to have on my calendar, but I'm fine taking baby steps with this woman. For now. Plus, I might get another job out of this.

"For the roof repair estimate. You never know—I might be too expensive for you ladies next door."

I grin at her and start to close the door. "Night, Hillary. Thanks for the bread." The last thing I see is her drawn-down eyebrows as she frowns at the door closing in her face.

———

"OKAY," I admit the next day. "I might've been a little rude to her." I toss another package of nails into my cart while Aaron is pushing the flatbed in front of me.

"*Might* have been?" He narrows his eyes. "What did you say? And why can't I know who it is?"

I shake my head, my smile internal as I check the list on my clipboard. I'm mostly tearing out the existing kitchen at the Summerwoods today, but I like to have the majority of my supplies either bought or ordered before I actually need them. It's my father's prepper genes in me, and I actually like this about myself.

"Liam, if you want a girlfriend, you have to actually be nice."

"She wasn't nice to me." I nod him forward down the aisle. "I need tarps and drop cloths." He gets moving again, and I add, "I just said she had to apologize before I would consider her job. She still hasn't, by the way."

Hillary did text last night, about thirty seconds after I'd shut the door in her face. She'd surely sent it from my front porch, and when I checked my doorbell cam, I'd seen her there. Puzzled and oh-so-cute as she tapped out the message, sent it, and then glared at my metal works wreath.

Then, she shot a glance to the camera, huffed, and stormed out of the frame. Just thinking about it makes me smile.

Her message had said,

> This is Hillary. I work until five almost every evening. Any time after that, any day this week, is fine.

She'd told me so much with that text. One, she went to work and came home. No stopping at the gym on the way home, no classes she takes in the evenings, no volunteer organizations she needs to attend meetings for.

Two, she doesn't have a boyfriend.

I haven't texted her back yet. The Summerwoods have vacated their home during my remodel, and I can literally work until sundown and then well into the night if I want to. Sometimes I've had to, because I overpromised on a timeline and then had to deliver.

Their project has been slotted for two weeks, and I actually do have another job after that lined up already. A playhouse in a backyard, but I don't mind that. I've built probably two dozen of them, and I get to design them myself, which I really like.

In fact...I have a meeting with the playhouse parents sometime this week. I start to check my schedule while Aaron loads indoor tarps and drop cloths onto my flatbed cart. "What else?" he asks just as I locate the meeting.

"Wednesday," I say.

"We don't sell days of the week," he deadpans.

I roll my eyes at him and say, "I need hard delivery dates on the paint I ordered last week."

"It's here," he says. "You can pick it up any day you want."

"Wednesday?" I say, though that'll probably be too early. But it covers me for what I just said, and then I don't have to explain anything else to Aaron. Not that he ever pushes me.

"Whenever," he says. "It's paid for, and you just pull up to the back, and Nate will help you."

I've been working in the suburbs of Charleston for a few years now, and I always bring my business to this small-town Cider Cove hardware store. Aaron's dad has always taken good care of me, and Aaron's been my best friend since I moved here and started fixing up the farmhouse on my own property.

We head for the oversized cart checkout, and he starts to scan my items, glancing at me every other second.

"Just ask already," I bark at him.

"Who is she?" he asks point-blank.

I fix my gaze on him, but he's used to my surliness and dark-eyed glare. "You don't know her."

"What if I do? A lot of people come through the store." He works here full-time, as he's going to be taking over the store as sole owner and manager by the end of the year. His daddy is retiring, and I can't help a wash of missing as it rolls over me.

"She's my neighbor," I mutter as I glance left and right, like perhaps one of Hillary's roommates will be standing nearby. Of course, they're not. The hardware store isn't even open to the public right now. Only contractors with a paid membership, which I have, are allowed in this early.

"Hillary Mays?" I ask, like maybe Aaron will know her.

"Fine, I don't know her," he admits, and then he smiles

at me. "But if she's bringing the mighty Liam Graff out of retirement, she must be something special."

I think of her pink pj's and her sexy sundress. Those nude lips and all that wild, auburn hair. I say nothing, but my pulse bumps through the veins in my body in a rhythm that says, *Yeah, she's pretty special.*

I tell it to calm the heck down, because it doesn't even know if Hillary is special or not. I don't even know her. I know she pushed some of my buttons over the weekend, and I did the same to her. That's it.

So, after I checkout and load everything I need into the back of my truck, I sit behind the wheel and let the AC blow on me as I respond to her message.

> Tonight? Six? Six-thirty? If that's prime dinner time and you'll be starving, I know a great place to get wings… We can talk business over barbecue.

Now I just have to wait and see what she says.

Part of me feels a little skeevy for asking her out but not really asking her out. Masking everything behind this roof repair estimate feels a little silly, but maybe I imagined all that blushing in her face last night. Maybe she really just doesn't like me, and maybe the biking bodysuit was too much for her.

"That's not a maybe, Liam," I grumble to myself. Still, I sure hope a bodysuit doesn't sink me before I've even begun to swim.

CHAPTER FIVE

HILLARY

Liam's text comes in while I'm in the middle of my morning meeting with Michelle. I glance at my phone, marveling at the wonder of eyeballs. They can scan something so fast, and then I'm back looking at my boss, totally listening to everything she's saying about Prime National Bank, Catarina Morgan, and the "real questions" I should be digging for answers about.

I know my questions, and I'm not going to deviate from them. But I smile and nod, even jot down a few notes, because I just need this meeting to end so I can re-read Liam's text.

It sure seemed like he'd just asked me out...

My brain must be on the fritz from the lack of sleep I got—or rather, didn't get—last night. I never did apologize to Liam, and I'm not sure what game he's playing by offering his time tonight.

Plus, doesn't he need to get up on the roof and *look* at it in order to give me an estimate on what it'll take to fix it? How can he do that from some wing shack?

I scoff. Wings. What a perfectly male thing to suggest. Does he seriously want to see me eating like a cavewoman, with my hands all saucy, and my face covered in orange goop?

No way. Wings are a meal—and I use that term loosely —best eaten after the I-do's are said. Long after.

"Sound good, Hillary?"

"Yes, ma'am," I say, taking back my sheet of paper, where I've typed up my notes, topics, and questions. Michelle has marked it up in red pen, just like my high school English teachers used to do, and I do my best not to frown at her cramped handwriting.

"So tomorrow afternoon," she says as she stands, her gaze dripping down my butterfly blouse and black slacks. "Don't...wear that."

"What's wrong with what I'm wearing?" I look down at myself, and while I can see the food baby from the entire loaf of zucchini bread I binged after I made it safely back to my third-floor bedroom, surely Michelle can't.

"Cat Morgan is a billionaire," she says as if I don't know. "You have to wear a dress at the very least. And not one of those maxi-things you young people are wearing now."

I raise my eyebrows. "My mama wears maxi dresses," I say. "They're popular with all age groups." They flatter all body types too, which is why I also love a good maxi dress. I love my cute sundresses with wide belts around the waist too, which is what I wore to Liam's last night.

Liam Stupid Graff. Why does every thought pattern come back to Liam?

"Do you have any skirt suits?" she asks.

I stare at her, horrified. I want to tell her I'm thirty, not eighty, but instead, I just say, "I bet one of my roommates does." Lizzie is a compliance officer for a chemical company in the city, and she's definitely the bunned, skirt-suit-wearing type of personality. I'm a little bigger than her, but I can send her a text after this meeting ends. If it ever ends.

"Great," Michelle says. "A shoe with a heel. Minimal makeup." She nods like that's the end of her personal stylist suggestions, and that's my cue to exit her office. Instead of going back to my desk, which is a partial corner office if offices only have three sides and it is stuck in the corner, I duck into the ladies room.

Liam's text shines at me in the dimmer light. *Tonight? Six? Six-thirty? If that's prime dinner time and you'll be starving, I know a great place to get wings... We can talk business over barbecue.*

My heartbeat flails against my ribs for a reason I can't really name. Surely Liam Graff is not interested in me. The very thought boggles the mind. I've always pegged him as a man who'd like someone more like Tahlia. Sunny and bright and blonde.

I'm the opposite of that.

I'm potato-shaped, with wild red hair with a touch of brown in it, and a "black cloud" demeanor—if I use my daddy's words. He's also the one who told me not to make assumptions about people, and I look back at Liam's text.

> Tonight is fine. But won't you need to be at the house to see the roof?

I'm just going to call a potato a potato, you know? I don't know what game Liam is playing, but I don't want to participate. If he wants to ask me out, he's going to have to do better than hiding it behind a business meeting.

> Oh, and I hate wings. They're so messy. Do you seriously take women on a date to get wings? Do they ever go out with you a second time?

My phone rings, and in the stillness of the bathroom, it's shrill and startling. I jump, my pulse spiking with the movement and the sound, and then it really starts to hum when I see *Handyman* on my screen.

That's the nickname I've put in for Liam, and I swipe quickly to answer the call. "What?" I hiss like I'm in the middle of watching a ballet and how dare he interrupt me?

"You hate wings? What kind of person hates wings?"

"The kind that likes to get second dates," I shoot back. "Dear Lord, tell me you're not serious about the wings."

He pauses for a moment, and I know I've won. I smile

to myself as I sit down on the toilet, praying he never finds out where this conversation is taking place.

"Maybe not the first date," he finally admits.

"Thank you," I say as diplomatically as possible. "So? Tonight? At the Big House? You need to get up on the roof, don't you?" I can already see him up there, the evening sun glinting off that bare chest...

I stomp hard on the brake pedal of my thoughts. Of course Liam isn't going to be doing a strip tease from the roof. Why would he come over without a shirt on? Fantasies really are so unrealistic.

"Yes," he says. "Do you guys have a ladder?"

"Um."

He sighs like I'm the last person on Earth he wants to talk to, and says, "I'll bring mine."

"Thanks, Liam." He says nothing else about taking me to dinner, and I knew he didn't really mean it. He probably just had a craving for wings and type-blurted it all out. Men.

"See you tonight," I chirp, and then I hang up before I have to endure any more dead silence on the phone with a man who clearly doesn't want to talk to me. A man who literally shut the door in my face last night. A man who's probably used to getting his own way—and that includes taking a woman to a wing shack on their first date.

I shudder, glad I've dodged that bullet, and make my way back to my desk. I have a little office space with two real walls and one partition—thus a "corner office" with no windows, no view, and no door.

Hey, at least a hot handyman can't slam it in my face.

My phone lights up, and I catch another text from Liam.

> You still haven't apologized. So I might be busy tonight.

"Might be busy?" I grab my phone, my blood boiling with less than ten words. I start to type furiously, slowing when another message comes in.

> And don't bother typing out I'm sorry now. I've just decided it has to be an in-person apology. So…see you tonight at six? Or would you like to reschedule?

"You can't just decide," I say, jamming my thumb on the backspace button to delete everything I've started to say. "He doesn't just get to change the rules whenever he wants." I tell him as much, and he sends back:

> Sure I can. You decide, Miss Hillary. I am the best general contractor in Cider Cove, but I'm sure you can find someone decent enough to patch a roof.

I nearly launch my phone over the partition, but a man

named Edward works there, and he'll probably go crying to Michelle if I hit him.

"Miss Hillary," I seethe as I slide my phone across my desk. It very nearly topples off the end but stops just in time. I stare at it, almost willing it to fall to the floor and crack into a million tiny pieces. Then I won't be able to text him back and continue this war between us.

I can usually think pretty quick on my feet, and I lunge for my phone again. Liam said he was starting a new job today with... "Who?" I ask myself, my fingers swiping to get back to his text string. He hadn't put the name there in our meager text string, and I sit back in my chair frustrated.

I should be going over my interview notes and reviewing the file on Prime, but I tell myself I have it all memorized anyway.

"Summerwood," I say, the name popping into my head. And Liam is a general contractor, so he must be buddy-buddies with his supplier... Three minutes later, I say, "Yes, hi, I'm wondering if you can tell me if there's something that needs to be picked up for Liam Graff?"

My brain splits again, and then out of nowhere, I say, "With Blue Ladder Builders? I know he just started a project with the Summerwoods today, and he'll fillet me alive if I don't have everything ready for him."

Silence pours through the line, and then the man who answers the phone says, "Who is this?"

I press my eyes closed as I clench my teeth too. The

little white lies are gone, and I can't think of any name but my own. "Hillary?" I guess.

"Ohhhh," the man says, and I'm not sure what that means. Is he sighing? Has Liam said something about me?

What a ridiculous thought. Of course Liam hasn't told someone at the hardware store about me.

"Sure, he's got paint here if you want to get it," the man says.

I don't really want to load up paint in my sedan. "I— do you know where the Summerwoods live?"

"Are you going to take him lunch?"

"Yes," I blurt out. "I'm going to take him lunch, but I want it to be a surprise." The surprise would be me knowing what Liam likes to eat.

Wings, comes into my head, and the whole plan develops in front of me, the way I see some documentaries too. I just know them from beginning to end, and I can't wait to put this one in action.

"The Summerwoods are just over in Sugar Creek," the man says. "Do you need the address?" He's being so agreeable that I know something is up.

I simply don't care. "Yes," I say. "Yes, I'd love that address…"

An hour later, my GPS says, "You have arrived," and I ease my car to a stop in front of an enormous house in a gorgeous neighborhood. A big white truck has been backed into the driveway, and I catch the Blue Ladder Builders logo on the side.

The scent of buffalo wings and bleu cheese fills my car, and I'll probably never be able to get it out of the upholstery. I glance over to the plain white plastic bag, take a deep breath, and say, "Now or never, Hill."

My phone chimes out a sound I barely recognize, and I use it as a distraction. An M sits at the top of my screen, and I pull it down, finally putting the dots together. It's from Matchmakers, the dating app I'd signed up for yesterday afternoon as a procrastination tactic to stall going to see Liam.

A man named Karl H. has messaged me, and I first tap on his profile. Oh, he's cute with his perfectly symmetrical smile full of white teeth and that big, dark beard.

You work in film? he's asked, and that tickles me the right way too. I smile as I message him back, and I kind of lose my head—and track of time—using the app.

A sharp knock on my window jolts me out of the flirt-fest I've perpetuated, and I drop my phone as I look to my right.

Liam has bent down and is frowning through the passenger window. Before I can stop him, he's opening the door, picking up the plastic bag with his wings, and sliding into the seat. "What the devil are you doing here?" he asks, his voice set to Growly Bear.

I leave my phone right where it is—at my feet, buzzing with a new message from Karl H-for-Hottie. "Bringing you lunch," I say sweetly, as his manly-muscley scent seeps into the car too. Great. I'll never get that out.

He doesn't buy my act for one single second, but I've come this far. Buoyed by the last several minutes of talking to a man who doesn't make me want to punch something, I smile at Liam. "Listen, I just wanted to come by and personally and *in-person*-ally apologize for yelling at you over the weekend."

He blinks, but at least he's not growling.

"I was *way* out of line, and totally sleep-deprived, but hey. That's just an excuse, and I—" I stop when he starts to laugh.

"All right," he says through his deep chuckles. "I got it."

I nod to the Styrofoam in his hand. "Wings for lunch. I heard they're one of your favorite foods."

He grins and grins at me, and I may not have been on a date with a man in a while, but I've been engaged twice. I *know* when the male species is interested in me—and Mister Liam Graff shows his interest in spades.

Latkes with sour cream.

I lean away from him, almost wanting to get out of the car. He *can't* be interested in me. What reason would I have given him for that?

"They are," he says, ducking his head and actually opening the Styrofoam. As his face is concealed a bit behind his ballcap, he lets out the stench of buffalo wings. I am so never getting it out of my nose, and I'm a little peeved that it's covering his cologne and construction scent.

He doesn't look at me as he asks, "So...tonight? Six, at the Big House?"

"Yes," I say. "Now, can you get out of my car with those things? I'll have to drive back to work with the windows down just to get the smell out."

CHAPTER SIX

LIAM

I know I'm a complete moron for going home to shower and deodorant up before heading next door to the Big House. I can't help myself, even though Hillary literally kicked me out of her car at lunchtime.

Still, she did it with a flirty tenor to her voice and a glint of desire in her eyes. I'm not an expert on reading women, for sure, but Hillary brought me lunch. At my worksite, which she'd called Aaron at the hardware store to get the address to.

That takes effort, and I'm not blind to that.

I stand in the master bathroom looking at myself, and I am blind to what I need to do to convince Hillary to go out with me. My attempt to get her to dinner tonight failed, and foolishness runs through me.

"A hat," I tell myself, and I wish I knew if Hillary had grown up here in South Carolina. I have numerous choices, and I move into the closet to survey my shelves of ballcaps.

I've got fedoras too, but I'm not going for the preppy-golf-guy look tonight. I'm dressed in dark blue jeans and a T-shirt the color of wet cement. It's got a bootprint on the front in jagged white lines, and I got it at a mountain bike rally I did last summer.

I've offered to take Hillary biking, but it was a casual mention, and I'm sure she's forgotten by now. I haven't, and I select a dark gray hat without an insignia. Then I won't be picking a sports team or affiliation that will offend Hillary.

I snort to myself. My very presence seems to offend Hillary, and that brings me more of a thrill than it should.

"Just go," I tell myself when I find myself standing back in front of the mirror. I am what I am. Bearded and beautiful, mountain bike and hat enthusiast, general contractor always looking for my next job.

I'm thirty-two years old, and as the clock clicks closer to six, my phone rings. My pulse jumps, thinking it's probably Hillary calling to cancel.

But a smile fills my soul when I see it's my momma. "Momma," I say, not embarrassed that I'm her boy. She still lectures me every chance she gets, and she invites me over for Sunday dinner, and she loves me without end.

"Liam, baby," she drawls out. She's from Alabama, but when she met and married Daddy, she moved to South

Carolina and made it her home. "What are you doing tonight?"

"I have a roof consultation," I say. "Why? What do you need?"

"Oh, this pesky dishwasher is leaking again," she says. "And Tabitha misses you."

I grin at the mention of her cat. She's really my cat, but when I got the house only a couple of months after my father died, I could barely keep myself alive, let alone a feline.

My sister had come to stay with Momma for a few months, and the two of them had taken in Tabitha and cared for her.

"I can come after the consult," I say. "I'll text you when I'm on the way." Momma lives about twenty minutes from me, through a couple of other suburbs and small towns that bubble up against Charleston.

"Thank you," she said. "I made chicken pot pie if you haven't eaten yet."

"Momma, you get me." We laugh together, and it's been a couple of weeks since I've been by her place. I went mountain biking this weekend, and last Sunday, I went to Aaron's to watch a ball game.

With that arranged with my momma, I don't have any other reason to loiter around my house. I go out the back and get in my work truck to make the quick drive to the Big House.

Nerves fire at me, but I pull into the driveway behind

a couple of sedans and an SUV, hoping none of the women who live here need to leave while I'm here. There are still hours of daylight left, but my feet are heavy as I get out and climb the steps to the front porch.

As I reach for the doorbell, I hear voices behind the still-closed front door that make me pause.

"...Liam Graff?"

"Just let me answer the door."

"He's *so* handsome. I can't believe you called him."

I glance to my right, where the voices are actually leaking from the house, and I see the window is open. So are the blinds, and no less than three women peer out at me. One of them is not Hillary, and I don't see Tahlia either.

I reach up and touch the brim of my ballcap just as the door opens. Hillary stands there in a pair of cutoffs and a sleeveless shirt that looks like her grandmother once owned it. Somehow, it suits her, and I've heard my sisters talk about thrifting items from a second-hand store. Apparently, it's fashionable and cool, but I know nothing about it.

I know Hillary makes my mouth dry, but somehow I get my lips to curl up into a smile. "Hey." I let my hand drop to my side.

"Why are you always saluting us?" Hillary folds her arms and cocks that sexy hip.

"I was saying hello to your roommates," I say, nodding to the side where I know they're standing. "That's all."

She scans me down to my work boots, which are the only thing I kept from my attire from earlier. When her eyes meet mine, oh, there's that spark. To me, if feels hot and electric, but Hillary's face doesn't give away too much. Those eyes, though...

"Something smells good," I say, lifting my chin as if I'll be able to see to the back of the house where the kitchen is.

But I don't smell anything baking or cooking. It's Hillary's perfume, and the floral scent is making my head spin.

"Did you bring a ladder?" she asks without commenting on anything I've said.

"In the truck." I indicate the whole world behind me, because I can't look away from her.

"I'll meet you around back," she says, and the door starts to close. I stand there and let her practically slam it in my face, and then the squabbling starts again.

"You shut the door in his face?"

"What?" Hillary asks. "Am I supposed to have him bring the ladder all the way through the house?"

"Maybe you can ask him to stay for pizza."

"No way," Hillary says. "Besides, Claudia, you're going out with that guy from Matchmakers. Why do you care what I say or do to Liam?" Her voice fades then, and I chuckle to myself as I turn and go get the ladder.

Only Hillary waits for me in the backyard, and I position the ladder against the house and look at her. "You think the leak is on this side?"

"Tahlia says it's above my room," she says, her gaze flitting around all over. "She also made pizza tonight, and you're welcome to stay and eat with us if you'd like."

My chest fills with something I can't name, because she's invited me to something, whether she wanted to or not. "I can't tonight," I say. "My momma needs help at her place, and I promised her I'd come after this."

"Your momma lives around here?"

"In Cherry Heights," I say.

She nods. "That's nice, Liam."

I'm not sure if she means it or not, because my conversations with Hillary have been full of sarcasm, taunts, and jabs.

"Well, let's see what's going on up here." I start to climb the ladder, and when I gain the roof, the full heat of the evening sun practically boils my flesh right off my bones.

I've worked on plenty of roofs, and sure enough, this one needs new shingles. That's apparent by the numerous bare spots. I bend and flip up one shingle, and it comes off in my hands.

Still, I go up the crest of the roof toward where Hillary's room is. "Oh, yeah, I see what's happening here." There's water damage along one of the piping vents coming out of the attic, and every time there's any moisture at all, there's going to be water going into the house.

This is a big house, as it's nicknamed as such, and this is a big job. I can't do this after hours. This is a whole job in and of itself, and I have things on my schedule for at least the next month. We're moving into May, so it shouldn't be too terribly rainy, but we do have storms from time to time.

I pull out my tape measure and get the numbers I need. Just as I start toward the ladder, Hillary pops her head up.

I yelp in surprise and try to skid to a stop. That sends me to my butt, and I slide down a couple more shingles until I come to a stop on the hot—flaming hot—roof.

"What are you doing?" I bark at her.

"I got worried," she says. "You've been up here for a while." She doesn't look away from me. "Is everything okay?"

"I'm good," I say. "The roof, however, needs a complete replacement."

Hillary's eyebrows draw down the way I expect them to, and there's the sultry look I've seen on her face before. She also doesn't move.

"Can you get down?" I ask.

She rolls her eyes like I'm the one doing something wrong, and then she disappears as she goes down the ladder. I booty-scoot to the edge of the roof, put my leg over the edge, and wait for Hillary to reach the ground.

She takes the ladder with both hands and steadies it for me, and I twist, turn, and step down.

When I reach the ground, she sighs. "How bad?"

"You have no weatherstripping along your pipes and

vents coming out of the attic." I dust my hands along my thighs and adjust my ballcap. Hillary's eyes drop my from head to my face as I lower my hands. "And the whole roof needs to be redone. Shingles. Some of the wood underneath."

"This sounds expensive."

"And it's not something I can do after hours in a night or two." I start to lower the ladder so I can carry it back to my truck. When I move, Hillary comes with me. "It's a whole job, Hillary." Her name comes out of my mouth smoothly, and while her phone chimes a few times at her, she ignores it.

"Cheese fries." She shakes her head, but I smile.

"Cheese fries?" I ask. "What does that mean?"

That gorgeous blush fills her face. "It's just...a spuddy swear word." She takes a deep breath. "I'll talk to Tahlia. Necessary things must be done."

"That they must," I agree as I muscle my ladder back onto the rack in the back of my truck. I once again clap my hands together and look at her. "I'll put together a bid. You're welcome to contact other roofers, but since I know you guys, and Tahlia's always been good to me, I'll do it for cheap. I promise."

I'm toying with quoting her only the cost of materials and donating my labor, but I manage to bite back that offer before I make a fool of myself. I'm still thinking about her "spuddy swear word" and what that really means, because it's given me a layer of Hillary I haven't seen before.

"Nice hat," she says, and my chest does that swelling thing again.

"Thanks," I say. "I'll text you a link to the bid by the weekend, okay?"

"Okay," she says, ducking her head. She looks up at me through her eyelashes, and there's no way she'll tell me no if I ask her out right now.

Her phone bleeps out a series of chimes, and she finally pulls it from her pants pocket and looks at it. Her face lights up with a smile, and I realize I haven't seen the full wattage of Hillary Mays at all.

The smile she'd just given me was coy, and a tiny bit flirty. The grin and gaze on her phone is full-out interest, and I want to slap the device away from her.

"Okay," I say loudly. "Well, my momma needs help, so I'll see you later."

She doesn't even move. "Yeah," she says, her voice that of a woman completely distracted by something or someone better than who's in front of her.

Annoyance sings through me, because *I'm* the loser in this equation. I open my door to get in the truck, but she's standing in the way. I nudge her with the door, and she finally looks up, her eyes broadcasting her displeasure.

"Move, then," I say as I get behind the wheel. Hillary has still barely moved, but her fingers fly like the wind. I start up the engine of my truck and press on the gas pedal, really giving it some roar.

Hillary glares harder, finally lowers her phone, rolls her eyes, and turns back to the Big House.

I drive away, my invitation to dinner lodged somewhere behind a pinch in my throat.

―――――

"ALL DONE," I say to my momma, who's got evening game show re-runs blaring from her TV. "I put on the new gasket." I lean over and press a kiss to my mom's forehead. "It shouldn't leak again."

I take a seat in the recliner where my daddy used to sit and read the paper in the morning, do his Sudoku in the afternoon, and watch Momma's TV shows with her in the evening. I sigh, and that alerts Momma to me. She gives me the Eagle Eye, which is a look all women over age sixty-five develop. I swear they can see things no one else can, especially if they birthed you.

"What's goin' on with you, Liam?"

"Just tired, Momma. Lots of jobs right now." I scoop up a bite of her chicken pot pie, and I swear, everything is right in the world with that creamy sauce, the chicken, and the flaky crust in my mouth.

"Did you get hired on the roof?"

"Maybe," I say with a frown as I feed Tabitha a teensy bit of chicken from my bowl. "I don't care if I get that job." Though I do, but this time it's not all about the money. "This woman that might hire me..." I take off my hat and wipe my hand along my forehead. "I'd like the job to be closer to her."

Momma's smile widens like I've just told her I'm going to ask Hillary to marry me. I shake my head before she can get started. "Don't."

"You haven't dated in a while," she says airily. Most women have that skill down too. I've even heard Hillary talk like that.

"Nope," I say. "And I'm not dating her either."

Yet, my mind says, but I still see the look on her face when she started texting. And I've never gotten a look like that.

"I'm thinkin' of doing some more architecture classes," I say as I finish my pot pie. I set aside the bowl and pat my lap, a clear invitation for my cat to come sit with me. Tabitha is a pretty calico, and she jumps right up onto my thighs. I smile at her and give her a healthy stroke down her back.

"Oh, that'll be good," Momma says, which is a statement I've heard her say plenty of times over the years. Usually to something she doesn't want me to do, but she's not going to try to influence me one way or the other.

"I just...never finished," I say. Part of me feels like I never really got to do what I wanted to do. Daddy died my junior year of college, and the perfect trifecta of Things happened to keep me from enrolling again.

The farmhouse. My finances. The support my family needed from the only male Graff left.

"Tell me more about this woman who's caught your eye," Momma says, a very Momma thing to do—get me talking about something else so I'll forget about the deeper things that plague me.

"Well," I say, a smile I wish would stay dormant coming to my face. "She's really pretty, but I don't think she likes me much..."

CHAPTER SEVEN

HILLARY

TONIGHT, IT'S ME AT THE CENTER OF THE COUCH, MY phone in front of me as the others crowd around.

"I can't believe he's a veterinarian," Emma says. "You've always wanted a doctor."

"It's not a requirement," I say, shooting her a glance that tells her not to say stuff like that. I love each of my roommates in different ways, and I've told them all a lot of the same things. But Emma and I have talked a lot about the type of man we want, mostly starting after my last failed engagement. My fiancé at the time wasn't a doctor, and he's still nothing but a trust fund baby. His family knows mine, and my parents only care about appearances. I'm sure my mother tells her friends, acquaintances, neighbors, and strangers too that I'm a big-city filmmaker.

I still love her—as long as she's not trying to set me up

with Charles Vaughn the Third again, or any of her other Southern high society friends' sons.

Karl Hunsaker, however, has proven to be an excellent match for me. We left behind the limited Matchmakers messaging system and moved to texts right after Liam left, and I push aside the concerns about the roof. Tahlia is the only one of us not home yet, and I'll talk to her about it privately.

Karl works at a vet clinic on the north side of the city, loves to travel, and says he's been watching his brothers get married and start families—and that he really wants to do the same.

It's like he knows my personal checklist for the perfect man, and he's just going *check, check, check.*

I've enjoyed messaging with him for the past couple of days, and I'm just waiting for him to ask me to meet in person. The excitement wears off as Karl's texts wane, and me and my roommates start to drift away to our bedrooms.

I do the same, promising Karl I'll text him after my interview in the morning. A text comes in after I've wrapped myself like a mummy and closed my eyes, and I sigh as I roll over and reach for my phone.

I'm expecting Karl, but I get Liam. My heart skips a beat at the thought of Liam. The mental image of him sitting on the roof makes my breath catch, and I'm not sure what that means.

After three years and two failed engagements, how can I have a crush on *two* men?

"Semi-crush," I say to my dark bedroom and brightly lit phone screen. Liam has said,

> I can at least put a patch on your pipes and whatnot before I start. If you hire me, that is, I won't be able to start until May 3rd.

"May third," I whisper. That's almost a month from now.

> Do we need the patches before you can do the whole roof?

> I'd say so, yes. They'll at least hold you if it rains, and I looked at the forecast, and it's supposed to storm for a couple of days next week.

He's looked at the weather forecast? Why does that make my heart turn into melted chocolate? Maybe he's just being a nice neighbor, or better yet, a savvy business-man. He wants the roofing job, because a six-bedroom, five bathroom house isn't small. The roof on the Big House is intricate, and it'll be thousands to fix and replace it.

I don't know what to do with these feelings swirling inside me. I even caught myself flirting with Liam after he'd loaded up his ladder, and thankfully, all the texts from Karl had distracted me enough to get Liam on his way.

I'm not sure why I've put him on a yo-yo, only that

sometimes I want to throw him far from me, only to pull him back in even closer. I sigh and close my eyes, the brightness on my phone calming into darkness as I rest it against my chest.

I wake up like that in the morning, only a few minutes before my alarm. I sit straight up, my pulse jackhammering at me. "I'm not late," I tell myself, but I lurch from bed and hurry to pull up my hair and cover it in a shower cap.

I skip everything but coffee for breakfast, and I arrive at work twenty minutes early and buzzing already. I should've gone with decaf, but I've been running on Autopilot-Hillary since I woke, and she orders regular coffee on her way to work.

"Morning, Michelle," I chirp as I walk by her office.

A crash sounds inside it, and she yells, "Hillary."

I slow my step—I'm wearing the heels she told me I should—and carefully turn around. "Yes?" I had to shave my legs this morning and everything, just to wear this pencil skirt.

Michelle scans me from head to toe and back, nods her approval, and gestures for me to enter her office. She's got a bit of a flush in her face, and I'm not sure if that's good news or bad. I've only taken one step into her legit corner office when she says, "Good news and bad news: which would you like first?"

"Can I guess them?"

She sits as she gestures for me to do the same. Has she

always said so much with her hands? Right now, I can't remember. I sink onto the edge of the single chair in front of her desk. "Cat canceled the interview," I say. "That's the bad news."

Michelle actually wears a sympathetic look. "She did, but Kevin said it's because she woke up ill. He says we're still on. It's still an exclusive. He just needs to take his mother to the doctor this morning."

I feel like a boss who doesn't believe her employee is sick after she's called in to get the day off. I imagine Catarina out on the beach, soaking up the rays and wearing thick sunglasses so I won't recognize her should I happen by.

"Okay," I say with a sigh. "If that's the bad news, what's the good?"

Michelle's face lights up again, and she says, "I just got an email from a Mister Tanner Bridgestone himself."

I search her face, sure she's lying to me. "And?" squeaks out of my mouth. Tanner Bridgestone is a legendary documentary producer. He's the gold standard for those in the industry, and as far as I know, he's never cold-emailed Michelle.

"And, he's heard rumors about the Prime National Bank scandal, and your name came up. He's interested in speaking with you, and perhaps...acquiring the documentary."

All of the air leaves my lungs. I want to speak, but I can't.

"Not only that, but if he did acquire this project, Hillary, he's made it clear he always works with the journalist and writer of the film during production." She leans back in her chair, her fingers coming together in a steeple. I usually see this move from a villain in a cartoon, but honestly, nothing is computing too well right now.

"That means you'd have to be in LA," Michelle says. She waves her hand now, dismissing everything she's said. "This is all if he likes the proposal, acquires it, and asks for you." She twists in her chair and plucks a piece of paper from the printer on the counter that runs behind her desk. "I printed the email for you. He did ask for you to contact him. Perhaps you could do that this morning instead of the interview."

"Yes," I blurt out as I take the paper from her. "Yes, I'll do that." I stand without squeeing, which is what I want to do, and I nod oh-so-professionally at my boss. Every potato dish known to man runs through my head as I leave the office, and I dang near twist my ankle in these stupid heels as I push into the ladies' room.

I run the last few steps to the biggest stall on the end, and I lock myself inside. "This is insane," I say as I scan the paper. "That's Tanner Bridgestone's *email address*." It's just sitting there, like he gives it out to everyone.

I pace in the oversized-yet-still-small stall, and then I sink onto the toilet, still fully clothed. I don't know why I can't process in my semi-corner office, or why the place I can happens to be a restroom, but as I finish reading the email, I look up to the ceiling tiles.

"This could be big." This could be the break I've been working for. His email said he'd tried to get an interview with Catarina, and he'd been told someone else had the exclusive already.

Me.

I giggle and pull out my phone to tell the girls. I see I've missed a few texts from both Karl and Liam, and as distracted as I am, I start to answer them first. I do manage to get a text off to my roommates' group chat.

BIG NEWS: A TOP-NOTCH DOCUMENTARY PRODUCER HAS ASKED TO MEET ME.

Texts from my roommates start flying in, like *Oh, boy, let's go!* from Claudia, and *That's amazing, Hill!* from Emma.

Tahlia will be in class already, but even she sends, *Let's party tonight!* before dropping off the thread. Lizzie congratulates me and then asks if, when I'm rich and famous, I'll still remember them, which makes me roll my eyes. I don't stop smiling, though, because this is absolutely giddy-grin-worthy.

Ryanne is the last roommate to answer, and she sends a bunch of party favor emojis and then, *This is amazing, Hillary! I'm in for the party tonight. I can check the shredder?*

She's a co-manager at an office supply store in the city, and she manages all the employees, payroll, and more.

She's around a lot of paper, and every time we need confetti at the Big House, Ry brings home an enormous garbage bag of shredded paper in a variety of colors.

I hate cleaning it up, but it sure is fun to watch it rain down in the living room or kitchen—sometimes the backyard, though Tahlia doesn't like how it takes weeks to get out of the grass.

I have good news! I text to my mother. I repeat the message to Karl, and then tap over to Liam's text string. He's said that he had some time that morning to work on the bid, and he's sent me a link. I'd sent him a thumbs-up emoji before moving on to another thread, and now, he's responded with,

> An emoji, huh? I didn't peg you for that type of texter.

I want to scoff, but instead, I say,

> What kind of texter do you think I am?

I send that, my thumbs already flying again.

> Follow-up question: There are types of texters?

> You're the proper kind,

You use capital letters and punctuation. You spell out every word, so yeah. The emojis seem a little out of character for your texter type.

I don't know if he's being cheeky or not. With Liam, it's impossible to know unless I'm face-to-face with him. And even then, I'm left guessing at least half the time.

I tap over to Karl's string, and he hasn't answered yet about my good news. I feel electric and alive, and I decide I don't want to wait for him to ask me out. I start to type out the fact that I have a little black dress sitting alone in the back of my closet, and maybe he'd like to help me get her out on the town that evening when my phone rings.

It deafens me in the bathroom, what with the echoing and the amplification of sound in the small space. "Mom," I say after I've swiped on the call as quickly as possible. "I'm at work, so I don't have much time."

"Let's go to lunch this weekend," she says, and I'm reminded of why I moved two hours away from my parents. Then, I can't just pop-in on them, and they certainly can't do that to me. If we want to have a meal together, schedules must be checked and plans must be made. "You can tell me all about it then."

"I can if you drive down here," I say, and I know that will take the wind out of her sails. I'm not trying to be rude or mean, but lunch with my mother is never just lunch with my mother. She'll pick some restaurant that has a man working there who she wants me to meet.

I've got more men on my plate than I know what to do with right now. My phone buzzes in my hand, the indication that I've gotten another message.

"Let me talk to your father," my mom says, and that's as good as a no. I try not to smile, but it really feels like everything is going my way today.

"Okay, well, I do have to run," I say. "I'll call you tonight with more details?"

"It's Tuesday, dearest," she says.

"Oh," I say. "Right. It's bridge night." We say the last few words together, and of course, my mother won't change her card-playing habits to take a call from her only child who has good news. I stuff the bitter sting down my throat and say, "Love you, Mom. I'll call you later."

I do love my mother, but I lower the phone and see I spoke with her for three minutes and twenty-four seconds. That's three minutes and twenty-four seconds too long, and I'm more exhausted now than I was before she called —for no reason.

My enthusiasm for meeting Karl hasn't waned, and I tap over to his thread. The message I'd started before my mom called isn't there, but I focus and quickly get it typed out and sent off. I sigh, my grin starting to hurt my cheeks, when I look up to the messages above what I've just sent.

> You've got your Teen Texters. You know the type, Hillary. The ones who use ur for your and can't capitalize for some reason, even though it's literally an autocorrect thing on your phone.

A smiley face sits above that.

I have not texted Karl about my slinky black dress that needs a night out on the town.

But Liam.

My smile disappears completely. The air leaves my lungs. Pure panic builds inside me, because how do you delete a text from someone else's phone? The damage is done, and I can't even imagine what the fallout will be.

"No," I say quite loudly. "No, this can't be happening." Today was *my* day, and now I've ruined it by messaging a horribly grumpy man. Horribly handsome and grumpy, sure, but as I'd told Claudia last night, good looks don't make up for a bad attitude.

I can fix this. I'll just tell Liam I mean that text for Karl. Simple. Easy.

I start to whip out another text about how that message was meant for someone else. I only have five words typed—*Hey, I'm so sorry but*—when another one lands below my very flirty and sultry invitation to dinner that night.

> What time should I pick you up?

CHAPTER EIGHT

LIAM

Hey, if you're not busy tonight, I'd love to get together. I have a little black dress that's been gathering dust in the back of my closet, and she needs a night out on the town to celebrate something. What do you think?

I HAD VERY NEARLY SPIT MY CREAMED WHEAT OUT OF my nose, that's what I thought.

"I knew it," I say as I wait for Hillary to confirm what time I should pick her up. The fact that we were going back and forth pretty rapidly, and now she's not answering, isn't lost on me, but I'd only given her one other type of texter before she'd laid the little black dress at my feet.

"I knew there was something between us." I pace away from my breakfast, leaving it uneaten on the table. I'll probably regret it later, but I can't sit here, waiting for an answer from Hillary. I have more demo to do on the Summerwoods' kitchen, and I tuck my phone in my back pocket, pick up my lunchbox, and head for the door.

Part of me hopes Hillary will stop by with another round of wings, though I do love eating out of my vintage lunchboxes. Today's lunch was actually made for yesterday, but I figure a turkey sandwich is a turkey sandwich, and it doesn't go bad in a single day.

My phone chimes as I leave the garage, and I swear I'd ram my tailgate right into a tree if it means I can check my messages faster. Relief paints my ribcage, because Hillary's texted back.

> Is seven too late?

"Seven is not too late," I dictate to myself as I type for her. "I'll see you then." I don't want to get into the nitty gritty of what we'll do tonight. I can ask her when I pick her up, because it's a Tuesday night, and while Charleston always seems to be a hopping place, it's *Tuesday night*.

I have a first date with Hillary Mays on a Tuesday night, and my stomach swoops. I remind myself that Momma and Daddy met at a dance, in the small town where she lived but he was just passing through.

"Probably wasn't Tuesday," I mutter to myself, though I'm not sure why it matters what day of the week it is. Maybe because there's nothing special about Tuesdays, and I want this date to be made of magic, unicorn horns, and high heels.

And kissing.

I shake my head. "No, you're not going to kiss her on the first date." I'll settle for holding her hand—anything to break the physical barrier between us.

That decided, I spend the morning ripping out the last of the cabinets and getting everything swept up and moved out of the way, all while letting my fantasies of Hillary in a little black dress play on repeat.

———

WHEN I ARRIVE on Hillary's doorstep for the second night in a row, I first check the window next to the door. The blinds are closed, as is the glass. So they've figured out how to be more discreet.

I ring the doorbell, but I don't hear anything chime through the house. Reaching up, I run my hand down both sides of my beard, though I trimmed it and made sure it's perfectly in place for tonight. I've got three restaurants on my short list, and none of them require eating with our hands, or slurping pasta, or anything that might be embarrassing on the first date.

I haven't told anyone about this date tonight—not even my momma—but as the door opens and three of Hillary's roommates stand there, it's clear she's told them about tonight. I'm not sure what I expected; she lives with five other women, and I live alone.

Maybe not three grown women ogling me, clearly making judgments in the time it takes for Claudia's eyes to travel to my cowboy boots and back to my face.

"Evening, ladies," I say, reaching to tip my hat. Yes, I've chosen a cowboy hat for tonight. I'm not sure why. A ballcap seemed too casual for a date with a woman wearing a little black dress.

"Manners earn him a point," Lizzie says, smiling. She tucks her dirty blonde hair behind her ear and looks over her shoulder before focusing on me again. "I didn't know you were a cowboy, Liam."

"I have the clothes," I say, wondering if this is a quiz or an interview I have to pass before I can see Hillary. "Once upon a time, I thought I might be a cowboy, but, well, let's just say the boots didn't fit."

"Looks like they fit mighty fine to me," Claudia says, and I whip my attention to her. Is she flirting with me? She smiles, but it seems friendly enough. I smile back, though I keep my lips closed over my teeth.

"Is, uh, Hillary here?" I ask, scanning the area behind them. The Big House opens up into a wide foyer that has a large great room on my right and a doorway that leads somewhere on the left. I've helped Tahlia in the kitchen and laundry room before, but I've always come in the back of the house with my tools and dirty boots.

Ryanne shifts to the right, blocking more of my view,

and I look at her. She wears everything in her face, but I'm not quite sure what she's trying to tell me. Almost a warning, maybe? Something in her dark brown eyes, framed by heavy eyebrows she wears well. She's anxious about something.

My stomach drops to my boots-for-show. "Hillary's not coming, is she?"

"Of course she is," Ryanne says. "She's just had a little...hang-up with the curling iron."

I've literally never seen a stitch of a wave in Hillary's hair, despite the heat and humidity in South Carolina. Of course, I've never paid too much attention to the redhead before last weekend.

"How many points, guys?" Emma asks from the back of the living room. I know the kitchen is back there, as is the staircase to the second floor. Hillary's room is on the third, and surely she'll appear there.

Tahlia edges into the living room too. "You're making him stand on the porch?" She shakes her head and gestures for me to come in. "Liam, get in here."

I smile at her and look at the three female bodyguards still preventing my entrance to the house.

"I'd give him a ten," Lizzie says.

"Nine," Claudia says.

"Ten," Ryanne says. "The button-up is a nice touch, Liam." She barely smiles at me before she turns and breaks ranks.

"What's the scale?" I ask as I enter the house. Claudia

moves out of the way as Lizzie follows Ryanne, and once I'm in the house, Claudia closes the door behind me.

I feel like I've stumbled into a parallel universe, where my farmhouse still sits next to the Big House, but all of the people are warped and different. There are far too many eyes on me, and I'm here under completely different pretenses than before, and I have no idea how to act or what to say.

Thank the heavens for Tahlia, who doesn't seem to have fallen into the alternate reality as she eases into me and hugs me hello. "You clean up for a date real nice," she says with a smile. "Ry, will you see if Hillary is hovering on the bottom step? She was right behind me."

"I'm not hovering," Hillary says as she comes around the corner. But she so was. I grin at her, because she's absolutely stunning in a flowered jumpsuit in navy blue and white.

It's not a little black dress, but I can't help thinking this is better. She wears a wide, white belt around her waist, making her hips swell in the best of ways, and my mouth goes dry at the sight of the white high heels.

Check.

Now I just need to find some magic and a unicorn.

"Hey," I say in one of the softest voices I've ever heard myself use. I talk to my cat like this, and I clear my throat. "Wow." I look back to her face, which she's done up nicely. Not too much makeup, and again, her lips bear almost no color. Why that's so hot for me, I don't know.

"Just wow. You look fantastic."

She has added a little wave to her hair, which is pulled back on the sides, but still hangs over her shoulders and down her back.

"Thank you," she says a little too diplomatically for me. She glances around at her roommates, and I startle when I realize they're all still there, watching. Listening. When Hillary had entered the room, all of them had fallen away.

She takes her handbag from Ryanne, nods at her, and then moves toward me. My heart pounds like a herd of wild horses have been let loose in my veins. Their hooves stampede through my body, making it hard to hear anything. Good thing my eyes still work, and I somehow know to lift my hand and slide it along her waist as she leans in and kisses my cheek.

"You look nice too," she says as she settles a safe distance away from me.

"You smell fantastic," I say without censoring myself. I'm used to letting my tongue run wild, but usually not with six women staring at me, and so much at stake. I force myself not to clear my throat again as I add, "I like that perfume."

Hillary smiles—actually smiles—at me and nods to Tahlia. "It's Tahlia's. She got it in Paris."

"Oh, nice," I say, though I don't really care where the perfume came from. Hillary and Tahlia and the other women clearly do, so I can pretend for a minute. "Should we go?"

"We should." Hillary waves and smiles to her friends, and finally, we escape back outside.

I take a big breath and blow it out, almost a laugh going with it. "Wow, that was tense." I hadn't even realized how tense until this moment. "I felt like I was underwater, trying to breathe."

"They can be a little much sometimes," she admits. She goes down the steps first, and I follow. I help her into the passenger seat of my SUV, to which she says, "You have more than one car."

"The truck is for work," I say. "My business pays for it." She nods; I close the door and hurry around to the driver's side. Once there, I start the engine to get the air blowing, and our eyes meet.

"What's your poison?" I ask. "I have a list of places I thought you might like." I manage to tear my gaze from hers, a tickle of excitement running through me. I swipe on my phone to get to my Notes app. I then turn the device toward her.

"Nothing you have to eat with your hands," I say. "Unless you love burgers, but they're not as messy as wings." I take a breath and tell myself to calm the heck down. I've been out with women before. Maybe not one as beautiful as Hillary, and maybe not on a first date that she initiated. But still.

"I figured Clancy's was safe," I say. "They have sandwiches and soups and salads." My throat is so dry. And why isn't she saying anything?

I glance at my phone. "Pizza is generally delicious and safe." I realize you eat it with your hands as I'm speaking, but I'm committed now. "Plus, a friend of mine owns this place, and they have the best dessert pizzas in the world."

"The whole world?" Hillary asks, something sparky and bright in her eyes.

She's teasing me, and that only gives me courage to continue. "Or there's an underground eatery done by this caterer. Tara Ward? She owns this place called Saucebilities, and my friend at the hardware store used her for a—I mean, he had her cater for their company party last year. It was amazing."

I realize how fast I'm talking, and I mentally command myself to slow down. "Anyway," I say when Hillary remains mute. "She's doing an Underground Dinner tonight. If we hurry, we could get in line and pray there's room."

I pull my phone back to my personal space, every cell in my body tingling in a weird way. Hillary watches me, and I wonder if she knows how much power she holds over me. She finally says, "I don't care, Liam. Pick somewhere you think will be fun."

"Fun?" I'm not sure how any of this is fun. I'm on the edge of a cliff, ready to plunge to my death just to end this. At the same time, I never want it to end. I flip the SUV into reverse. "Nothing about dating is fun."

"Nothing?"

"No." I shoot her a look, not sure where my dark cloud mood has come from. "What part of me being scrutinized by your five roommates do you think was fun for me?"

She opens her mouth and then snaps it shut.

"Yeah," I say. "Or me standing in the shower tonight, obsessing over where to take you. For the record, that wasn't fun either." I can't believe I'm talking about showering with Hillary Mays. I need a muzzle, and fast.

As I drive, I completely abandon the idea of any of the three places I've thought of. "You want fun?"

"I just—yeah," she says. "Dating is supposed to be fun. Getting to know another person you're interested in. Getting all dressed up. Putting your best foot forward. It's fun, Liam."

"Maybe," I grunt out.

She reaches over and takes one of my stiff and clawed hands from the steering wheel. There's this chemical reaction when our skin touches, and I wonder if she feels foamy and fiery the way I do.

"I'm sorry about the women at the Big House." She squeezes my hand, like maybe I forgot she was holding it. Such a thing is impossible, but I say nothing. "They were —none of us are dating right now, you know? And you're this—this—I don't know. I don't want to say it, because you already have a huge head."

"I do?" I scoff, the fire moving through me hotly now. "I do not. And even if I did, how would you know? We've barely spoken to each other in the years we've been neighbors."

"It's your *at-tit-tude*," she says, enunciating every syllable. If I wasn't driving, I'm sure I'd find her rolling her eyes.

"I have been nothing but nice to you guys," I say. "Tahlia hires me to fix the fridge. I come running. She needs the lawn mowed? No problem; I'll be there Saturday. You need the roof done? Sure, let me come over *after work* to check on it for you." I shake my head. "You have the completely wrong opinion of me."

"Fine, then," she says, plenty of bark in her tone now. "Change it for me."

I glare out the windshield, her hand still securely in mine. "I wanted to ask you out when you came over on Sunday night," I say, my words catching in my throat.

"Why didn't you?"

"Because."

"You shut the door in my face."

"You yelled at me from your third-story window, and then marched down to the lawn to chew me out."

"This is the attitude I'm talking about." She pulls her hand back and folds her arms.

I sigh and shake the frustration out of my bones. "Hillary," I say slowly, using all three syllables in a Southern accent. My mind whirs with something I can use to change her mind about me. "I have a calico cat named Tabitha."

She looks over at me, surprise etched in her eyes. "You do?"

"My momma takes care of her," I say. "She needed a friend after my daddy died, and I—well, I needed someone else to take care of Tabby. I was in a rough place for a while myself." I clear my throat again, and no one can blame me for that.

"I'm sorry about your daddy," Hillary says in a quiet voice. All of her bluster is gone too, and I wonder if we've been putting on a front for each other.

I make a turn and my "fun" destination appears up on the right. "What about you?" I ask. "What's something that will make me change my mind about your...sassy *at-tit-tude?*"

She looks lost for a moment, and I want to tell her I'll find her. Wherever she is, I'll get there. She just has to open the door for me first.

"I...I had a really important interview scheduled for today, and it got canceled." She reaches up and plays with the ends of her hair. "My job drains me dry."

Ah, I know this feeling. "I understand that," I say quietly. Tonight is not the night to get into all my short-comings, my college dropout, or my unrealized dreams. I make the turn into the bowling alley, and say, "All right. This is where we're going to have fun."

"The bowling alley?" She sounds completely dubious. "Really, Liam? What are we? Ten?"

"It's Tuesday night," I say, seeing the big banner hanging from the roof. "It's Galaxy Night."

"I didn't bring socks," she points out.

"No problem," I say without missing a beat. I pull into a parking space, noting all the minivans and other SUVs. I have a feeling the bowling alley is going to be hopping with ten-year-olds, but I don't back down. She wanted fun? Bowling is fun.

"We don't have to bowl," I say. "There's food here, and pool tables, and darts." With the SUV parked, I look at her. "Do you play darts?"

She cocks her head at me, those eyes flaming now. Oh, I like that, and I decide a little sassy fire between us is perfectly okay. "Do you really think I know how to play darts?"

"It's throwing a sharp object," I say with a grin. "I think you'll excel at it pretty fast." I get out of the SUV and go to help her down. My Southern manners earned me some points at the Big House, after all.

I take her hand as we walk toward the door, which is covered with black paper or a black curtain, making it impossible to see inside. "What was the scale at the Big House?" I ask. "I got a couple of tens and a nine."

"Ten," Hillary says in a perfectly normal voice. "Just think, if we don't work out, you can try Lizzie or Ryanne." She shakes her hair over her shoulder. "Claudia got a date on that singles app, so she'll probably tell you no."

"She did only give me a nine," I tease as I reach for the

door handle. I look at Hillary, and time pauses for us. "You ready for this?"

She looks at the blacked-out door and back to me. "It's Galaxy Night. Should be fun."

"Should be." I open the door. "Let the games begin."

CHAPTER NINE

HILLARY

THE BOWLING ALLEY IS DARK, WITH GLOW-BRIGHT
stars and planets and spaceships all over the walls and ceiling. Every lane to my left is occupied, and children run,
play, laugh, and shout. It's loud, with music pumping
throughout the huge space.

"This way," Liam shouts over the chaos, and I grip his
hand tighter as he leads me along the back of the lanes.
Moms and dads sit at the chest-high tables there, plenty of
food and drinks in front of them.

"It's like a children's league," I say. But I've spoken
almost to myself, and Liam doesn't hear me. He's a lot like
I thought he was—going from hot to cold in two seconds
flat—but he's also already showed me a sweeter side of
himself.

And it's not because of the cat, though that does help.

It's because he made a list of restaurants he thought I

might like. Despite my words about chicken wings being a bit sassy and lashed at him, he heard me. He knows I don't want to eat messy food on the first date, and he'd come up with a list of places I might like.

A sigh moves through me internally, and not only because he's leading me away from the Galaxy Night Party and toward a lit area of the building. "Howdy, Davy." He laughs and releases my hand as he man-hugs the guy behind the counter. "What are the chances of pool or darts tonight?"

Davy looks to his right, and I follow his gaze. There's a door that leads into another room, and beside it is the "Bowling Bistro" where I can get fried chicken, tater tots, or a hamburger. I'm starving, and I want all three—as long as they come with a side of Liam.

"We've got a table open," he says. "Then you can play whatever's free in there. We don't do assigned tables or boards on weeknights."

Liam glances at me, seeking permission, and I nod. "Great," he says easily, our exchange over in a matter of two seconds. "We'll take the table. What's the special tonight?"

"Hot chicken wings," Davy says, and Liam chortles.

"Great," he says. He passes over some money, though I'm not sure what for, and Davy gestures to the room.

"Won't be hard to see the table," he says. "Shirl's in there, and she'll help you if you need it." He grins at Liam, nods to me, and tucks the two twenties into the till while Liam nudges me toward the room.

"Go on," he teases. "We made it this far, and I'm pretty sure there's not going to be any children in there."

I go toward the room, and sure enough, this is the calmest place in the bowling alley. Five or six pool tables stand in the space in front of me, with dining tables and booths lining the wall to my left and to my right. There's more seating that way, as it wraps around toward the far wall.

A partition raises up in the middle of the room, with four dart boards on this side that I can see. Lines have been painted on the floor, and more of those chest-high tables mark each dart-throwing station.

My heartbeat throbs in my throat, and I don't even know why. I've played pool before. Darts, too, and Liam's right. It's just throwing something. I don't need technique to do it, though I'm sure there are plenty of people who disagree with me.

"This way, beautiful," Liam says, and I stumble after him in Ryanne's heels. The tables we pass have men and women at them, but significantly more men. Liam seems to know someone at every table, and he shakes hands and laughs and nods over to the other side of the room.

By the time I slide into the booth, I'm breathless and impressed all at the same time. Liam picks up a laminated half-sheet of paper and hands it to me. "The menu isn't big, but everything I've had is pretty good."

I don't look at it, but instead watch him. Power and confidence ooze from him, and how he doesn't know that baffles me. "I like the cowboy hat," I say, and that gets him to look up.

He swipes it from his head and sets it on the bench next to him. "I'm not really a cowboy, but it makes me feel dressed up." He smiles, and he's so gorgeous when he does. No wonder Lizzie gave him a ten just for his smile—something she told me before he'd rung the doorbell.

"I'm not wearing anything of my own," I tell him. "You don't have to be a cowboy to wear a cowboy hat."

He nods, something sparkly in his eyes. My feelings for Liam are confusing, and convoluted, but the fact is still the fact. I do have feelings for him. Maybe I texted the wrong guy earlier today, but this is not a waste of my time.

At least I hope it isn't. When I'd texted my roommates about it, they'd all said to give Liam a chance. *What can one date hurt?* Claudia had asked.

I'd go out with him in a heartbeat, Lizzie had said.

He said yes really fast, Tahlia pointed out. *He's obviously feeling something too.*

You don't even know Karl, Ry said. *Chatting online is not the same as face-to-face dating.* She'd steadfastly refused to get online to find a date, and I'd been in her camp until two days ago. Her point stands, too. I do know Liam, at least a little bit, simply by being around him in-person.

It had taken Emma most of the day to answer, as she'd

been up to her elbows in flower arrangements today for a big wedding tomorrow. She'd barely made it home before Liam had arrived. She'd said, *I agree with Claudia. It's one date, and who knows? You might really like him.*

I'd scoffed at that, because, well, because what Liam said on the drive over is right. I *have* formed an opinion of him, and it's not a good one. He's also right that he has been there for us ladies in the Big House whenever we've needed him, no questions asked.

"What'll you have?" a woman asked, and I look up at her, drawing myself back to the present.

"Do you have Diet Coke?"

"Diet Pepsi," she says.

"That's fine," I say, though it's definitely not as good. "With a lemon, please, if you have it." I glance at the menu, but it's pretty standard stuff. "I'd love the piggy pork fries, please." Done, I set down my card-menu and look at Liam.

He's wearing stars in his eyes, and somehow that makes him hotter and softer at the same time. "What?" I ask.

"The piggy pork fries are my favorite," he says.

Another thing we have in common. Maybe I shouldn't be making a list of those things, but right now, it feels like I have to.

He looks up at the waitress and says, "I want the fries too, and a bacon cheeseburger. No pickles, okay, Shirl? You always say there won't be, and there always is."

"No pickles," she says, scribbling on her pad. "You want your original drink?"

"Yes, please," he says, and he sets down his card too.

"Give me ten minutes." Shirl walks away, and I gaze across the table to this man I'm out with. It almost feels surreal.

"I have so many questions," I say.

"All right." He leans back. "Let's do Dating Twenty Questions. Then maybe we can just talk and eat and have that *fun* you wanted."

"Dating Twenty Questions?" I wait for a woman to walk by our table, noting that Liam doesn't look at her at all. "I've...uh, I haven't dated in a while. I'm not sure what that is."

"How long has it been since your last date?"

"Three years," I say. "You?"

"Maybe a little longer than that." He speaks in a rough voice, and I sure like the way it rumbles in my ears and chest.

"And we're off," he says. "We just get to ask questions back and forth like this, and if you want to follow-up on anything, you can. But it's back and forth." He nods to me. "So you just asked, and I answered, so I get to ask now."

I wave for him to do that, my chest a little tighter than it was before. I want to learn things about him without having to share anything of myself, and I know that's not going to fly with Liam.

"Will you get to reschedule your interview?" He again surprises me with a sentimental, sweet question.

"Yes," I say. "I should hear by the end of the week, but this past week, they waited until after hours to say we could have a day this week. Then they canceled." I shake my head. "I don't want to talk about work."

"Okay."

"What's your original drink?" I ask. "You must come here a lot to have something like that."

He smiles and plays with the edges of the laminated menu. "It's just peach-mango-cherry sweet tea, but it's got this trifecta of colors in it, so it gets a lot of attention."

My mouth waters as a round of cheering rises up here in the room. Something exciting is happening over at one of the pool tables, but the partition and the people playing darts obstructs my view.

"Where are you from?" he asks.

"Columbia," I say. "My parents still live there." I don't want to talk about my family either, and I cross my legs, my left heel dangling now, as the shoes are a little too big.

"They have great biking trails in and around Columbia," he says, growing a bit more animated. "I love that city."

"Yeah," I say. "It's got its own vibe, I guess." I smile back at him. "Where are you from, and why do you love mountain biking so much?"

"Ah, you're cheating," he says with a chuckle. "Sneaking in two questions at once." He draws in a breath.

"I'll play your game, beautiful. I'm from right here in Charleston. My momma still lives in the house where I grew up, and I love mountain biking, because I don't like sitting still and doing nothing. I like the outdoors, and biking takes care of both of those."

"Do you really think I'm beautiful?"

"Eeeeent." He makes a buzzing noise, and I startle at the volume of it. He leans closer and says in a much milder tone. "I gave you a pass on the asking-two-questions thing. You don't get to skip me and ask another one." He grins and takes both of my hands in his. He looks at them, a sense of wonder on his face though I can't quite see his eyes.

When he looks up, I can, and this man definitely has feelings for me. "Why do you like me?" I ask.

"A fourth question." He shakes his head. "Unbelievable. I didn't think you could lose at Dating Twenty Questions, but you, Miss Hillary Mays, have definitely disqualified yourself from the game."

"That's it, then? Game over?"

"We can circle back to your questions if there's time." He glances out into the rest of the room, and it sure seems like he's hoping Shirl will return with our food before he has to answer my questions.

"What do you do for a living?" he asks. "You know I'm a general contractor, but I don't even know what your interview was for."

"I'm a documentary researcher," I say. I shrug, the

movement rippling from one shoulder over to the other. "Well, I'm hoping to be a documentary producer one day. I have a degree in film and journalism, and I want to do more than write. I want to bring the stories to life."

I hear the passion in my own voice, and I want to downplay it, so I duck my head. "Maybe one day," I say. "Right now, I'm a researcher and investigative journalist for Bibliostar."

"You don't have to be embarrassed of what you want," he says, and I look up.

"I'm not."

"You drooped," he says.

"What does that mean?"

"It means, you were talking about your dreams of being a producer, and then you...just sort of folded into yourself, like what you were saying wasn't valid. You drooped." He pulls his hands back. "That's what my daddy used to call it. My sisters do the same thing sometimes."

"How many sisters do you have?" I ask.

"Is that your final question?"

I think of the other two I asked, and I'm honestly not sure I want to know the answers to whether he truly thinks I'm beautiful or not and why he likes me. I can't identify why I like him, but I just know I do.

So I say, "Yes."

"Two," he says. "They're both younger than me. Stella is married; Rebecca isn't."

"Any brothers?"

He bursts out laughing, and I know exactly why. I don't join him, but instead pull a napkin from the dispenser and lay it in front of me while he does. "You're really bad at this game."

"Maybe it's a dumb game," I shoot at him.

"No brothers," he says. He's grinning and sunny and perfectly in control of himself as he adds, "And yes, I think you're absolutely beautiful, whether you're wearing that sexy jumpsuit or those pink pajamas. I like you, because—well, you make me feel alive in a way I haven't in a long time, and I thought that was worth exploring a little bit."

"Bacon cheeseburger," Shirl says while I'm still blinking and reeling through what he's said. "Piggy pork fries, times two. Diet Pepsi, with lemon, and the Maui Sunrise." She sets everything on the table in front of the right person and adds, "I took those pickles off myself, Liam. Hope you're happy."

"Thank you, Shirl." He grins at her, and she smiles right on back.

"You two enjoy."

I look down at my dish, which is a mountain of French fries—that alone overjoys me—covered with barbecue pulled pork and a healthy mound of cole slaw. I'm definitely going to enjoy this, but more than that, I'm enjoying the man across from me far more than I anticipated.

Can it be possible for two grumps to find happily-ever-after with each other? Shouldn't one of us be the happy-go-lucky sunshine part of this relationship?

"Are you just going to stare at that, or are you going to eat it?" he asks.

Irritation licks through me as I raise my eyes to his. "I'm going to eat it, you—you—" My eyes land on his cowboy hat. "You cowboy."

He laughs again, a bite of pork and potato on his fork that only adds to the amazingness of this night. "That's a compliment, beautiful, not an insult." He nods to my fries. "Go on, try them. They're delicious."

"I love potatoes," I tell him, revealing one of my darker secrets.

He doesn't even seem to notice how far I've let him in as he nods and says, "This is way more than just potatoes."

I fork up a bite that has some of everything—French fry, pulled pork, plenty of sauce, and a few shreds of slaw. I put it in my mouth, and it's a creamy, tangy, salty party. I groan, my eyes rolling back in my head as Liam laughs again.

We may be on our first date at a loud Galaxy Night bowling alley, with people everywhere and clacking pool balls and bullseyes being aimed for. But this is absolute perfection, and now Liam has a high standard to meet for our future dates.

CHAPTER TEN

LIAM

"I can't believe you hit that triple twenty," I laugh-say as Hillary and I spill out of the bowling alley. Tonight has been the best hundred bucks I've ever spent, and I push my financial thoughts away to focus on the woman I'm still with.

She's giggling and walking like she's slightly drunk, though she didn't have anything more that Diet Pepsi tonight. She comes back to my side, her grin absolutely infectious. This is the Hillary who was looking at her phone the other night. This is the way I want her looking at *me*, not whoever she was texting then.

I sober, because I want to ask her about that. After our game of Dating Twenty Questions, we ate and talked about pool—which she learned how to shoot from her daddy—and darts—which really is just throwing a sharp, pointed object at a target. We laughed with others at the pool table and dart board, got the hot wings as a dinner follow-up, and I'm nearing desperation to ask her out again.

Technically, it'll be the first time, as she asked me out tonight.

"So," I say, really dragging out the word. "We've had some fun tonight, so I'm going to submit we have to each say one serious thing on the way home." I cut a look at her out of the corner of my eye. Her smile fades, but the joy lingers in her eyes.

"All right," she says, her arm in mine slow-Southern-fine and our pace casual and even. "Did you want to start?"

"Sure." I smile over to her. "So..." I exhale out my breath and take a fresh one. "My daddy died about ten years ago, and when that happened, I had to drop out of college." My chest turns a tiny bit tight, but the pinch doesn't stay for long.

"I was studying architecture, and I miss it sometimes. I have to work pretty hard to make ends meet, and I don't know. Sometimes I question my life choices."

"You don't like being a general contractor?"

"I like it okay, yeah," I say. "Don't you ever just some-times feel like you have a dream that hasn't come true?"

She nudges me with her hip. "Yeah, every day." She gives me a smile, and I reach into my pocket to pull out my key fob to unlock the SUV. The car beeps, and I guide her to the passenger side.

"Is yours about becoming a documentary producer?"

She turns back toward me, apprehension written across her face. "Sort of. Sort of not."

"So tell me."

Hillary sighs and looks past me, though she's got one hand resting on my hip, right on my belt. I'm hyper-aware of the weight there, of her whole body in front of me, of the scent of that flowery, dusky perfume.

"After my second failed engagement, I had to stop and really take stock of what I wanted," she says. "And that's when I realized it wasn't healthy for me to live too close to my parents. That's when I moved here, because Tahlia had just inherited the Big House, and she needed room-mates, and I needed something new, and yeah."

Her eyes flit all over the place, but once she finishes talking, she looks at me. "There you go."

"There's a lot to unpack there," I say slowly. "I'm gonna start with the obvious: You've been engaged twice?"

"You heard that part, huh?"

"Oh, I heard that part." I pull her into my arms, feeling that hand on my waist slide all the way around to my back. "I think that's the part you wanted me to hear," I whisper as I lean closer to her ear. Her hair smells fantastic, like peaches and cream and cucumbers, and maybe a little bit like the hot grease from the bowling alley.

"Maybe," she whispered. "It's just...if we start dating, you'll be the first guy I've been out with since the last engagement ended."

"I look forward to hearing more about it," I say, pulling back. There's plenty of light pouring from the lamps in the parking lot, and she can't hide from me as close as we stand. I've got my cowboy hat on, but if I duck it, the brim will hit her forehead.

There's so much to say and so little at the same time, and I find myself leaning forward to brush my lips across her cheek. Her eyelids flutter as they close, and I bring her closer and into a tighter embrace.

"When can we get together again?" I whisper-ask. "That is, if your opinion has changed about me." I pull back, suddenly horrified. "Has it?"

"Slightly," she says with that teasing glint in her eyes. "Do you still think I'm too sassy for my own good?"

"Only slightly," I say. "Is, uh, slightly enough to get a second date?"

She reaches up and trails her fingers down the side of my face. "Yeah, I think so."

"I'm working late tomorrow night," I say. "Thursday?"

"I take French classes on Thursdays."

My eyebrows fly up. "Wow. I wouldn't—wow. Okay."

"*Oui*," she says with a giggle.

"Friday?" I suggest.

"We're having an appetizer party at the Big House."

She looks up at me. "I'd invite you, but that would be complete chaos."

"Yeah, I'd pass on that," I say. "Not that I don't like your roommates. I do. Of course I do."

"I know you do." She turns and opens the door. "We all lived together for a year in college. It was Tahlia's senior year, and I don't know. We just had a good connection, and it just worked out that most of us were looking for a fresh start when she got the Big House. It took a few months for all of us to get there, and I was one of the last. That's why my room is on the third floor."

"Oh, the third floor is drawing the short straw?"

"That's a lot of steps to climb every time you want to go to bed," she says. "And can you imagine moving into that third-floor bedroom?" She gets into the SUV, and I laugh as I close her door.

We haven't solidified a second date, but I mutter to myself, "Don't push this," as I round the vehicle and get behind the wheel.

"Saturday?" she asks as I settle into my seat.

"Saturday...for?"

"Our second date."

"Oh, sure," I say. "Except my momma is having Sunday dinner on Saturday this week, because she thinks I'll come that way."

Hillary smiles. "You ditch your momma on Sundays?"

I chuckle and start the car. "Not always, but the past

few I have, yeah. It's prime mountain biking weather." I put the SUV in reverse and start to back out. A horn sounds, and I slam on the brakes.

"You weren't even looking," Hillary says through her laughter.

I wait for the car I almost hit to go behind me, and then I back out. "I can't help it if your beauty distracted me."

"Oh, I'm not taking the blame for this." She shakes her head. "And you need to work on your pick-up lines."

"I do?" I laugh again and shake my head. "I don't know about that. I feel like I've done okay tonight. You said you'd go out with me again."

"Now you're pushing it."

"How so? By calling you beautiful and letting you win at darts?"

"*Letting* me win?" She practically howls out a scoff. "I beat you fair and square."

"So Sunday," I say. "Do you go to church? Oh, I remember now. You sleep in on the weekends."

She gives me a growly-sexy glare. "Funny," she says. "Just for that, I don't think I'm available until next week."

I laugh, but part of me is terrified I really will have to wait a week to see her again. "All right," I say, deciding to call her bluff. "Well, I have your number and you have mine." I get us on the road back to the quieter streets of Cider Cove, and Hillary leans her head back against the rest.

We've both said a lot tonight, and I don't feel the need to fill the car with chatter on the way home. I walk her all the way to the door, and she turns toward me. "Before next week," she says.

I'm better able to keep up with her random conversation topics now, and I grin at her. "Maybe on Friday night, I can sneak over and steal you away from your roommates for a few minutes."

"If you bring cookies, I won't even tell my roommates where I'm going." She puts both hands on my chest and leans into me. "I had a good time, Liam."

"Same," I say as her lips brush my beard up by my cheekbone. "I'll call you."

"Oh, don't strain yourself," she teases. She opens the door and puts one heeled foot inside. "A text is fine."

"Hillary, I know you want more than *fine*." I tip my hat at her and wait for her to put both feet inside the house, and then I lift my hand in a wave as she gently closes the door. She didn't correct me on the fact that she wants more than fine, and I seriously wonder on the short drive home if I can give a woman like Hillary what she wants and deserves.

"You've got this, Liam," I mutter to myself. That was definitely the best first date I've been on, ever, and I don't want to give up on happily-ever-after without truly giving it a shot.

So I won't.

———

I FINISH PUTTING in the spark plug and straighten. After wiping my hands on a gray rag, I toss it to the side. "Moment of truth," I say to the garage. I've been working on this truck for a couple of weeks now, and I'd like to get it out of my hair.

I'm dirty from head to toe, and I need a shower desperately. But not if this vehicle doesn't start. I climb into the cab, press the brake, and say a little prayer before I turn the key. The engine sputters for a moment and then roars.

"Yes." I pump my fist out of the truck. I pull my left leg in and close the door. "Let's go for a ride, Gerald." I don't know why I name every car or truck I work on Gerald, but I do. He chugs along down the dirt lane out of my mechanic shed and toward the road. I'm the last house on this road, and fields take up the land to my east of me.

To the west is the Big House—bordering my land and orchards. Twilight has fallen as Gerald and I rumble past the house, and I don't see Hillary's car. She could be parked on the other side, but she did tell me she usually parks in the driveway off Cherry Lane.

Gerald performs all his proper functions, and I park him in front of the farmhouse. It's too dark for pictures tonight, but I'll get some good ones in the morning, and I'll get the for-sale listing online during my lunch hour.

I've just closed my front door when Hillary texts.

> Home from French class.

I lean against the kitchen counter and grin at the thought of her learning French.

> Say something to me in French.

It takes her a few seconds, but then I get:

> Je veux manger le dîner.

I grin, then long-hold on the text and copy it into Google translate. It spits out, *I want to eat dinner*, and I navigate back to my texting app.

Chuckling, I type out,

> After I shower, I could bring you some wings.

> I'll pass on the wings.

I can't think of anything witty to say, so I order a pizza and jump in the shower. Twenty minutes later, I'm mostly grease-free, and my all-meat pie is on my doorstep. I grab it and start the quick walk to the Big House.

I'll have to ring the doorbell again, and who knows who'll answer. Instead of doing that, I head around to the back of the house, where I settle on the top step of the back porch. Then I text Hillary.

> I have pizza on your back porch.

A soft light comes out of the window behind and to my right, which I know is their kitchen. But no one seems to be moving around or cooking.

> You do not.

> I'm a lot of things, but a liar isn't one of them.

> I'm in my pajamas.

> I've seen those before.

She doesn't text again, and I flip open the box and pull out a slice of pizza. I don't normally spend so much money on eating out, but I'm pretty sure the ladies here in the Big House will hire me to fix their roof, and I have another consultation next week for a deck build—one of the Summerwoods' neighbors who's seen me working at their place this week.

Right when I finish my first slice of pizza, the back door opens, casting more light onto the porch, onto me.

"You're really here," Hillary says, and I twist to see if she's really wearing her pajamas. She is not.

"You're never wearing what you say you will be," I say.

She comes over and hands me a bottle of water before she sits beside me. "I don't normally show men my pajamas on the second date."

"Again," I say. "I've already seen them."

"That was an accident," she says.

I snort, because that so isn't what happened. "I think you need a vocabulary lesson." I pick up another slice of pizza and hand it to her. "I don't think you know what an accident is."

"I do too."

"Then you know it's not yelling at someone out of a window, and then coming down three flights of stairs—in your pajamas—to yell at them."

She takes a bite of her pizza, and her non-argument tells me I've won. "So you're not wearing your pj's tonight, and you teased me with a little black dress the other night too, and I never got to see that." I look at her, but she seems fascinated by the darkness spilling across the back lawn.

When she swallows, she says, "I'll make it up to you."

"Yeah? How are you gonna do that?"

"I don't know," she says. "I'm still working on that part."

"Mm, I look forward to the making up," I say. "And seeing the dress." I reach over and take her hand in mine. "It's good to see you. Did you hear on your interview?"

She smiles and leans her head against my bicep. "Not yet."

"Tomorrow, then," I say, and I press a kiss to her hairline. "I might be able to come do the tarring around that pipe tomorrow night. But I'll check with you, so I don't ruin your roommate appetizer-fest."

"Okay," she says, and then we sit there together, our fingers intertwined and the night sky speaking when neither of us wants to. It's serene, quiet, and just...perfect. I can't help feeling some of the magic between us, and now all I need is that elusive unicorn.

CHAPTER ELEVEN

HILLARY

"Okay, okay, okay," Tahlia says as she gets up on the couch in the big den off the front foyer. She's got her blonde hair down tonight, and it looks like she straightened it and blew it out before our appetizer night. "I want to do announcements. I know a few of you have them."

Her eyes meet mine and claw in for a moment. I blink, and now she's looking at Claudia. My heartbeat bumps a little strangely in my chest, but nothing too crazy. I do have a couple of announcements, and yes, I've held them close to me for a few days.

I sincerely hope Liam is okay with going slow. He didn't seem disappointed on Tuesday that I slipped into the house without kissing him, and last night on the back porch, with fireflies, silence, and pizza...that was perfection.

I'm surprised a man like Liam knows how to burrow straight into my heart, but so far, he's doing an ooey gooey cheesy-potatoey job of it.

"We've got our food, so eat what you need to in order to tell us a few things." Tahlia gets down off the couch and picks up her plate. It's loaded with chips and guac—which is her specialty—the garlic-lime shrimp skewers Ryanne always makes, a few of my loaded potato skins, a couple of Emma's pimento cheese pita triangles, at least one of Claudia's fried green tomatoes, with Lizzie's black bean stew in a bowl on the side.

I've taken some of everything too, and I pop a perfectly crispy-on-the-outside-soft-on-the-inside potato skin into my mouth. It's buttery, and cheesy, and bacony, and salty, and sour creamy, and the most delicious thing in the world.

"Claudia?" Tahlia asks, and she hands her a fake microphone made out of a tennis ball atop an empty paper towel tube. Tahlia made it for Big House meetings, so we didn't all talk over one another. She's a teacher at heart, and she's very good at crowd control, even among us.

"All right," Claudia says, her plate balanced on her lap. "One, I'm going out with the guy from Matchmakers. His name is Greg, which I'm not holding against him, and we're meeting at the mall tomorrow night."

"The mall?" Lizzie asks. "That's not very romantic."

"It's a public place," I say, smiling at Claudia. "It's smart—and." I dunk my fried green tomato into a pool of homemade ranch. If there's anything better on a potato than ranch dressing, I don't want to know about it. My mind would be blown wide open.

"They have that Chinese restaurant Claudia adores," Tahlia fills in for me, also smiling. "That's great, Claudia."

She nods, tucking her dark hair behind her ear. She has a literal mane of hair, and she spends as much time complaining about it as she does loving it. Tonight, she's braided back the sides to keep it out of her face, but plenty spills over her shoulders.

She picks up a pimento pita but holds it instead of taking a bite of it. "And, there's a rumor around my office that the City Planner might retire soon."

I pull in a gasp, as do a few others. "Claudia, that's the perfect job for you," I say.

"It really is," Ryanne adds, the words barely discernible through her mouthful of shrimp. I'm just glad there's a little protein to our appetizers tonight. Everyone knows Ry is always going to make something with seafood. She's done scallops before too, but none of us liked them all that much.

She made a paella that we devoured, but that's more of a meal than an appetizer, and I'm not complaining about the tangy, garlicy shrimp, that's for sure.

"So if-when that comes up," Claudia says. "I'm going to apply for it." She nods and holds out the microphone. "Who's next?"

Lizzie takes it, and I pop a chip loaded with guacamole

into my mouth, glad I'm not next. I have two pieces of news too—one personal and one professional. Liam isn't even a secret, though I've said very little about our Tuesday-night date to my roommates. Contrary to what Liam probably thinks, we don't gather every evening in our pj's and tell each other everything.

"Okay," Lizzie says, and she's actually holding the fake mic to her mouth. She's freshly showered, as she said she was out "in the tanks" today. She works at a chemical research company, and I honestly have no clue what she does all day.

She's the nicest human ever, I know that. She sends me private texts about how I'm smart and funny, and she asks for my grandmother's best potato recipes like she really wants to have them and make them someday.

Only Lizzie really cooks in the Big House. Tahlia bakes. The rest of us get by with convenience foods and eating what they make and put in the fridge.

"I've been talking to the CEO of Fashion Plus. You know, that plus-size clothing box I get every other week?"

"Oh, I know about it," Emma says. "I almost stole that purple flowered blouse you got a month ago."

Lizzie's mouth drops open. "Is that why I can't find it?"

"No." Emma focuses on her plate of appetizers and lifts a spoonful of stew to her guilty lips.

"I am raiding your room after this," Lizzie says matter-of-factly. That's the best way to describe her—very matter-of-fact. "Anyway. Winnie and I have been talking, and she wants me to be a model for the service."

A pause of silence fills the den, and then a roommate-explosion fills the room with sound. "Congrats," is heard, and I say, "That's amazing, Lizzie."

"Do you even *want* to be a model?" Ry asks, and Lizzie doesn't have to answer. The glow on her face says it all.

"I want to be a model," I say. "Who doesn't? They do your makeup all cute, and fix your hair in ways you'd never think to, and you get to wear amazing clothes."

Lizzie hands me the mic, and I'm holding the glittery pink paper towel tube before I even realize it. I look down at the tennis ball, which was also painted pink, though I can see some of the yellow-green fibers starting to show through.

"All right," Tahlia says. "Hill's got the mic."

I look up, all five pairs of eyes on me now. They're still eating, but I know they want details about Liam.

"Okay." I clear my throat. "First, I too have some exciting news about work. Catarina has set another interview time for Monday. First thing, so hopefully she won't cancel again."

Everyone nods, but they say nothing. A tremble rumbles through my stomach, because normally, they'd all shout their congratulations at me the way we did for

Lizzie. I tuck my burnt auburn hair behind my ear and look at Claudia. She takes a bite of her potato skin, though they're meant to be eaten in one bite, and grins at me.

"All right," I say. "I'm not giving details about Liam."

"Oh, come on," Emma says. "I see him going into the hardware store all the time, and Hillary, that man is *hot*."

I'm not going to deny that. "He's an acquired taste," I say instead.

"Yeah, and did you *acquire* him?" Ry asks, her eyes holding a devilish glint.

"Okay, gross. No." But I smile as I shake my head. "We had a...great date, actually. He asked me out again, and I said yes."

"Oooh," Emma says. "You're dating him."

I haven't put that label on us yet, but I don't have anyone else asking when he can see me again. Karl-from-Matchmakers was fun to flirt with and talk to, but he hasn't made a move toward wanting to meet me in person. Not even a little bit. When I accidentally texted Liam instead of Karl, I would've been the one to initiate that.

Part of me wonders how Karl would've reacted. It doesn't matter now, because I sent the text to Liam instead, and we did have a pretty amazing date a couple of nights ago.

"She's gone into her head," Claudia says, taking the mic from me. "Hillary? Are you there?" She's speaking loudly only a few inches from my face, her smile big and knowing.

"I'm dating Liam Graff," I say out loud. "In fact, he might want to meet up on the roof later." I glance at Tahlia. "I think we'll be done by then."

"The roof?" Ry's eyes are like full moons. "Is that some secret hiding place?"

I shake my head. "No. He just...I don't know why he suggested it."

"Because he wants the job on the roof," Claudia says.

"Oh." I snatch the mic back from her. "He sent over the quote too. It's a lot, but he's offering us half-price on the labor."

"I'll bet he is," Lizzie says suggestively. "You'll be paying the other half in kisses." That causes everyone to giggle, but I shake my head, refusing to join them.

"No," I say. "I haven't kissed him."

"Yet." Tahlia plucks the mic from my hand and hands it to Ry. "Take his offer, Hillary. I'll file a claim with the home owners insurance, which should cover it."

I nod at her as Ry tells us that she's considering firing some of the employees at the office supply store she manages just so she can hire some new people. "Then maybe I can get myself a hot date too."

"Just join Matchmakers already," Claudia says. "Both Hillary and I met someone in minutes."

Ry shakes her head, because she's not an app-type of woman. She passes the mic to Emma as my phone vibrates against my thigh. I ignore it, though the urge to see what Liam's said pulls at me like gravity.

"The Rose Petal went up for sale," Emma says, her voice as calm and kind as ever. She's a honey-blonde, and her personality is just as sweet as her hair color. "I put in an offer, and now I'm waiting on the financing."

"You're going to own it?" Lizzie asks.

Emma nods, and that causes another round of shrieking and congratulating. Then, a collective sigh moves through us, and I pick up my last shrimp and pop it into my mouth.

"You haven't gone, Tahlia," Ry says, and she leans forward and picks up the mic from where Emma's dropped it on the coffee table. She extends it toward Tahlia, who takes it reluctantly.

"I don't know if I want to say mine."

"You started it," I say. "You can't not follow your own rule." Tahlia meets my eyes, and I see her trepidation in full. "Just give us the gist," I say, amending my statement.

She nods, her throat moving as she swallows. I need more potatoes for this, as I don't think it's going to be something I want to hear. I stand up and return to the table of food behind the couches and load my plate with only cheesy, bacon potato skins. I take a big dollop of ranch, which is technically for the fried green tomatoes, and return to my spot.

"You know how the schools get fliers for after-school programs and community classes?" Tahlia asks. No one answers, because yes, we know that. "I looked into some of the adult programming, and there's a business class. I signed up for it."

"Like Hillary's French class," Claudia says, shooting me a nervous look.

I know exactly why Tahlia is taking a business class, but it's not my news to tell. My phone buzzes again, but I drag a potato skin through the ranch and put the whole thing in my mouth.

"Yeah," Tahlia says slowly. "Like Hillary's French class."

"All right," Ry says. "That's announcements."

Tahlia gets up and puts the mic back on the shelf behind the speakers for the surround sound system. "What are we watching tonight, ladies?"

With the mic gone, it's a free-for-all of opinions on what movie we should watch tonight. I add my voice when there's something suggested I absolutely don't want to watch. Otherwise, I let them argue it out.

I pull my phone from my pocket and see Liam has indeed texted a couple of times.

> Cookies are out of the oven!

He's sent a picture with the message, and the cookies look perfectly browned and delicious. Surprise darts through me, because Liam doesn't seem like the type of man who knows how to cook.

Color me impressed.

Ready when you are. The ladder will be against the back of the house where it was the other day. Come up whenever you can.

My pulse thumps harder and harder. He's outside already? I glance toward the big front windows, and the sun has definitely set. It's probably dusky or twilighty outside, and I don't want to be too obvious about sneaking out to see him.

I'll be another twenty minutes.

I hope that's true.

And I can't stay long.

I love my roommates, and while Tahlia's business class is so she can learn what it will take for her to turn the Big House into a bed and breakfast one day, she won't make any of us leave before we're ready.

So with my potato skins gone and my paper plate in the recycling bin, I snuggle into Tahlia's side as Claudia starts *Boss Baby*. "I can't believe we're watching this," I whisper-complain, but Tahlia doesn't answer me.

"It's good," Ry hisses at me, and I roll my eyes at her.

A little while later, I get up and refill my sweet tea and

fill a plate with some of everything that's left—which is everything. As I walk behind the couch, Tahlia leans her head back and catches my eye. "Behave," she says.

"I will," I say. "Be back in a jiff."

Climbing a ladder three stories with a paper plate of appetizers isn't the easiest thing I've ever done. I almost lose them twice before I poke my head up over the rain gutter.

Liam sits all the way up at the pinnacle of the roof, an electric lantern casting his face into sexy shadows. He's lit enough for me to see his smile, and he gets to his feet easily.

"I brought you some food," I say, lifting the appetizers and holding where I am until he can come and get them from me.

His boots land loudly on the roof as he leaves the circle of light cast by the lantern, and he reaches for the paper plate. The ladder feels like it's swaying left-right, right-left, and I release the paper plate when I think he has it.

"Oh," he grunts, and the paper plate tilts toward me. I grab onto the side of the ladder, sure I'm going to topple backward, shrimp skewers, potato skins, and pimento cheese coming after me.

I'll be splatted on the perfectly mown grass below, all the best Southern foods plastered all over me.

Liam kneels and grabs the ladder, the plate of food a

lost cause. It's half on the cusp of the roof and half on me, and when I look up at him, I feel something thick on my eyelashes. He wears a horrified look on his face which I can only see because he's so close to me now, and then he starts laughing.

Laughing.

CHAPTER TWELVE

LIAM

"I'm glad you find appetizers on my face so amusing." Hillary's voice is like a whip, and the snap of it makes my chuckles fade into silence.

"Can you get up the rest of the way?" I ask, still gripping the ladder. She'd worn panic in her expression a few moments ago, and she'd dropped the plate of food before I had ahold of it.

"Maybe," she says. "I never got all the way up the other day."

"You've come this far. It's just a couple more steps." Leaning over her is awkward, as I'm already on the roof. So I back up a little, which causes me to release the ladder. It's not like I was single-handedly holding it against the roof.

Hillary comes up another step, then another, and half of her body is above the top of the ladder now. I smile at her encouragingly and stretch my hand toward her. "One more," I say.

Her eyes meet mine, and oh yeah, she's freaked out. "There's nothing for me to hold on to."

"Take my hand," I say.

"How the tater tot am I going to get down?" She actually looks down, which is a huge mistake. She groans and presses her eyes closed. "This is bad. This is so bad." She's whispering that under her breath over and over, and she's frozen.

This isn't funny, and I tell myself not to laugh. Not that I want to, but she's really not in any danger. *Unless she flings herself backward*, I think.

"Hillary," I say in the calmest voice I can. "Open your eyes, beautiful. Look at me. Take my hand."

Her hands gripping the top knobs of the ladder shake she's clenched them so hard.

"Hillary," I bark.

That gets her to open her eyes. "Good," I say in my more commanding tone. "Look at me. Take my hand. It's one more step."

"It's two, Liam," she growls.

"Great," I say smoothly. "One more up, and then one to the roof. I've got peanut butter Reese's Pieces cookies. Come on now."

"Luring me with food won't work." She looks like she might murder me the moment she gains the roof, and yet, as she releases one of her vice-grip hands, I grab it and hold it tight.

"I've got you," I say.

She scoffs. "If I go down, I weigh enough to pull you with me."

"You're not going down," I say.

Hillary takes the step up, and she looks like a contortionist since she won't let go of the other side of the ladder. She grunts and takes the last step, and I grab her other hand, mine sliding up to her elbow and pulling her into me.

We're a good five feet from the edge of the roof, her chest practically pressed to mine, as she says, "You should've said 'of course you don't weigh enough to pull me from the roof, Hillary.'"

I grin at her, wondering if I can kiss her right here, right now. Something tells me I better not. "Of course you don't weigh enough to pull me from the roof, Hillary."

She gives me a wry look and presses into me enough for me to get the hint she wants to be further from the edge. I back up, which is hard to do on a slanted surface, and I turn back to where I've set up our dessert station at the top of the roof.

I keep a good hold on her hand as we climb up there, and I indicate the plate of cookies I brought. She sits on one side, and I retake my spot closer to the lantern. Now that she's here, I'm not sure what to say.

"You made these?" she asks.

I pick up the plate and hold it out for her. "I mean, I baked them."

She smiles, and oh, with that soft white light highlighting her face, it's one of the most beautiful things I've ever seen. We might not fall physically from this roof, but I still feel myself in desperate need of a parachute when I look into her eyes.

"I found them in the refrigerated section," I say. "You know, by the canned cinnamon rolls and stuff."

Hillary takes a cookie from the plate, and they don't look half bad. "I like those canned cinnamon rolls," she admits before she takes a bite of the cookie. "Mm, I like this too." Crumbs linger on her lips, and all I can think is that they're the luckiest things in the world right now.

I take a cookie and put the plate down. "Your mama didn't cook?"

"Heavens, no," she says. "We had someone to do that for us."

"Do you buy the things you take to appetizer night, then?" I look toward the mess I left near the ladder. That has to be cleaned up, or there will be birds attacking this house with the first rays of light. "I can climb up here and hose off the roof."

I look over to Hillary and find her wiping her face with the hem of her T-shirt. I catch a glimpse of the skin along her stomach. Maybe the bottom band of her bra before she quickly covers herself.

Heat fills me from head to toe, and I look away. My

voice grinds through my throat, and my mind has gone blank. I can only see that image of her body, and my word, I've lost my ever-loving mind.

"I made the potato skins," she says. "It was my grandmother who cooked. She taught me a few things."

"Mm." I nod to the night, not sure why *I'm* the uncomfortable one. "What did you learn to cook?"

Hillary takes my hand, and something inside me relaxes. "You're tense."

"You almost fell off the roof."

"You dumped the food I brought for you down the front of me."

"You showed me your—" I want to reach over and switch off the lantern, but I leave it shining. I'm sitting up higher than her, and I'd have to turn almost all the way toward her to truly see her.

"You're not wearing a hat."

"It's nighttime," I say.

"That hasn't stopped you before."

I can't think of a pithy comeback, so I say, "True."

The night twinkles and chirps back at us for a couple of moments, and then Hillary coughs. At least it sounds like a cough. Maybe a snort. A scoff?

Then her laughter paints the deepening night in brighter colors, and I have no choice but to look at her. "What?"

She grins in that way I like, the lantern-light making her eyes shine like diamonds. "You claim to own hundreds of hats, and you didn't wear one tonight? That's funny, number one. Number two, you always have something to come back at me with."

I reseat my fingers through hers and use my other hand to swipe it through my hair. "I just showered. Sometimes wearing the hat makes me feel like my brain is being squeezed out of my skull."

"I showed you what?" she asks.

I squint into the night, almost like maybe the correct answer to this will be written in the stars. "You were wiping your face with your shirt."

"Do I have nice abs?" she teases.

I look at her then, because she obviously doesn't care that she flashed me. Maybe she does. It's hard to tell in the shadows and with the way she's smiling. "Maybe," I say.

She laughs then, tilting her head back and letting her hair fall down her back. She's also showing me the perfect column of her neck, and I suddenly feel very vampiric. The urge to touch my mouth there is almost more than I can contain, and I remind myself that Edward somehow controlled himself around Bella. I can keep my lips to myself for now.

Hillary leans into my bicep, and I move the plate from between us so she can scoot closer. She does, and after she's quieted, she says, "Talk to me about mountain biking."

"What do you mean?"

"You said you'd take me. Do I need to...I don't know.

Get some special gear? One of those bodysuits you have? Beef up my abs to hold me on the bike?"

Surprise fills me again, and I tell myself to get used to it. Hillary is a surprising woman—and not at all like I thought she was. "You really want to go mountain biking?"

"Yes," she says. "And for our next date, I'd love to cook some of my grandmother's recipes for you. It'll feature my favorite food."

"What's that?" I ask.

"It's a surprise."

I hear the smile in her voice, and I lean down and try to see her face. I can't, so I just press a kiss to her temple and wrap my other hand around hers. She doesn't stay for too much longer, and I help her over the lip of the roof and down the ladder without incident.

Thankfully. I take everything down with me that I brought up, and I re-climb the ladder with their hose. I grunt and groan and spray down the roof with my eyes mostly closed, getting myself completely soaked in the process.

When I reach the ground for the second time, I roll up the hose and rehang it on the handle sticking out from the house. I strip off my shirt, and it might just be water in my ears, but I swear I hear a collective gasp.

I look to the Big House, but I don't see anything. My phone chimes, and I pull it from my back pocket of my totally wet jeans. Gross. I hate wet denim more than anything—which is only another argument for the biking bodysuit. No one wants to ride a bike with jeans and get wet or muddy.

The chafing that would cause...

Nice abs, Hillary's texted me, and I yank my eyes back to the kitchen windows. There's still no one there, and I barely dare to let my eyes roam upward. Ah, there. Second-story window, so not Hillary's room.

"Thanks for cleaning the roof, Liam!" Tahlia calls, though I can't see her.

I reach up and salute, and a cacophony of voices start whispering and talking back and forth. The moment I round the corner of the house, I press my back into the siding and answer Hillary.

> Back atcha.

———

"WHAT IS WITH YOU?" my sister asks the very moment she lays eyes on me. I swear, I'm so sick of women looking at me and making judgments.

"What do you mean?" I toe the front door of Momma's house closed and give my oldest sister, who is still three years younger than me, the stink eye. "I brought the iced tea, Momma."

"Good boy," she calls from the back of the house, and I preen like a canine who's fetched the ball for his master.

"You were whistling on the walk up the driveway," Stella says, planting her hands on her hips. She narrows her eyes and won't let me by her to put the bottled iced tea my momma prefers in her fridge. "Something's going on."

"He's dating someone," Momma says, completely selling me out.

"I am not," I say quickly. "It was one date, Momma." And maybe pizza on the back porch and a stolen moment on the roof. Those aren't real dates. Are they?

Stella's hands fall away from her hips, her eyes rounding. "You're dating again?"

"It's not a crime," I tell her. "Can you let me by?"

She moves, and I go into the kitchen giving my mother the stink eye now. "You just had to say something, didn't you?"

Momma only smiles, and I load her fridge up with the iced tea.

"See?" my younger sister says as I straighten from my momma's ancient appliance. "I knew I heard his truck."

"I didn't even drive my truck," I say. "I brought Gerald, just to see how he'd do with all the stopping and going." I grin at Rebecca, who was only sixteen when our daddy died. I open my arms to her and ask, "Did you know dating is considered a crime around here?"

"I did," she says soberly as she walks into my embrace. "Stella's given me the lecture about dating sixteen hundred times."

"I'm sure it was only fifteen hundred," Stella says.

I grin at Becca as we part. "Who were you talkin' to?"

"Oh." She grins and holds up both hands. "I didn't know you were dating anybody, so..."

"You brought a friend for me to meet." My mood falls to the ground and dives in deep.

"She's nice."

"I'm sure she is," I say in a deadpan. No matter how many times I've told my sisters not to set me up, they still think they can. I'm capable of getting a date—clearly—but what they have never grasped is that I didn't want one.

"There you are," Becca says as she opens the back door. "Sorry, I forget this screen just slams shut."

In walks a brunette, and sure, she's pretty. She's way too young for me, though, as Becca is six years younger than me and that means most of her friends are too. "This is Juliet."

"Hey, there." I smile and shake her hand. "Liam."

She stutters something that sounds like a "Hello," but I'm honestly not sure. And not to be totally rude, but I don't care. I turn back to Stella, hoping she can salvage tonight's dinner. "Where's Stan tonight?"

"It's tax season," she says, though April fifteenth was at least three weeks ago.

"So does that mean he's working?" I ask, because I'm the grump in the family and I can.

Stella gives me a sharp look. "Yes, he's working."

"It's Saturday night," I say.

"I know what day of the week it is." The doorbell rings, and we all turn toward it.

Momma starts toward it, which makes sense, as it's her house. She would never order dinner for us, and I know she's made something bubbly and delicious by the scent of cream and browned meat hanging in the air. I have no idea who would be at her house, ringing the doorbell, so I follow her through the arched doorway and into the living room.

She gets to the door and opens it, and there's another woman standing there. Probably a decade older than me, and she lifts a brown paper bag toward Momma. "I see you have company," she says. "But I made you some bread, and I thought you might want it for dinner."

"Thank you, Mary." Momma takes the bread and hugs Mary, whose eyes never leave me. I don't know her, and a frown pulls at my eyebrows. I'm satisfied she's not here to do anything nefarious to Momma, and the whole exchange takes less than thirty seconds.

"Who was that?" I ask as Momma reaches me again. I take the bagged bread from her, and it's warm along the bottom.

"She just moved in down the street," Momma says. "She just got divorced and has two boys." She pats my chest. "Her house needs work, Liam, so wipe that distrustful look off your face and come slice that bread."

I scoff at my momma's assessment of whatever my face looks like. I'm also not going to slice this bread, but I do take it into the kitchen and give it to Stella to get that job done. She does it as Momma dishes up her famous chicken and dumplings.

"Momma, I love you," I say with a grin as I sit down. My sisters and momma join me, and Momma looks around at the three of us, plus awkwardly, Juliet. I try not to think about who should be here with us, but I still look to the spot beside me where Daddy would most likely be sitting.

"All right," Momma says. "Liam will say grace, and then he's going to tell us about his girlfriend."

"Oh-ho," I say. "We're not to that level yet."

"Well, get the deal sealed," Stella says. She grins at me as she reaches for my hand. I sweep my ballcap off my head, surprised Momma didn't chastise me for wearing it at the table, and I take Juliet's hand across the table from me.

There's absolutely no fizzle there, and that's when I know I have something real with Hillary. Or at least chemical. I say grace and settle my hat back on my head. "Momma, I want to hear how you and Daddy met."

"Again?" Becca whines. "Come on, Liam."

"It's a sweet story," I say.

"How did you meet—what's her name?" Stella asks.

"Hillary." A grin comes to my lips. "She yelled at me out of a third-story window."

"Why am I not surprised?" Stella asks, and everyone at the table—including Juliet—bursts out laughing.

As we eat, I imagine bringing Hillary here to meet Momma. I think they'd get along real nice, and I have to tell myself to push on the brake a little. Hillary and I are brand-new. So new, the tags haven't even come off our relationship yet.

Heck, we barely *have* a relationship. Still, I make Momma pose for a selfie with me, and my thumbs fly as I send it to Hillary.

> Talking about you tonight.

Cute!

Her, not you.

> You don't think I'm cute?

No, sir, you are not.

> What am I, then?

You know what you are.

I actually have no idea, and I want Hillary to spell it out for me. Instead, I tap out something else.

> Tomorrow. Me and you on a second date. Breakfast? Brunch? Lunch? Afternoon tea? Dinner? Dessert bar somewhere?

It sounds kind of desperate when I read it back, but I hit send anyway. Then I just have to wait for Hillary to answer. She takes her sweet Southern time, and I'm driving Gerald home, the sun long gone, when my phone finally brightens with a message from her.

> Can I decide when I wake up in the morning? I'm taking a sleeping pill and turning off my alarm.

I pull to the side of the road.

> I won't be mowing the lawn in the morning, I promise.

> I guess we'll see if you break your promises then.

> Like the little black dress you promised me?

> I told you I'd make that up to you.

> Starting tomorrow?

> I'll decide when I wake up.

I chuckle to myself and Gerald, and I can't help looking to the third floor of the Big House when we drive by. "I hope she wakes up in a good mood," I mutter to myself as I try to see if Hillary's window is lit up. I can't, because her bedroom is on the back of the house.

No matter what, it seems like our date tomorrow will be predicated by whatever mood she wakes up in. So I pray for sweet dreams for Hillary, because selfishly, I'd like to see if I can kiss her on the second date and not get punched.

CHAPTER THIRTEEN

HILLARY

THERE IS NO LAWN MOWER GROWLING WHEN I WAKE up. Sunlight streams through the closed slats in my blinds, slanting across my bed as I stretch my arms up above my head.

"I slept in," I say to myself and the softly blowing ceiling fan above me. I reach for my phone, startled to see my alarm is going to go off in two minutes. I'd set it for nine a.m., sure I wouldn't sleep that long.

But I've had another busy week, full of stressful waiting on Catarina, a magnificent mid-week date with Liam, then French class, appetizer night, with appearances by Liam in between all of that.

Oh, and I went to the gym yesterday in attempt to make the abs Liam claims he saw into actual muscles. That's going to take more than one trip, for sure, but I find

I do want to go biking with him, and I can't remember the last time I rode anything.

I'm not a boat person, or a scooter, bike, or ATV person. I ride and drive in a car, and I can walk around my office. Even as I swing my legs over the side of my bed, I feel muscles in my calves I haven't used very often—until yesterday morning.

"That was a mistake." I groan as I stand up, and I take a moment to lunge a little to try to soften up my sore muscles. After I brush my teeth and run wet hands through my hair, I head back to my room to text Liam.

> Is ten too late for breakfast? Is that more of a brunch time?

> Did you just wake up?

An idea pops into my head as I strip out of my pj's and put on a pair of shorts and a T-shirt.

> Let's do afternoon tea. I'm going to make you one of my grandmother's quick breads.

> I have never been on a tea date.

> Really? That shocks me.

I grin to myself as I abandon my phone and kneel down to dig in my bottom desk drawer. My granny's recipes have gone with me from home to college, back home, to an apartment in Columbia, and then to the Big House. I just know she has a couple of bread recipes with potatoes in them, and I find the green and black binder and pull it out.

With it open on my lap, I flip through the sheet protectors until I find the bread section. Sure enough, there are four potato bread recipes, but one of them is a potato rosemary focaccia, and I don't have the time or skill for that today.

"Potato bread," I say. "Or onion potato bread." I suppose it'll depend on what we have in the kitchen that I'm allowed to use. I know I have spuds; I panic when I get down to four left, because I can eat potatoes for every meal on any given day. And have, several times, thank you very much.

Downstairs, only Lizzie nurses a cup of coffee in the breakfast nook, and she smiles at me as I breeze into the kitchen. "I slept late," I say as if everyone needs to know.

"Probably dreaming of those abs," she says with a grin.

I didn't actually dream at all, but I don't tell her that. When I take a sleeping pill, it's like my mind goes blank. I hardly ever take them, because I've seen what they do to people, and I don't ever want to be too much like my mother.

I get my red hair from her, but it's muted with brown from my daddy. I like to think I'm far more accepting and inviting than either of my parents, and I push them out of my head as I dig through the pantry to find all the baking ingredients I need.

I should tell my mama that I got the interview rescheduled, because she does like hearing about my job. I've heard nothing more about Tanner Bridgestone, and therefore, I've told no one anything more. I haven't said anything to my mother about the opportunity at all. When it becomes a real opportunity, then I might.

"What are you making?" Lizzie asks.

"Potato bread," I say. "Liam and I are going to have afternoon tea together."

"How very proper," she says in an English accent. I grin at her and start putting the dough together. It's not the assembling that takes long with a bread. It's all the waiting. Once I have it resting and rising, I head upstairs to shower.

Climbing those three flights makes me think of Liam again, and I lean against the counter in the bathroom, panting and with screaming calves, as I check my phone. He's texted again, and it says,

> What do I need for this tea party? I don't actually own any tea...

I smile.

> I'll bring everything. Can you provide the venue? Maybe in your glorious orchard or something?

My thumbs have a mind of their own, and they fly across the screen.

> I just put together our snack for this afternoon and came back upstairs to shower. This third-floor bathroom can really make a woman breathless.

It takes him a moment, but he comes back with,

> You've said shower and breathless in the same text. What are you trying to do to me?

I laugh, the sound really more of a giggle.

> What are we having for our afternoon snack? Also, are we in kindergarten again? Who has an afternoon snack?

> I have one every day. And it's one of my granny's potato bread recipes. You won't be disappointed.

> Bread never disappoints, you're right about that.

A moment later, another text from him comes in.

> I can provide the venue. I'll send you a pin.

> I can't just come over and knock on your door?

Nope.

I'm having so much fun texting him, and I had no idea the grouchy, usually silent Liam would have this fun, quick-witted side to him.

I shower; I bake the bread; I go over my notes for the interview in the morning. Before I know it, tea time is at hand, and I pack up the potato bread, a pair of teacups, a couple of bottles of water, and the instant sweet tea packets that you can empty into a water bottle and *voilà*! You have tea.

Or as the French would say, "Voilà Tu as du thé."

Look there—you have tea.

I choose to walk next door to Liam's, which turns out to be a mistake before I even reach the boundary between our two properties. It's hot today, with plenty of humidity, and my hair is sticking to my forehead, my ears, and the back of my neck. I fear the bread is going to be smashed, as I don't have a cute picnic basket or anything to carry our tea in, so I threw everything in a plastic grocery sack.

It swings awkwardly as I walk, and I go all the way to his front porch before I remember he sent me a pin. I mutter-swear under my breath and pull out my phone. The pin directions lead me past his house, a freestanding, three-car garage with the doors all down, and out into the orchards. I glance left and right, wondering if there might be danger out here.

"Like what, Hillary?" I ask myself almost under my

breath. "A rabid scarecrow?" Scarecrows aren't even the right thing. This isn't a cornfield. I also realize my mistake of leaving the venue up to Liam, because he's definitely chosen somewhere outside.

And I'm already sweating buckets. My mood worsens the longer it takes me, and my phone rings before I reach the pin destination.

"I'm coming," I growl into my phone.

"You're late," Liam says, plenty of amusement in his tone. Maybe I'm wrong about him. Or us. Maybe he's the sunshiney one when I thought we were both grumpy grumps.

"I went to the house." The plastic bag loops are starting to wear against my palms. "I think I'm almost there. Tell me there's air conditioning."

"It's sort of breezy today," he says.

My steps turn into stomps, and then I see a flash of red. "I think I see you."

"I see you too. I'm hanging up now." He ends the call, and sure enough, I catch sight of him again. He's wearing a pair of navy shorts and a red tee that seems to cut off the circulation from the bicep up.

He's got a red ballcap on backward, and a grin, and he takes the bag of tea supplies from me without me even handing it to him. "Hey." He scans me down to my flippy, strappy sandals. "Not the best footwear for an outdoor tea party."

"I didn't get the outdoor part of the memo."

"I sent you a pin two hours ago," he says as he lifts the bag to the table he's set up in the shade. It smells like peaches, leaves, and joy out here, and some of my dark mood lightens.

"Oh, we have bread." He lifts it out, his dark eyes seeking mine. "You made this?"

"Yes." Sudden shyness overcomes me, and I sit down and let him set up the afternoon tea.

He smiles as he dumps in the packets and shakes up the bottles, then pours us each a little teacup-full of tea. "This is great." He takes a seat too, then looks at the bread. In the bag. Back to me. "I suppose I'm supposed to cut this with my laser mind?"

I blink, realizing I'm the worst at planning outdoor tea parties. "We can just rip off a chunk."

"Like cavemen?" He seems aghast at this, like eating with his hands is completely unacceptable.

"Please," I say. "You hold saucy wings in your hands and gnaw the meat off the bones. You can rip off a hunk of bread and eat it." I reach for the bread and snatch it out of his reach. "Or don't. I don't care. It just leaves more for me."

He chuckles and after I've torn off the end of the bread, he takes a chunk too. His face lights up with the first bite, and he says, "This is really good."

"I don't appreciate the tone of surprise."

"Come on," he says. "I didn't have a tone of surprise."

Maybe he didn't, but I don't concede the point. He's

male hotness in a red T-shirt and a ballcap, eating the bread I made like he's actually enjoying it. I enjoy sitting with him far more than I anticipated, a fact I'd felt a few times on Tuesday too. I'm not sure what it means, or why I keep getting reminded that I actually like Liam.

"So," he says between bites. "I just have to ask. What made you want to go out on Tuesday night?"

I laugh-wave and say, "It was an accident, actually. See I was texting this other guy, and I..." My voice fades to nothing at the same time Liam's eyebrows get higher and higher and higher.

He polishes off the last bite of his bread and dusts his hands together, assumingly to dislodge any errant crumbs. "You were texting another guy," he says, and it's a statement of fact. No question mark in sight.

"Uh, no. I mean, yes. But—" I don't know what to say, and a truckload of guilt crashes into my lungs.

"Did you—why did you go out with me then?" He leans back in his chair. "Ah. That's why you didn't wear the little black dress. It wasn't for me. It was for him."

"No," I say, but he's not wrong.

He folds his arms, and he should have a license to do that. The action makes his muscles bulge, and my mind goes a little blank just looking at him. Totally not fair, and thus, a license should be required.

"And you went out with me, because...? You didn't want to pay full price for the roof? What?"

"You hadn't even quoted me on the roof yet," I say.

"But you knew I'd give you a good deal." His eyes blaze with something that isn't quite anger, and isn't quite hurt. It's a horrible combination of the two, and I hate it with everything inside me.

He picks up his teacup, looks at the amber liquid inside, and tosses it to the ground. "I have work to do." He stands, sets down the teacup, and walks away. Just like that. One foot after the other, moving further and further from me.

"Liam." I twist to watch, sure he's going to come back. He does not. "Liam!"

"I'll be on the roof at dawn," he calls over his shoulder. "Gotta get that pipe tarred up before it rains this week."

He leaves me sitting in the middle of his orchards. Legit leaves me there to pack up my sad, ripped up loaf of bread and the tea-that's-not-really-tea. And here I thought we'd hammer out our schedules for the week to find a time —or times—we can see each other again.

Now, he's going to be hammering on the roof bright and early.

"What a mess," I sigh-say. I look up into the leaves and branches, getting only a hint of the blue sky beyond. "Why did I say that?"

And the better question is: Why *did* I go out with Liam when I'd sent him that text meant for someone else?

CHAPTER FOURTEEN

LIAM

"I can't believe this," I hiss to my peach trees. They say nothing back, but the universe is filled with my own foolishness. It streams through the space around me, and I think of the way Hillary's face lit up, that special smile she had—and none of it was for me.

Some other guy. She's been texting *someone else*, and her Tuesday night little-black-dress-date-night was for *him*.

I yell into the sky, every defense, every wall, every foul thought about women I've ever thunk right there in my head.

"Liam," I hear her call behind me, but I have much longer legs that her. I know where I am on my own property. And I have strong locks to keep redheaded beauties out of my house.

I thump the garage door where my vehicle projects

wait for my spare time, and stomp into my farmhouse through the back door. I have a security system that I traded for, and with one touch of a button on the app, I can lock every door and activate every window alarm.

I do that, thinking I might be taking things a bit to the extreme. A five-foot-five-inch woman is not going to come barging into my house, a gun blazing. Still, I feel like I'm in the same amount of danger, and I pace along the length of my island.

It's mid-afternoon on a Sunday. My whole day and evening lay in front of me, and I actually thought I'd be spending the time with Hillary. "Stupid," I mutter to myself. It's times like these that I wish I had Tabitha here with me. Then at least I wouldn't be talking to myself.

My stomach growls, and I take that as a sign to get the heck out of my house. Hillary isn't the type to back down from a challenge, and I need some space and time to get some clarity. I snatch my keys from the hook by the back door, and I leave the farmhouse.

I'm not moving as fast as I was before, because Danger in the Form of Hillary Mays can come around the corner at any moment. I don't see her in the back yard, or along the sidewalk that runs to my detached garage.

After managing to slip inside undetected, I start my SUV, open the garage door, and leave the property—all without a Hillary sighting.

My lungs finally remember how to breathe, and I steadfastly refuse to look at the Big House as I go by it. I can't stop my thoughts from running wild, and I keep wondering if she's still out in the orchard, ripping off hunks of her potato bread and sipping her tea from that ridiculously flowered teacup.

Longing streams through me, and that only adds fuel to my already raging irritation. I shouldn't be longing to be out in the orchard with a woman who didn't want to go out with me.

"Then why did she go out with you?" I wonder aloud. She didn't even put up a fight. She didn't try to get out of it. Nothing. Did she?

Maybe I'm insane. Maybe I missed all the signs of her rejection.

Yanking the wheel to the side, I pull off the road a little faster than I should. I don't care, and the vehicle comes to a stop a mere breath before I put it in park. My phone will tell me the truth.

I scroll back up, because we've been texting a lot this week. Tons and tons of messages—flirty ones too. Would she do that with someone she didn't want to go out with?

I finally reach the text about the little black dress, and I slow down to really go over every message.

I've said:

> I had some time this morning to go over your bid. I'm sending you a link to it via email. It'll lay everything out for you. Since we're neighbors, and I've known Tahlia for a while, I'll take 50% off the labor costs.

An emoji, huh? I didn't peg you for that type of texter.

What kind of texter do you think I am? Follow-up question: There are types of texters?

You're the proper kind. You use capital letters and punctuation. You spell out every word, so yeah. The emojis seem a little out of character for your texter type.

That smiley face emoji. I actually hate myself for sending it in this moment, but it is what it is. I guess we all send texts we don't mean to sometimes.

You've got your Teen Texters. You know the type, Hillary. The ones who use ur for your and can't capitalize for some reason, even though it's literally an autocorrect thing on your phone.

Hey, if you're not busy tonight, I'd love to get together. I have a little black dress that's been gathering dust in the back of my closet, and she needs a night out on the town to celebrate something. What do you think?

What time should I pick you up?

Is seven too late?

Seven is not too late. I'll see you then.

I let my phone fall to my lap. What am I supposed to think? Yeah, the invitation for a night out with her in a little black dress came out of left field, but so what? I'm supposed to somehow know that she meant that for someone else?

"She changes subjects rapidly," I say. "I learned that on our first date, and in all of our texting convos since."

My phone rings, and Hillary's name sits there. My heartbeat thumps and bumps, and while I want to talk to her, I really don't at the same time. I let the phone ring too long, and the call goes to voicemail.

She obviously doesn't leave a message, because my phone is only silent for four seconds before she's calling again.

"Okay, so she's going to be a pain in the butt." I stab at my phone to answer the call, and I put her on speakerphone. "What?"

"You're not home."

"Nope. Do you want a medal for figuring that out?"

She sighs, and I pull back on the rudeness. Still, she's the one who has explaining to do. *Then let her do it.*

I hate that thought, but I'm right. I take in a long breath through my nose and slowly exhale it. "I needed some ice cream," I say. "If you have something to tell me, I could meet you back at my place in like, I don't know, thirty minutes."

"Okay," she says quietly, and I hate that I've upset her. At the same time, she owes me an explanation, and after I end the call, I ease my car back onto the road and continue toward my new goal—the grocery store.

Twenty-eight minutes later, I pull into my garage and close the door behind me. I gather the two pints of ice cream I've bought, along with the two bags of cookies, and exit through the side door.

Hillary's sitting on my back deck, her knees almost all the way to her chest, and her head resting in one hand as she spots me. She lifts her head, almost the way a golden retriever would if their master asked them, "Do you want to go to the park?"

She's perked up now, but she doesn't get to her feet. I've got ice cream melting in the bag I carry, so I can't stand here frozen in the doorway of the garage for long. I force myself to take the first step, and by the time I've gone three or four strides, Hillary is on her feet.

She's wearing a pair of tight black shorts and a V-neck tee with ruffles along the sleeves in bright purple. It plays well with her hair, and I wish I could rewind time an hour and ask her a different question as we sit down for afternoon tea.

"I have cookies and ice cream," I say when we're only ten or fifteen feet apart.

"I went out with you because I wanted to," she says. Her chin lifts a good three inches. Maybe more. "Yes, I was texting someone else too. Yes, I was asking him out.

But I didn't get the message in the right string. It went to you. Yes, I was mortified. I was going to tell you I meant it for someone else, but you were..."

She pauses there, but I have to hear what comes next. Maybe *I'm* the golden retriever too eager to go to the park. She texts about a little black dress and a date, and I'm like, salivating over myself, panting *yes-what-time-should-I-pick-you-up*, and jumping to obey her every command.

"You were sweet," she says, and I don't expect that word to come out of her mouth. "You wanted to go, and I found that...interesting. I had no idea what you saw in me that you liked, because I hadn't been very nice to you."

"You really weren't," I say.

"And, I don't know. I figured we'd go out once, and I'd deem you too grumpy for me, and that would be that. No harm, no foul."

"You're grumpier than I am."

She sends a soft smile across her face, where it just brushes along but doesn't truly stay. "And yet, I wasn't the one who ran from the orchard and then left his house to get ice cream."

"I didn't run," I say, rolling my eyes.

"You didn't saunter," she throws back at me.

"You told me you meant to ask out someone else!" I shake my head. "What would have done, huh, Hillary?" I start toward her again, because while my back yard is shaded, it's still blazing hot outside. I brush by her, glaring all the way, only freezing when her hand latches onto mine.

I'm already past her, mostly, but I turn slightly. Our bodies make a T, with mine being the long part that reaches down to touch the bottom line on a piece of paper. I'm not looking at her eyes, but I can still feel the weight of them.

"Maybe you should've asked me out," she says.

I scoff. "Maybe I was still feeling out the situation between us." I do look up at her then. "I thought you were just a little ahead of me. That you must've been feeling the same spark I had, and were just—just—ready sooner to act on it."

"You have an answer for everything, don't you?"

"Yes," I say almost over the top of her. "Like you don't."

"You irritate me."

"Join the club." My eyes drop to her lips, and oh, that's a mistake. I try to pull them back up, but they feel like they've been hooked with sinkers and thrown into the lake to catch bottom feeders. When I finally manage it, Hillary is looking at my mouth.

Oh, boy.

Do I wait for her to initiate this too? Will she even allow me to kiss her?

"Sometimes I'm only annoyed for a second," I say.

"Same." Her eyes meet mine, and I don't give anything a second thought. I drop the ice cream and cookies to the sidewalk and take this gorgeous redhead into my arms. It's been a while since I've kissed a woman, and the gasp of surprise that flies from her mouth almost stops me.

But I've got momentum on my side, and I press my lips to hers at the same time my eyes drift closed. I've wanted to taste this mouth since the moment she came barreling across the lawn at the Big House to chew me out, and since she barely wears lipstick or lip gloss, I feel like I'm getting the pure essence of Hillary Mays.

All the heat in the atmosphere fires between us, filling my veins with lava and then fireworks. She kisses me back, and it almost feels like a wrestling match for a moment. Then she gives in, lets me set the pace, and I kiss her like I've never kissed anyone before.

Because she is unlike anyone I've ever been out with before, and all I can do is pray this smooths over the speed bump we've just hit. Oh, and that she won't punch me when she realizes what's happening.

CHAPTER FIFTEEN

HILLARY

Kissing Liam is like the happiest, most sensual, best thing that's ever happened to me. My vision is colored with rainbows, and the air smells like chocolate. His arms around me will shield me from anything bad in the world, and his mouth... Oh, that mouth.

From what he says to the things he can do with it, I'm in love with his mouth.

He finally pulls away, his breath a bit ragged, and I pull in the biggest breath of my life. I need oxygen to reason through the past hour.

I open my eyes and find him gazing at me. He says nothing, and part of me wants to push him away, push this moment away. For I can't be here again.

Panic builds beneath my breastbone, and I breathe through it. Once, then twice. I grab onto Liam's collar and study the ribbing there.

"Hey," he finally says, and his voice is soft and careful. One of his hands is on my lower back, the pressure steady and strong. The other rests on my outer right bicep, and he moves that one to push the hair out of my face. "Not a good kiss?"

"No." I whisper-shake my head. "It was great." I look up at him, needing him to understand. "It's...me, Liam."

"What about you?"

"I...I've been engaged twice, right?"

"Mm." He backs up and bends to pick up the dropped groceries. "Let's go inside, okay?" He doesn't wait for me to agree; he just turns and goes up the few steps to the beautiful back deck I admired while he was off shopping. I follow him, cross the deck, and enter his house.

He closes the door behind me gently, but I still jump at the very final clicking sound. The sound of locking me in this house with him. The feeling of being trapped overwhelms me, and I'm not sure why. I'm not engaged to this guy. I can leave any time I want.

I keep telling myself that as he unpacks the two pints of ice cream he bought, along with a package of Chips Ahoy cookies and one of mint Oreos. "I wasn't sure what you liked," he says as he rips back the top of the Oreo package. "But I got mint chocolate chip and peanut butter fudge tracks." He glances over to me, but he doesn't let his gaze stick. "I figured since you like peanut butter cookies, it might be a universal dessert flavor."

"I'd like that one, yes," I say.

"So not a mint fan?"

"I think you are." The Oreos plus the ice cream is a dead giveaway.

"I like it all," he says easily, like he didn't just give me the best kiss of my life a minute ago. Like nothing out of the ordinary has happened today at all. He opens a drawer in the island and gets out two spoons and with one, he points across the island. "You can sit. I'm not going to bite you."

Yet, hangs in the air between us, but neither of us say it. It's probably only my deranged fantasies thinking it.

I round the island and pull out a barstool, finally noticing my surroundings. Liam's kitchen is beautiful, with dark wood cabinets that reach all the way to the ceiling. Some of them have glass doors, with bright blue dishes behind them. His appliances shine with silver, and he's got a bowl of green apples in the middle of the island, almost like he's staging this place to sell it.

It feels used and lived in, while being clean and functional too. There is no art on the walls, no wooden sayings. Just a pot rack that hangs above the island, where his gas stovetop is too. If I had to guess if a man or a woman lived here, I'd guess a man, and one look at Liam tells me I'm right.

He's pure male, and a lot of it. My lips tingle with the memory of kissing him, and I reach for the spoon so I won't reach to touch my mouth. He comes to sit beside me, but he doesn't get too close.

"So, you've been engaged twice," he says.

"Yes." I peel back the top of the ice cream, and it's started to melt around the edges. Perfect. It's vanilla ice cream, with fudge swirls, and little football-shaped chocolate tokens that are filled with peanut butter. It's joy in a two-cup container.

I take a bite, which gives me courage to keep talking. That's one thing I realized in the few minutes I sat out in the orchard alone: if I don't want to lose Liam, I have to tell him what I'm thinking.

And funnily enough, I don't want to lose Liam.

I look over to him. "I wasn't good at listening to my gut when I was younger. That was a hard lesson to learn, because I found myself hanging out with the wrong people, for the wrong reasons. Or listening to someone, just because I thought I should."

He nods, but otherwise gives me the space to keep talking. I fish out another peanut-butter filled chocolate and eat it. It's almost frozen inside, and I let it melt with the ice cream around it before chewing.

"I said yes to both proposals, when I knew—I *knew*—I didn't want to marry my boyfriend at the time. I knew I wouldn't be happy long-term, and I don't know. I've had to really be honest with myself and figure out what I want."

"Okay," he says slowly.

"So when I realized I'd texted you instead of—instead of this other guy I'd been messaging, yeah, I panicked. I almost backed out. But then...the date was fun, Liam. Tell me you didn't have fun."

"It was fun," he whisper-admits.

"I did find you slightly less acidic." I bump him playfully with my shoulder. "You did change my mind about you, and yeah, I can admit I'm attracted to you, and I can't even remember that other guy's name right now."

He scoffs and gives me a dark glare. "You can too."

"Fine," I say. "I can, but I don't want to go out with him. I stopped messaging him days ago."

"Did you?"

"Yes." I pull my phone out of my pocket. "You can check my phone if you want."

"I don't need to do that." He looks fully at me. "I'm learning how to trust women, and I figure I might as well start with you."

I nod my gratitude, hoping he understands my Hillary-Non-Speak. "For a while there—maybe until this afternoon, actually—I didn't think love was in the cards for me. The white picket fence? The husband who gets up and goes to work, mows the lawn, brings me meds when I have a headache..."

I shake my head, because my thoughts are coming out uncensored, and that's never good. "It hasn't been on my radar for a while."

"And now?"

I shrug and take another bite of ice cream. "It's early stages still, but I feel like I've been in a cocoon for a few years, and it might be time to spread my wings and try flying again."

He reaches over and takes my hand in his. "I feel the same way."

"You do?"

He nods. "I've felt like a failure since my daddy died. Dropping out of college, it...it broke me somehow. I didn't even realize it until later, and yeah. I struggle with self-doubt. Some insecurity."

"You?" I almost laugh but quickly cut it off. "Liam Graff, if there's anything you shouldn't be, it's insecure."

He gives me a closed-mouth smile and then pulls his hand back so he can spoon some mint chocolate chip ice cream onto a Chips Ahoy. He eats it as an open-faced ice cream sandwich, and maybe, just maybe, I fall in love with him a little bit right there in his kitchen.

After he chews and swallows, he asks, "Why not?"

"Because you're incredibly good-looking," I say without censoring. I'm in so much trouble. "And smart. And strong. And handy." I cut a look over to him. "You own your own house, your own company. You spend time with your momma. You do work for others when they ask and give half-off on the labor. Heck, you probably win mountain bike championships I don't know about and kiss babies when they're born just for good luck."

He bursts out laughing, and that's such a glorious sound that I allow myself to smile too. I take one of his cookies and dip it in my melted ice cream. I don't normally like soggy cookies, but the cream has barely started to sink in before I pop the whole thing into my mouth.

"I'm just saying that I think you're great," I say. "More than enough for any lucky woman out there—myself included."

"Looks who's being insecure for no reason now."

I lift one shoulder in a slight shrug. "Well, there are the two failed engagements... They mess with my mind sometimes." I can't look at him when I ask-add, "Does it bother you that I've been engaged twice?"

"Yes, and no," he says.

That gets me to swing my head toward him, my eyes widening in unexpected surprise. "Yes? And no?"

"It bothers me that those other guys didn't know who they had," he says, real quiet-like. Almost like he doesn't want to say anything too loud. "It bothers me that you think not marrying someone you don't love is a bad thing. Otherwise." He makes himself another open-faced ice cream sandwich but holds it in his hand as he looks at me. "No, it doesn't bother me."

It's true that I haven't allowed myself to think past life in the Big House, with five roommates, all of us chasing our dreams. But now, sitting in Liam's house, with him, my thoughts expand in ways I haven't allowed them to before.

I see myself married, with a family, and all of us forging our way toward our own definition of success.

"I bet if you hadn't dropped out," I say. "You'd have more regrets than you do now."

"Probably," he says. "Just like you'd regret marrying either of those other guys."

"Totally." I smile at him, and he grins back at me. My throat closes, and that means I still have something hard to say. "I really am sorry," I choke-say. "I don't want to go out with Stupid Karl." I lean closer to him, and he reaches over and grabs my barstool and pulls me flush against him. "I want to go out with you."

"Mm," he says. "I guess that's okay with me."

I smile to my pint of ice cream, then dunk another cookie into the melted bits and eat it. "My interview is tomorrow."

"You're going to crush it."

I like his confidence, and I want to swim around in his support. "Maybe we can get together for lunch afterward," I say. "I'll be hopped up and talking a mile a minute, but you should probably get to see that side of me before you decide if you want to keep seeing me."

He chuckles as he reaches over with his spoon and takes a scoop of my peanut butter delight. "You can't scare me away with a little hopped-up excitement over a big interview."

"What does scare you away?" I ask.

He lets several seconds of silence go by, and then he asks, "Can I get back to you on that?"

I don't press the issue, and instead, we finish our afternoon treat in companionable silence, side-by-side, and then I ask him to go over my interview questions with me.

The best part of the afternoon is that he agrees, and he doesn't seem put out by my work or my desire to want to be good at making documentaries.

He's charming and sweet, and yes, by the time I leave his house, darkness has fallen, and he's kissed me a few more times. In fact, I stumble-step along the side of the road that leads back to the Big House, the tips of a few fingers touching my lips—where he's just kissed me goodnight.

I definitely can't remember my own name at this point, and I certainly don't know who I was messaging on Matchmakers before Liam took me to the bowling alley on Tuesday night.

————

I'M WEARING the shiniest pair of black heels in the world when I arrive at Silver Linings, the assisted living facility where Catarina Morgan lives. My pencil skirt is straight and tight, and I borrowed Lizzie's brand-new designer blouse. It's light blue, with sailboats all over it. I'm not usually into nautical ware, but Lizzie says it brings out the dark red in my hair and the flecks of blue in my eyes.

I've put a wave in my hair, and I wear way more makeup than normal as I step up to the reception desk. "Good morning," I say pleasantly as I reach for the pen to write my name on the check-in sheet. "I'm here for—"

"You must be Hillary Mays," a man says, his voice made of gold and silk.

I turn toward him, knowing instantly I'm looking at Kevin, Catarina's son. He's wearing a designer suit at nine a.m. on a Monday, and I need to pull my A-game out of a hat.

I straighten and take a couple of steps toward him. "I am. Good morning, Mister Morgan." I grin at him and extend my hand. "I'm Hillary Mays." I clutch my over-sized briefcase, which carries my notebook with my approved topics and questions.

"Wonderful to meet you in person." His words almost ooze from him, and after he shakes my hand, he takes me through the door to the right of reception. I haven't signed in, but the secretary doesn't call me back.

Kevin may have a lot of money and good taste in clothing, but he is no small talk aficionado. He simply walks along the sidewalks, with their trimmed bushes and perfectly tended-to flower beds. The sun shines, and the air is clear. My stomach boils, the only indicator that something might not be one-hundred-percent right here.

I clutch my bag and watch every step, because I don't wear heels every day. Or even every week.

Kevin doesn't take me to one of the resident's residences, but instead to a clubhouse. He holds the door for me, his smile plastic around the edges. I see it now when I didn't before, and oh, he doesn't want me here. I flash him a bright smile, hoping that will ease his concerns.

I haven't done a ton of interviewing, to be sure. But Kevin doesn't know that, and I stitch on my Confident Skin as I step past him.

Inside, there's a group of men and women seated around a table, playing cards. I think of my parents, and they would never do this. Mama's bridge nights come with champagne and lightly playing classical music.

In fact, she's even told me to make sure I don't allow anyone to put her "in a place like this." She and Daddy still have full-time, live-in help. It's just one person, but Roderick does all the cooking, shopping, and cleaning around the estate. If Daddy dies first and leaves Mama behind, Rod will be right there to take care of everything.

I push my parents out of my head and smile at the circle of older people playing cards. Then I follow Kevin into a conference room that has all of the blinds drawn. He waits inside the room this time, and pushes the door closed behind me.

There's hardly any light in here—only what's coming through the windows behind a seated woman on the side of the oval table. Because of that, it's hard to see her face, but I keep a smile on mine.

"Mother," Kevin says smoothly, but his voice reminds me of fish oil now instead of silk. "This is Hillary Mays."

"It's so amazing to finally meet you," I say as I go around the end of the table. The chairs are oversized and rolling, and I can just see myself skidding and slipping and falling right out of one of them.

Catarina stands and I swipe my lips across her papery cheek a moment later. I take both of her hands and kiss her other cheek, and then she's gripping my fingers so hard I can't pull them back. "It's lovely to meet you too, dear." She wears dark red lipstick—at least it looks dark from my perspective and with the limited light.

She can't weigh more than a hundred pounds, but she's remarkably strong. She glances past me to her son. "Thank you, Kevin." It's a clear dismissal, but Kevin doesn't immediately bow his head and duck out of the room.

"Mother—"

"I'm fine," she says over him. "We promised Hillary an hour, and you can come and collect me at ten o'clock." She nods, and this time, Kevin does leave the room.

I twist to look over my shoulder at him, and I catch the look of distaste on his face. Suddenly, I know who the problem is, and it's not Catarina. It's not that she may have been ill last week. It's Kevin, and his issues with letting me speak to his mother.

Once he's gone, I say, "It's a bit dark in here, don't you think? Do you want it that way, or can I turn on the lights?"

"The lights will be fine," she says as she re-settles into her chair. It doesn't buck and spit her back out, and I move over to turn on the lights with a bit of hope running through me. When I face Catarina again, I realize what power I hold.

I know exactly who she is. I know exactly the life she's led.

I was raised by a woman almost identical to her, and I know how to get past my Southern Socialite mother's defenses to find out what's really going on behind the scenes. Now I just have to do the same with this mega-millionaire...who may have been involved in one of the biggest financial scandals in South Carolina's history.

CHAPTER SIXTEEN

LIAM

"IT WAS INCREDIBLE," HILLARY TELLS ME AS THE SUN sets behind her. She dunks a fried piece of cheese in a mixture of mayo and ketchup. She lights the whole restaurant, and all I can do is bask in her glow. "She told me everything, and I can't wait to go through the tape, write it all out, put the pieces together."

She grins and pops the sauced cheese into her mouth.

"That's so great," I say. "Sorry I couldn't make lunch work."

"It's fine." She waves her hand. "If you have an opportunity, I can wait."

I reach across the table and cover her hand with mine. "What did your boss say?"

"Mm." She reaches for her napkin, the words almost bursting from her before she can get them out. "She's thrilled. Just thrilled, Liam. She's going to help me go through everything and put together the parts we'll recommend for filming, that kind of thing."

I really have no idea what her job looks like, but a lot of people don't get my work either. "So what'll you do next?" I ask, wanting to feast on her energy for the rest of the night. She's like a beautiful phoenix who's risen from the ashes, grown a glorious set of wings, and is just now ready to flap them.

And I get to watch.

"I'll spend time in the tapes," she says. "And the facts we've put together from other sources." She dunks another piece of cheese, then looks up as our waitress arrives with our food. Our conversation pauses while we get our soups, salads, and sandwiches put in front of us.

Tonight's date is sponsored by Stella, who I called after work to ask how I could be the best support for Hillary. Stella has a good career too, and it's important to her. Mine is to me too, but I just needed another POV so I can be the best boyfriend, so I can be the man Hillary deserves.

Her words from our yesterday afternoon ice cream binge still run through my head. *I bet if you hadn't dropped out, you'd have more regrets than you do now.*

I would, and I know it. My momma needed me. Stella and Becca needed me, and while I still have dreams of being an architect, I also feel more at peace with the career I have. I did have a chance today to meet with another general contractor during my lunch hour, but I've held onto how the meeting went and what Nathan Knight wanted.

"And we'll write a script," she says. "We'll go through everything, and we'll make recommendations for the length of the documentary, put together all the contact information, type up the quotes." She's stirring her ranch dressing into her salad now, and when her eyes come back to mine, she says, "What about you? What did you and Nathan Knight talk about?"

I look down at my Rueben sandwich, which has been cut in half and makes my mouth water. About like the woman across the table from me. "Uh, he's putting together a proposal for a forty-four-unit condo and town-home complex over in Riverside Downs. He can't manage it all himself, and he wants to know if I can come on with him."

"Liam." Hillary gasps out my name so hard I look over to her to make sure she hasn't choked on a mushroom. Those fungi. They'll get you one way or another.

But she hasn't choked. She's blinking at me with big, round eyes. "That's amazing."

"I don't know," I say. "I've never done a huge build like that."

"But...you can, right?" The size of her eyes normalizes, and her pretty hair bounces from the high ponytail she's put it in.

"I don't know," I say. "I'm the handyman next door, you know? I do kitchen remodels and deck builds. I fix roofs and tear out flooring and put down new stuff. I don't typically have to work with a whole hosts of subcontractors, though I suppose I do know several, yeah."

She finishes her bite of salad and wipes her mouth with her napkin. "So this'll be a stretch for you. Something new."

"Yeah." I don't want to talk about work anymore for some reason. "So, what are you doing this weekend?"

"Well, my amazing new boyfriend is going to wait until nine to mow the lawn on Saturday, so that's my sleep-in day." She smiles at me with stars and glitter in her eyes, and I want to give her the world. "Sunday...I don't know."

"What about going mountain biking with me?" I ask. "We can go Saturday or Sunday."

"Really?" she ask-teases. "Your momma isn't going to demand to see you again?"

I duck my head, though I'm only wearing a baseball hat tonight. "I think she'll survive."

"Well, I don't have a bike."

"I have several," I say.

"Of course you do." She tucks her hair and gives me a mock glare. "I don't have a helmet."

"Again, I got you covered."

"And...what about the body-suit?" She really hits the T on the word suit, and for some reason, I feel like I'm standing in front of her in my clingy Spandex.

"You're going to have to provide that yourself," I say. "I don't have any extras of those."

"Yeah, and the crotch would probably hit my knees."

I burst out laughing, because she's not wrong. She grins, and then her phone rings. She's still smiling as she pulls it out of her purse, which sits on the chair beside her. I see the moment her grin drops, and she holds up one finger, and I sober too.

"It's my mom."

"Get it," I say, because Hillary has said a few things about her parents, and none of them have been all that complimentary.

"I can talk to her later."

"No, go on." I say, waving to her. "I'm going to stuff my face with this corned beef, and I won't listen in."

She cocks her head, and the phone continues to ring, and I pick up my sandwich. "If I don't answer it, she'll just call me back."

"Oh, you mean how you did to me yesterday?"

Her mouth fishes open and closed, and I love it when I say something she doesn't have an instant comeback to. I grin and chin-nod to her phone. "Oh, too bad. You've poked the bear."

"Maybe she won't—" She cuts off as her phone rings again. She sighs loud enough for me to hear it above the ringing of her phone, and she swipes on the call and lifts it to her ear. "Hey, Mama."

Her voice is perky and bright, and I notice how easily

she can fake being happy to hear from her mom. Maybe she is. For all I know, she just doesn't want to interrupt our date to talk to her mom. Maybe they have a better relationship than I've assumed.

"No, I remember," Hillary says, and the falseness in her voice will likely be heard in California. I raise my eyebrows, but Hillary drops her eyes and shakes her head. "I'll be there, Mom."

A few more seconds go by, and I can hear tinny talking coming through Hillary's phone. Her head stays down, and she runs one hand through her ponytail over and over. "Yes, Mom. I said I'd be there."

She twists toward the restaurant, but I still hear her say, "I'm not going to repeat it to you. I'm thirty years old." A mighty sigh comes out of her mouth, and she lifts her head as she rolls her eyes. Ah, there's the sassy redhead I know. "Fine. Friday night. Seven-thirty."

She meets my eyes and gives me a ghostly face, like she's going to die if this conversation continues for much longer. I chuckle and mime for her to give me the phone.

Horror enters her expression and shrinks back in her chair. "No," she says next, quite loudly too. "No, Mama. I'm not staying for the weekend. I—can't."

She shakes her head, her eyes begging me for help now. But she won't give me the phone, and I'm not going to lunge across the table and take it from her. "I'm busy," she says. "I'm going mountain biking with my boyfriend..."

She really drags out that word, her pretty eyes rounding again.

Mine do too, and I point to myself. "Is that me? Am I your boyfriend?"

She picks up a piece of fried cheese and tosses it at me. "Yes, Mama. No, you can't meet him this weekend. It's new, and I haven't even introduced him to my friends." She instantly presses her eyes closed as her shoulders sink down. "No, Mama. Of course you're more important than my friends."

I finish half of my Rueben, and Hillary's practically got steam coming out of her eyeballs. "You know what? I have to go. No, really, I have to. There's a fire in the house, and I have to get out." She hangs up and tosses her phone on the table. It slides toward me, but neither of us make a move to stop it or pick it up.

She stuffs another bite of salad in her mouth, and I'm not sure if this is serious or if I can tease her. "I'm actually surprised she's not calling again."

"She won't now."

"You told her there was a fire in the house and you have to get out."

She looks up, and I grin at her. "A *fire* in the *house?*" I lean back in my seat and fold my arms. "And she won't call again?" I laugh right out loud. "What other excuses have you given her to get off the phone?"

"I don't know," she mutters.

"Oh, come on," I say. "Have you, I don't know, cut off

your finger? Found a serial killer in your closet? Oh, I know." I grin and grin at her. "You've just gotten arrested, and the cops are taking your phone."

"Stop it," she says crossly.

"Just give me one excuse."

She sighs at me the same way she did her mama. "I may or may not have told her once that the lifeguards were clearing the beach because of a recent shark attack."

I laugh again, because only Hillary would go to sharks to get off the phone with her mom. She finally relinquishes her sassy mood and giggles with me. She hasn't touched her sandwich or soup yet, and she makes no move to do so now.

"Liam," she says. "Uh, this might be totally off the wall, and it's totally fine if you can't. Or you don't want to. Or this is just totally insane."

I reach for my cola and take a sip. "I can't wait to hear this."

She rolls her eyes at me, and I have to admit, it's not as cute when the gesture is aimed at me. "Forget it."

"No, say it."

She switches out her fork for a spoon and stirs her soup, all of her attention there. Then those hazel eyes lift to mine. "My parents live in Columbia."

"Okay."

"Where are we going to go mountain biking this weekend?"

All the dots line up, and I see a road trip in my future.

A road trip with Hillary. "Columbia," I say slowly. We study each other for a few seconds. "You're thinking an overnighter?"

"What? Absolutely not," she says. "I'm thinking a road trip."

"With a stay overnight," I say. "I mean, what? You're... I don't really know what you're thinking. Why don't you just tell me?"

"I swear," she mutters. "You and me in Columbia. We're gonna be there this weekend anyway, and it's a long drive. Why don't—could you—?" She exhales like this is obvious, but I'm not going to jump in again.

"What's this weekend?" I ask.

"My dad's sixty-fifth birthday party," she moan-says. "I obviously can't miss it."

"And it's on Friday," I say. "So you want me to..."

"Come with me," she blurts out. "I want you to come to my dad's birthday party with me, so I don't have to deal with my ex-fiancé *and* my mother on the same night."

I have no idea what to say, because she literally just said it was too soon for me to meet her mama. And now she wants me to go on a weekend trip with her to do just that.

Wow, Hillary moves even faster than me, and I'm not sure if I should be impressed or scared. Right now, I go for silent, because there's a storm brewing in her redheaded head, and I can't wait to see what she says next.

CHAPTER SEVENTEEN

HILLARY

"It's just that Charlie will be there, and among all the other terrible things my mom said, one of them was that he'd be there, and she insinuated that we could get back together."

Liam simply stares at me from across the table, and frankly, I feel the same way. A little blank and a little bit like I've been hit with a hot frying pan.

Overnighter rings in my ears, and I'm not super enthused by the fact that Liam hasn't immediately agreed to go to my dad's birthday party with me.

"And we can go mountain biking on Saturday," I say. "That would leave Sunday with your momma, and you won't even have to make an excuse."

"Well, now that I have the shark one and the house fire, I think I'm good for a while."

I roll my eyes, but that's only the surface of the excuses

I've used over the years to get off the phone with my mother. "We don't all have Southern mommas who make —make—make *jambalaya* and insist we come over for Sunday dinner with the sibs."

Liam's smile slips. "You don't have siblings."

"So I have a heavy load to carry," I say. "Are you going to make me beg?"

"I'm going to make you explain what exactly the schedule will be like this weekend." He leans forward, those dark eyes hooked so deeply into mine, I could close mine and still see him. "And, I'm going to need you to define what we are." He gestures between the two of us. "Me and you. You said the word *boyfriend*."

I lean forward too, not about to give him the advantage. "Yeah, because you've been kissing me for a full day. Do you think I go around kissing all the men I know?"

"I hope not," he says, those eyes turning even darker. "Because then I'll have to find those guys and punch their faces in."

I laugh and shake my head. "You're not the violent type."

"What type am I?"

"We're so far off the rails," I say, though I normally love our back-and-forth and how derailed we get. "Listen, I'd love for my *boyfriend* to accompany me to my dad's birthday party, though I know that's really early for us in our brand-new relationship. But I really don't—" My throat closes at the mere thought of coming face-to-face with Charlie Vaughn again after almost four years.

"I don't want to go alone," I say bravely.

"Then I'll go with you," he says. "And you'll stay with your parents, and I'll find a hotel, and we can go biking on Saturday. Is that the agenda?" He says nothing of what this trip will cost him, but I know he doesn't have much extra money. He's told me about his excitement for every consultation he gets, and I know he's always looking for his next job.

"I—you won't need to get a hotel. My parents' house is enormous. There are probably eight guest bedrooms there."

"So I was right."

I glare at him. "It's a road trip."

"With an overnighter at *your parents'*." His eyebrows go up. "That's way more than even I said."

He's right, and I don't really have a leg to stand on. "Please?" I try.

"Are you going to introduce me as your boyfriend?"

"Yes."

"So I can call you my girlfriend." He's not asking, and he so cute, I only pretend to be annoyed with him.

"Yes."

"And we'll leave after work on Friday?"

"Yes."

"I just need a bag for one night?"

"And clothes for a fancy birthday party," I admit. "At my parents', that means a jacket, Liam. Bare minimum."

"I'll bring all the mountain biking gear," he says without missing a beat. "Minus your riding bodysuit. You'll need to pack your own biking attire, but I can take you shopping if you want." That teasing glint comes back into his eyes, and I can't help sliding a little bit on the slippery slope of falling in love.

I've been here before, and I tell myself to find a foothold and dig in. I can't fall for another handsome man too quickly. I simply can't, because I'll never recover from a third failed engagement.

"I can find my own biking clothes," I say.

"Then I'll pack the bikes."

"I'll buy us lunch on Saturday for our ride."

"I'll pay for the gas to Columbia."

Our eyes meet again, and this time Liam reaches over and takes my hands in his. "An overnight road trip with my girlfriend to her parents' house. Are you going to provide the gift for your father?"

I moan and roll my neck and my eyes at the same time, numerous potatoey swears coming to mind. "Crispy tater tots," slips out. "I need a gift for my father." I sigh and look at Liam. "What are you doing tomorrow night? Want to go shopping for a wealthy guy who buys everything he wants?"

Liam grins and squeezes my hand. "Sounds like the best Tuesday night of my life."

I lean forward, and Liam meets me halfway, his mouth absolutely delicious against mine. I so enjoy kissing him, and I love the way his hand slides up the column of my neck and curls warmly around to the base of my skull.

It feels like he's claiming me, like he's falling for me the way I am him, and I kiss him as long as I dare being in this public place with my hot, new boyfriend.

———

"KNOCK, KNOCK," Claudia says as she pokes her head into my bedroom. When she sees me sitting cross-legged on the bed, her ball of yarn almost untangled, she enters. "Wow, you're almost done."

"This is so therapeutic," I say. My Tuesday night shopping session with Liam ended about an hour ago, and I'd needed something to keep my hands busy while my mind works. No, I haven't found anything for my father, and honestly, I could show up with a scarf—in the summertime, in South Carolina—and he'd smile and hug me.

Claudia sinks onto the bed with me. She's just showered, and she brings the scent of the tropics with her. "Why do you need therapy tonight?"

I look up for a moment, my eyes leaving the dark gray yarn I've been focused on for so long now. When I look back to my lap, the lines cross. "Uh, my dad's birthday is this weekend."

"Are you going?"

"I have to."

Claudia makes a noise somewhere between a scoff and a groan, but I ignore her. "That's not the real problem, though it's a big one."

"Go on."

I pull the yarn and wind the freed part around the ball. "I asked Liam to come with me."

"You're kidding." At least she doesn't tell me how long I've been seeing him—exactly one week now—as if I don't know.

"My mama said Charlie's going to be there, and we were planning a Saturday bike ride anyway."

"In Columbia?"

"Yeah." I look at her again. "He knows all the trails there, and I haven't been mountain biking in ages."

"Ever, you mean," Claudia inserts.

"Fine, maybe ever." I glare at her and go back to her ball of yarn. I feel like each fiber represents part of my life, and I'll never get them separated enough to wind them together neatly. "But it sounded fun. A long drive with my boyfriend. We talk and laugh and get lunch. Then, a little bike ride. How hard can it be?"

"I'm seeing broken bones in your future," Claudia says with a perfectly straight face. She reaches over and covers my busy hands with hers until I still. "Liam can handle your parents."

"You think so?" I scoff, because while I really want to

see him try, I do not want to see him fail. And no one wins against my mama if she doesn't want them to.

"Of course. Liam is super successful, Hill."

"In the wrong way, Claudia." I sigh. "My parents..." I don't continue, because I don't have to. Claudia has met Don and Carolle Mays, and she knows their level of pretentious. "Maybe I should've protected him and said I'd meet him at the trailhead on Saturday."

"He can hold his own," Claudia says. "Worst case, you leave early."

"We're staying there." I don't have to look at her to imagine the wide, shocked eyes and the stretched-O-mouth. The choking noise she makes paints a great picture, thank you very much.

"Staying there?" she gasps.

"Separate rooms," I say. "The house has at least eight bedrooms." And my parents have me. Just me. My mom does own a fluffy white dog, who probably gets two or three of the bedrooms to herself.

"It's fine," I tell her as well as myself. "It's one party. One night. Then we get to go mountain biking. I can do it."

Claudia hums, and that's her way of saying she agrees, but she can't quite get herself to say the words.

"Besides," I say. "I might not be in the area for much longer, and then maybe I'll miss my parents so much, I'll be dying to come back."

"Wait, you're leaving?" She pulls her hands back, and

my gaze falls on the yarn again. The top couple of strands are a bit mucked up, and I unwind them to tighten them into place again. "Where are you going?"

"I mean, I scored the interview of the century," I say. "Michelle and I have been laboring over the storyboard, the script. We're going to pitch the documentary by the end of the month." I look at Claudia. "Tanner Bridgestone will surely be interested. He's already on the radar." I blink at her. "The studio is in LA, Claude."

"LA," she repeats. "You're moving across the country."

The dream blooms right in front of me, but I shake my head. I've never even been to California, let alone Los Angeles. To see where they've filmed movies, TV shows, and documentaries—the news! Game shows!—is a literal dream of mine.

But despite my parents having money, neither of them has been bit by the travel bug, and I spent my childhood right here in South Carolina. I went to college here. I now work here. In that moment, as I'm literally untangling yarn and rolling it into a neat ball, I realize how utterly boring my life is.

"Don't tell anyone," I whisper-say. "Okay? It could be nothing, and I want to keep my hopes to myself for a little longer."

Claudia leans over and hugs me, which is totally messing up the yarn. But I abandon it and hug her back, because right now, she feels like an anchor I need. "I'm thrilled for you. I hope it all comes to be."

When she pulls back, she's smiling, and I return the gesture. "Thank you." I know she won't say anything to the other girls, and it's not like she and Liam text back and forth or anything.

"What about Liam?" she asks, going right for my jugular.

I shrug and look back to the yarn. "This is why I need therapy."

"Maybe he'll go with you."

"The film industry either moves really fast or really slow," I say. "Even if we sell the documentary, it doesn't mean it'll get made right away. Or at all."

"But *Tanner Bridgestone* is on the radar," Claudia says.

I giggle and shake my head, the end of the yarn almost in sight. It just has a few more loops to work through. "You don't even know who Tanner Bridgestone is."

"No, but *you* do, and he's a Big Deal. He's going to buy this documentary, and you're going to move to LA to produce and direct it, and your life is going to be forever changed."

"Yeah," I say. A week ago, this would've have me giddy-baking so I could give my friends pie as we gushed over this great almost-opportunity. But now, with Liam in the picture, I'm not sure I can walk away from Charleston, from the Big House, from my life here, so easily.

CHAPTER EIGHTEEN

CLAUDIA

It's a perfectly normal Wednesday, complete with hot coffee and my computer agreeing with me, when everything blows up.

It starts with my secretary poking her head into my office with the words, "Did you hear?"

I glance away from the boring spreadsheet in front of me that spells out the various parks, pavilions, and paths in Cider Cove and what's been reserved already. I'm putting together the social media campaign for the city for the next thirty days, and I'd love to have some sort of statistic about how many parks are already reserved, simply to encourage more patrons to get online and save the space they want for the dates they want.

"Hear what?" My office at least has walls, but it's not located in the downtown government buildings. Public

Works gets relegated to a drab, gray trailer on the west side of town where the railroad yard is.

No joke.

It's almost like we're communists out here and might need to jump onto the next passing caboose to get out of town should we do something the citizens of Cider Cove won't like.

"There's a rumor flying around." Sybil glances over her shoulder and comes into my office. She gently pushes the door closed, but that won't last long. The AC in this place doesn't work properly if the doors are shut for long.

Beckett Fletcher, the man who works right next door to me, will likely kick the wall within five minutes and yell, "I heard you close that door, and now I'm suffocating!"

I'd like to suffocate him sometimes, but I think I've done a good job of putting on a professional front and working with him.

Sybil perches on the chair in front of me, which is so fitting, because she's a light blonde with blue eyes that flit everywhere, and she can't weigh more than a Thanksgiving turkey. She's definitely bird-like, and I internally giggle at my own joke about how she *perches* on the seat.

"Word is that Mike is going to retire."

I search her face for the missing information my brain needs. Mike is such a common name, and I probably know six of them. In a work capacity... I pull in a breath.

"Mike Bowing?"

Sybil nods, her bony chin going up-down-up-down.

I lean back in my chair as if she's winged the breath out of me. "He's been the City Planner for two decades."

It's the position I want, and everyone in this room knows it. I meet her eye, and she is my closest friend at work. We sometimes go to the gym together too, but she can spin like no one I've ever met, and I can't quite get my shoulders all the way to the ground in the alternative yoga class.

And let's face facts: Me and the gym aren't exactly sympatico.

Me and the City Planner position are made for each other, though. I have the training. I have the degrees. I have the experience.

"Where did you hear this?"

"Rhonda from Thomas's office just called. She heard it from Brenda, who heard it from Val, who heard it when she was walking by the board room on the third floor." She nods, her eyes wide and serious, like this chain of hearsay will hold up in a court of law.

The Secretary Scuttlebutt.

No one should *ever* underestimate what a secretary knows, as he or she often fades into the wallpaper, and higher-ups forget they're there.

"Any idea as to when?" I ask.

"Val didn't hear much more. I guess she flattened herself against the wall, and Mike was in a meeting with Winslow and Mayor Garvin."

"Just the three of them?" Winslow Harvey is the City

Manager—and my boss. I think his first name and last name got mixed up, but that's another private joke I keep to myself—and the girls in the Big House.

"Mm hm." Sybil jumps as the pounding kick I predicted fills the office.

"Ten seconds," I say, holding up my hand in a universal sign of Wait. I mentally count down while Sybil twists to look at my closed door. I focus on it too, and maybe I get a little too much joy out of annoying Beckett.

He certainly doesn't make life easy for me around here. He's one of the worst name-droppers on the planet, and he likes to pretend his job is more important than mine, because he has more meetings in the main government buildings downtown.

"So many, I might get an office over there too, Claudia." *Knock, knock.* He always punctuates his most irritating sentences with two knocks. He's not picky about the surface either. I've seen him do it on Sybil's desk, my doorframe, my desk, his own desk, the elevator door, and even his lunchbox once.

"Three...two...one..." I count down.

"Why is this door closed?" he demands, knocking loudly on it. It swings open a moment later, and he frowns at me and my secretary. "My office is five degrees hotter already."

"Were you on the phone?" I ask politely.

In front of me, Sybil's wingbones start to shake with

silent laughter. I can't see her face, but I would love to. Or maybe not. Then I'd start laughing too.

Beckett frowns deeper, his sandy blonde hair practically quivering over his forehead. He does have a great head of hair, which was the first thing I noticed about him when we first met. I've been in my position for five years, and he in his for four years and ten months. It's a fact I have to pull out about once a year to remind him he's not God.

His eyes hover between blue and aqua, and to be honest, I thought he was pretty good-looking upon initial glance. But his personality is so abrasive that all of his hotness is obliterated every time he opens his mouth.

"No," he says. "I wasn't on the phone."

"Oh, well, I thought that might be it," I say. "What with all the hot air you blow whenever you talk."

He realizes I'm goading him, and he rolls his eyes. The muscles in his face relax then, and fine, he's good-looking. I'm a female attracted to males, and I can admit it, if only to myself.

"Do you two really need this door to be closed?" he asks.

Sybil turns back to me, and I give an almost imperceptible shake of my head. We probably shouldn't even have discussed the Secretary Scuttlebutt here at all, because these walls are paper-thin, and Beckett doesn't respect anyone's privacy.

Once, I thought he'd bugged my office, and I spent an

entire Sunday looking for the electronic devices. Turned out, we both just had our windows open, and he could hear my conversations with Winslow. Then, he took the ideas to our boss first, and I'd nearly lost my mind.

"No, sir," Sybil says with more Southern charm than I could ever master, and she gets to her feet. "We're finished."

"Great," he says, standing back so she can slip out of my office. "Did that email come through from Play Now? They said it would be here today, and I need it."

"I haven't seen it, sir," she says, and because of those paper-thin walls, I hear him heave the sigh of the century.

I duck behind my computer screen and smile at the spreadsheet, though there's nothing sexy or exciting about it. Sybil doesn't usually work directly with Beckett, but his secretary is out on maternity leave, and her replacement is only part-time, which has left Sybil dealing with the Beast.

I click over to my open, standing messages with Winslow, and I start to type. If there is any chance—no matter how remote—of Mike retiring and the position of City Planner coming open, I want him to know I'm interested.

Extremely interested.

CHAPTER NINETEEN

LIAM

"All right," I say. "I've had enough." I reach over and brush her hands away from her mouth. Hillary's been gnawing her nails since we left Charleston. "Shouldn't I be the nervous one?"

I glance at her, and she's giving me a death glare. "Seriously," I say. "What is wrong with you? It's your dad's birthday party. How bad is this going to be?"

She found him a gift last night. It's wrapped and sitting on the back seat of my truck. The bikes are in the bed, and our bags ride comfortably on the floor in the air conditioning too. We've texted and talked all week, and she's not said anything else about her family.

"I'm just worried they're going to eat us alive."

"Okay," I say, my stomach starting to do this rumbling-nervous thing. I've been feeling that way all day, actually, but I haven't wanted Hillary to know. I packed a pair of slacks, a green polo, as Becca says green is one of my best colors, and a blazer I borrowed from my daddy's closet for tonight's party.

We've left in plenty of time to get there before the shindig starts, and I should have time to "freshen up," as Hillary called it.

"So let's come up with a code word or something," I say. "Then, we can use one of your brilliant excuses and get out of whatever conversation or situation we're in." I raise my eyebrows at her.

"We can't say the house is on fire and we need to get out." New hope lights her eyes. "Wait. We could actually *set* the house on fire..."

"Smashed spuds," I swear at her. "Are you serious?" I look to her and the road, her and the road, her and the road, before her face falls, and she shakes her head.

"You're scary," I say. "You're not going to light your parents' house on fire."

"What excuses are we going to use then, Mister Know-It-All?"

My fingers tighten around the wheel. "I can say I need to talk to you for a second. Oh, I'm so *sorry*, Mister Devereux. Miss Hillary has an *important* call with a *film producer* out of *California*. They didn't realize it was so late—time difference, you know—and they simply *must* talk to her."

I raise my eyebrows into the resulting silence. Hillary

gapes at me, but I say, "Your turn. Get me out of something tight."

Her mouth opens, but only a squeak comes out. I laugh, though I'm starting to get more and more anxious with every mile that passes. "That was great, baby. It's really going to work."

"Maybe you're allergic to pickles," she says. "Or seafood. My mama loves seafood, and I guarantee it'll be everywhere tonight."

"An allergy," I say. "Smart."

"Maybe your little brother is calling from prison and needs you to pick him up."

I snort-laugh, glad when she's smiling in the passenger seat too. "Keep going."

"Our code word could be *rooftop*," she says.

"And how would you work that into a sentence?" I like this game, and now that Hillary is out of her head and talking, my stomach begins to settle.

"Yes, I just love the view from a *rooftop*," she croons. "It's simply *gorgeous*." Her smile fades. "You'll see. Everything at this party will be simply gorgeous. I think those are the only two words my mother and her friends know."

"Well, you'll be there, so they'll be right about one thing."

Hillary's smile is soft this time, and she rewards my possibly-lame statement by reaching over and taking my hand from the wheel. "Thank you for coming, Liam."

"Yeah, sure," I say casually, but I'm definitely going to

need to swipe on another layer of deodorant during my freshening-up time.

The mood lightens, and she suggests another excuse for me could be that my sister needs help with her taxes, and she simply can't call anyone but me. Or that my momma has fallen and can't get up.

"Oh," I say, my stomach starting to hurt from all the laughing now. Fine, and a little bit because I haven't eaten since lunchtime. "One for you could be that the roof you hired me to fix is leaking, and your bed is wet."

Hillary smiles but doesn't laugh. "Liam, they'll already think you're not good enough." She swallows and pushes her hair out of her face. "This is going to be a disaster."

"It's fine," I say, though I already struggle with believing I'm good enough. *She's* the one who told me I'm employed, that I own my own business, and that I'm good enough for her. Her words have sunk in, but they're still new, still trying to find a good place to implant and grow.

"It's right here," she says, and my GPS says the same thing a moment later. I make the turn, and sure enough, what spreads before me can only be described with one word.

Wealth.

From the centuries-old live oaks that line both sides of the immaculately raked lane, to the emerald green grass that runs for a good two hundred yards before it hits a mansion, to the way the windows seem to hold the evening sunlight and beam it back to the guests, this estate is exactly that.

An estate.

"How big is this place?" I ask.

"Fifteen acres of land," she says. "The house is something like seven or eight thousand square feet." She sounds timid now, if not a little miserable, and I reach for her hand again.

"We're in this together," I say.

She squeezes tightly and echoes, "Together."

Though we're early, a valet—a legit man in a black tuxedo—comes toward me as my tires crunch over the gravel in the pull-through driveway.

"His name is Colonel," Hilary whispers as she presses a bill into my palm.

Surprise renders me mute, because I didn't know I'd need to tip her family's employees. "Colonel?" I ask. "Like Colonel Sanders?"

"In fact, he used to own a KFC franchise. He's retired now and says he works events for something to do. Mama loves him and hires him for all of her parties."

I don't know if I should snicker or simply let Colonel Sanders take my keys and park my truck. The man crosses in front of the truck, and I still haven't decided when he opens the door.

"Sir," he says. "The party isn't for another hour."

"Hey, Colonel." Hillary chirps as she leans toward me. "We're here for the weekend."

His face blips through shock and then smooths into joy. "Miss Hillary. I wasn't apprised of your arrival."

I look at Hillary, feeling like an unnecessary appendage between the two of them. "He wasn't *apprised* of *your* arrival."

"We can take in our own stuff," she says. "Can you put Liam's truck in the family garage? We'll need to get it out tonight, probably. For sure in the morning."

"Of course, ma'am."

I look at the Colonel, and he raises his eyebrows.

"Come on, baby," Hillary says loudly, and she gets out of the truck on her side. There's another valet there to help her, and I decide I can't sit in the driver's seat and stare. I copy every move Hillary makes, except I slip the Colonel the money Hillary gave me. I see the flash of a twenty as I do, and my heartbeat stutters a little.

"Thank you," I say as nobly as I can, and I hate myself for my tone of voice. This so isn't going to work for me. I'm not going to pretend to be something and someone I'm not every time we come to see her parents.

With that thought, I realize how long-term I'm thinking, and that has me frowning mightily too. At the same time, why shouldn't I be thinking long-term? I'm not a player. I'm not just looking for a good time.

"James," Hillary says as I come around the hood of the truck. "This is my boyfriend, Liam. Liam, this is James and Colonel. They usually come help with crowd control for things like this, don't you guys?"

"Every chance I can," James says with a smile. "Mrs. Mays is wonderful."

"Yes, just fabulous," Hillary says with her mouth, but her eyes tell a different story. I slip my hand into hers, because turns out, Colonel is carrying my bag for me. James has Hillary's, and they lead us up the wide, ornate steps to the front porch.

"This reminds me of a castle," I say. "The pillars, the carvings." They're not gargoyles, but flowers and cherubs —which are almost as terrifying as the monsters and dragons and serpents traditional gargoyles are patterned after.

"Yeah, all we need is a moat and an evil queen," Hillary mutters.

I stifle my laugh, because the grand double-doors have just been thrown open, and I have an entire house to marvel over. I've never considered myself that great of an actor, but I gasp and point and wonder at all the right things, until finally, Colonel deposits my bag on a king-sized bed in a room on the second floor in the West Wing while Hilary is led into the East.

"There's a balcony here," Colonel says as he opens the curtains. "Closet there." He nods to his left. "Full bath there." Another nod toward the corner door. "I'm sure Miss Hillary will come get you for the party."

"I'm sure," I say, and then Colonel bows himself out of the room, closing the door behind him. Relief fills me, and

I sink onto the bed before looking up to the ceiling. "What have I gotten myself into?"

The ornate crown molding doesn't answer, but there's a fluttering knock on my door. I barely have time to move my gaze to it before Hillary enters. She barely creates a gap wide enough to squeeze through, and then she closes the door silently before locking it.

I raise my eyebrows at her. "Are you playing hide and seek?"

She shakes her head as if I'm serious and tiptoes toward me. "It's a lot to take in," she whispers as she cuddles in next to me.

I lift my arm around her. "Yeah." I sigh. "I mean, you said they were rich, but I guess I just..."

"If you know, you know," she says. "If you don't, it's a culture shock, for sure."

"I'll give you that."

She sits up and looks at me. "I know just what to do to de-shock you." A devious smile plays with her mouth.

"You do?"

Her eyes drop to my mouth, and she says, "Mm, yeah," just before she kisses me. My pulse electrifies, and if I was hooked up to a heart monitor, there'd be a spike as high as Mount Everest.

But then, Hillary's right. I relax into kissing her, because it's slow, and easy, and fun, and by the time there's another knock on my door—this one much heavier-handed —I'm almost light-headed.

"Twice baked," Hillary swears, and she literally rolls off the bed and under it in one motion.

A woman calls, "Liam, dear, are you decent?" and I know I'm about to meet her mother while she hides under my bed.

CHAPTER TWENTY

HILLARY

"Give me a few seconds," I hiss to Liam, but I'm not sure he hears me. I scoot away from the edge of the bed where we were kissing and toward the far side. If I can get in the closet, I can come out with something and pretend I was looking for something for him to wear.

I slide out from underneath the bed and get to my knees. Liam is almost to the door. "Liam," I whisper-hiss.

He turns back, and I wave both hands like I'm applauding in sign language. Thankfully, he somehow understands my ridiculous sign language, and he kicks a grin in my direction.

"Did you seriously just melt like a puddle of Jell-O under the bed?" He's way too close to the door to be saying such things.

I gesture him closer, and he abandons his quest to get

the door. I locked it, or my mama would already be in here, Liam's decency notwithstanding.

"My mother is very traditional," I say as he nears the end of the bed. "She will not approve of me being in here unless I'm helping you get dressed."

His eyebrows go up, and they've been doing that a lot today. "Oh? So kissing she doesn't like, but you *dressing me* is okay?"

"I won't be dressing you." I roll my eyes as I gain my feet.

"That's what you literally just said."

"I'm helping you *choose* your clothes," I fire at him.

"Liam?" Mama calls again, and she really is relentless.

He looks toward the door and then back to me. "You're thinking about setting the house on fire right now, aren't you?"

He laughs, and I get such joy from it, especially if I'm the one causing his happiness. "So am I going to be getting the door?"

"Yes," I say. "Call to her that you're coming, and I'm going to duck into the closet with your bag." We both look at it lying benignly on the bed, and I grab it. "Just let me get in there first."

He watches me as I hurry across the room and disappear into the closet, calling, "Just a moment."

I'm safely in the closet for a good five seconds, Liam's bag ripped open and the contents of it flung over the floor of the bare closet, before I hear Liam's overly loud declaration of, "You must be Carolle, Hillary's mama. Hill?"

There's no way my mother buys this act, but as I go sailing out of the closet holding his suit coat, I say, "This is perfect, sweetheart. I think my—" I cut off dramatically when my eyes meet Mama's. My steps slow, and the jacket falls to my side. "Mother will love it."

I give her a big smile. "Mama." I shoot Liam a glance, and his eyes sparkle with amusement. How he can think this is fun is beyond me. "What are you doing here?"

"I heard you two had arrived, and I came to see how Liam was settling in."

"Did you go to my room first?"

Mama blinks, which means no, but she lifts her chin and says, "Yes. You weren't there."

I lift the jacket, my blood still a little heated from the kissing I'd been enjoying. "I'm helping Liam pick his jacket for tonight."

"That one's my daddy's," Liam says, and I've never been more grateful. Then I won't make a fool of myself by insulting it. Not that it deserves an insult, but I had been about to suggest we choose a different one, just to have something to say.

"It's perfect," I gush at him, thinking as fast as I can. "With that green polo I saw in the closet, you'll steal the spotlight tonight." I get my feet moving again, and I press the jacket to his chest and snuggle into his side.

He smiles at me, and a thousand conversations are had

in the look we exchange. I don't truly have time to appreciate that while we've only been dating for a short time, I have this moment with him. This ability to communicate with only eyes, because we have shared experiences and private, previous conversations to rely on.

"Yes, you'd look lovely in green," Mama says, and that pulls our attention to her.

I quickly step out of Liam's hooked arm around my waist and over to Mama. "You look fabulous," I say as I lean in to touch my lips to her cheek. She's already dressed for the party, of course, as it starts in less than an hour. "Where's Daddy?"

"He's on his way home from the golf course."

"Uncle Mark?"

Mama's lips purse for only a moment, and then they dissolve into a smile. "Yes, he came and kidnapped your father for lunch and eighteen holes for his birthday."

"I'm sure Daddy cleaned his clock."

Mama smiles, and I pray Daddy did beat Uncle Mark at golf, or the party will be off to a bad start. "I'm sure." She takes a deep breath. "Have you two eaten? We're not serving dinner at the party." She looks past me to Liam. "Hillary, why don't you introduce me?"

I press my eyes closed. I can't believe I didn't introduce Liam. I turn so I'm standing beside Mama, and we're both facing him. "Mama," I say. "This is Liam Graff, my boyfriend. Liam, my mother—"

"Carolle," we say together. His smile could light the

whole mansion-castle, and he steps forward. "I've heard a lot about you from Hillary." He eases into Mama and sweeps a kiss along both of her cheeks. His momma taught him well, and I can't help the appreciation pulling through me. "It's so great to meet you."

"You as well," Mama says politely, but I've known her for thirty years while Liam's interacted with her for thirty seconds.

He steps back to my side, his hand sliding into mine and holding securely. He's so...*sweet*, and I find my lips tipped up into a goofy smile. "We would love to eat," he says. "At least I would. I haven't eaten since lunchtime on the Summerwoods' back deck."

"Of course," Mama says. "Come down to the kitchen whenever you're ready. The party will be starting soon, and we'll be in the library, so the sooner the better." She lifts her skirt on the right side, and the shiny, silver sequins go up a couple of inches. She turns, and it looks like the dress has been stitched on her body, as I can't see a seam or a zipper anywhere.

She glides away, saying, "I have to go get my gems. Don't be late, Hillary."

"No, Mama," I automatically parrot. I move to the open doorway of Liam's room and watch her float away. Only when she reaches the staircase does she turn back and give me a look that I can't quite decipher but which sends a thrill of anxiety through me.

"Hill?"

I jolt as Liam's hand lands on my lower back. "Yes."

"Can we really eat?" He leans closer to me, his breath softly drifting across the nape of my neck. "I'm starving."

"Yes," I say. "Let's go now, and then we can come get changed and sneak into the party through the back door."

I can't believe I'm even here, and I wonder when I'll have to come face-to-face with Charlie Vaughn. I should probably be glad Mama came to Liam's room first—and that I was here with him. I can't even imagine the interrogation that would've happened had I not been, and if she'd caught me alone, I'd be hearing about how perfect Charlie is about now.

"We can sneak in through the back?" he asks.

I turn toward him and reach for his hand. "Let me show you the back staircase."

He laughs as I tow him along, and I feel like I'm sixteen again, trying to sneak my forbidden boyfriend out of the house without my parents finding out. I pause at the door that leads into the hallway, glance over my shoulder at Liam, and laugh as I push into the smaller corridor that leads to the back staircase.

That'll take us directly into the kitchen, so even if the party had started, no one would see us in our non-fancy clothes, sneaking dinner together.

"Wow," Liam laugh-says behind me. "This alley is a little sketchy."

I grin too, and he stops moving. Since we're holding hands, I do too, and he pulls me back to him. "Seems like the perfect place to sneak a kiss. Is that what you used to do, Miss Hillary? Sneak boys into your house and then lead them down this dark hallway?"

He presses me against the wall, and things get really exciting. "Maybe," I say.

"Mm." He leans down and kisses me, picking right where we left off in his bedroom.

"You're going to have to eat fast," I murmur against his lips.

"I hold the world record for eating dinner fast," he kiss-says, and then he matches his mouth to mine again.

I'm not sure what he saw in me in that exchange with my mama, but I saw him standing at my side. Being charming and Southern-gentleman, and while it's only been a couple of weeks, I find myself falling in one of the best ways possible.

Falling in love.

———

"WOW, WOW, AND TRIPLE WOW," Liam says an hour later. Yes, the party has started already. We're about fifteen minutes late, which is perfectly fashionable in my mother's eyes. I hear voices wafting up from downstairs, and perhaps I'll have Liam escort me down the curved staircase to my father's birthday party.

He'll be standing in the foyer with Mama for at least

another half-hour, greeting guests, shaking hands, and guffawing about how he can't believe he's this old.

I cock my hip and put one hand up on the doorframe. "You like my dress?"

"I didn't even know they made dresses like that." Liam's eyes roam down to the hem of my gown and back to my eyes. "The earrings are a nice touch." His voice sounds like he's swallowed sand.

"They're my gems," I say.

"Did you bring all this with you?"

"No," I say. "It's here, in my closet."

"Purple is your color, Hillary." He moves toward me and slides one hand along my waist. My dress has a very low V-cut that goes almost to my belly button and big, wide ruched straps that go over my shoulders. It has a swooping piece of fabric that hides the extra weight along my stomach, hugs my hips, and flares at my knees like a mermaid dress.

It's a deep purple that's not quite as black as eggplant skins, and yes, the color plays very well with my hair. I've braided that into a crown around my head, and I've only been wearing the diamond teardrop earrings for two minutes.

"I am the luckiest man in the world," he whispers as he touches his lips to my neck. Gooseflesh prickles along my shoulders and down my arms and back.

"Are you ready to meet my daddy?" I ask.

"Yes." He steps back, and he's wearing a pair of black

slacks, shiny cowboy boots, that green polo, and his daddy's jacket.

"You look amazing," I tell him. He's definitely not up to my daddy's standards, but I don't care. "No cowboy hat tonight?"

"You said a jacket was minimum attire, Hill. I didn't think I could wear a cowboy hat."

I reach up and gently push his hair to the side, though he's already swooped it that way. "It feels strange to be going somewhere where you're not wearing a hat."

"There's always tomorrow." He grins at me and takes me down the hall toward the main staircase. I feel the eyes of the people lingering in the foyer, sipping champagne and taking appetizers from trays, and I hitch my smile into place as I scan the crowd.

No Charlie Vaughn. Yet.

Enough people must be looking, because Mama turns to see what's going on, and she leans into Daddy. He finishes with the gentleman in front of him and turns toward me. His smile fills his whole face, and while I know he's a little stuffy and overbearing, he also loves me.

"Darling," he says as he reaches the bottom of the stairs at the same time Liam and I do. "You look stunning."

"Thank you, Daddy," I say. "Happy birthday."

He takes me from Liam and hugs me. "It's so good to see you."

"You too, Daddy." When I step out of his arms, I indicate Liam. "This is Liam Graff, my boyfriend." I smile up at him, and Liam stretches his hand forth to shake Daddy's.

"I'm so glad you came," Daddy says. "How did you two meet?" He flings me a look I know well, and one I don't like. While Daddy has always been more accepting of me and my choices, he does want me to "marry well," whatever that means.

"He lives next door," I say quickly.

"I'm working on the roof at the Big House," Liam says.

"He owns his own construction firm." I gaze up at him, a splash of adoration moving through me. "He's a small-business owner, Daddy."

"What about you, sir?" Liam asks. "Hillary's told me a few things, but I'm not sure I know exactly what you do."

My teeth press tighter together, though I manage to keep the smile on my face. "Daddy's a lawyer," I say. "Or he was, before he retired a few years ago."

"I sat on the South Carolina Supreme Court," Daddy says with a great deal of importance in his voice. Roasted rosemary wedges, we're going to be standing here talking about the law forever.

"Fantastic," Liam says without missing a beat.

"It's definitely a step up from roof repair," Mama says as she lifts a flute of champagne to her mouth with a gloved hand. She seems to be unable to look at any of us directly, and I wonder how much she's already had to drink.

Liam laughs like she hasn't just insulted him. "That it is, ma'am. It's definitely not for everyone."

Humiliation and regret sing through me, and my arm in Liam's tightens. "The world needs all kinds of people," I say.

"Has Hillary told you about the documentary she's doing right now?" Liam looks down at me, and I want to shout *rooftop* at him. We never did settle on a safe word though, and panic builds within me.

"Have you guys been on a rooftop?" I practically yell.

Liam gives me a side-eyed look and refocuses on my daddy. "I don't know everything about what she's working on, but she's really excited about it, and I love listening to her talk about the interviews she does, how she puts together a storyboard, and the whole filming process." He looks from Daddy to Mama. "Have you talked to her about it? It's fascinating."

I've never had a man say anything like that about me or my work. No one has ever cared about the research I do, and I stand there at Liam's side, feeling like a light bulb that shines light out onto the people around her.

Mama looks at me. "She did say she had some news, but she never called again."

"It's not quite news yet," I say with a laugh, realizing how true I've spoken. I glance up at Liam as guilt cuts through me. I've told him nothing about Tanner Bridgestone. Right now, I reason, there's nothing to tell. "He's just being kind."

"No, I'm not." He holds me tightly against his side while Daddy gazes around the party, his tell of boredom. He's never been super keen on my career, but I've never needed him to be.

I didn't realize how much I wanted it to matter until Liam's enthusiastic statements.

"She's really incredible."

"Thank you, baby," I murmur. "Let's leave my parents to greet the rest of their guests."

"Yes," Mama says with high importance in her voice. "Oh, look, Hillary. Charlie and his parents just arrived." She nods toward the front doors, which stand open. Lightly blowing fans keep the flies out, but sure enough, they don't stop my ex-fiancé from walking in.

He's wearing a dark suit with a white shirt and tie, just like my father. His parents look like they've flown directly here from the red carpets of the Country Music Festival, and my stomach lurches so hard, I put my hand over it.

"Oh, Hill," Liam says smoothly. "My momma's calling. She wanted to ask you about that charity fundraiser you're doing. Do you think we could slip out the back for a moment?"

"Yes," I say, despite my mama's poisoned look.

"You're doing a charity fundraiser?" she asks.

Liam holds up his phone, which somehow does have an incoming call. *Momma Mia* sits on the screen, and his eyebrows go up. "It'll only take a few minutes."

I nod and turn my back on Charlie Vaughn and his

approaching parents. "Be right back, Daddy," I say, but he's already absorbed into his Very Important Friends. It's Mama I'm going to have to answer to, but I reason it won't be tonight. She'll save face at any cost, and I quietly slip away with Liam and his phone call about a fake charity fundraiser.

CHAPTER TWENTY-ONE

LIAM

I WAKE TO SOFT, WHITE LIGHT PAINTING MY FACE. The mattress beneath me is way too soft, and my back protests as I lift both arms up over my head. I settle my hands behind my head and look up to the ceiling, which is at least twelve feet above me.

This house...

I actually really like it, because there's something about old Southern architecture that I really appreciate. It has good bones that have stories, and I wish I had longer— and the approval of Hillary's parents—to explore the house a bit more.

She and I escaped the party pretty early last night, and I wonder if she'll have a price to pay for that this morning. We didn't talk about breakfast or a wake-up time or make a plan as to when we'd leave to go mountain biking.

I'm not in a huge rush, because I rarely sleep anywhere but my own bed, and I almost never have nothing to do first thing in the morning. This lazy Saturday is...nice, and I sit straight up. "No wonder Hillary didn't like me mowing the lawn at seven-thirty on a Saturday."

I ruined this...this quaint, quiet, relaxing time for her with a grumpy, growling machine—with a surly, sarcastic me behind it. I've never really apologized for that, and I look toward the door. Can I sneak down the hall and past those yawning steps to her room?

I know where it is; I picked her up there last night for the party, as if I'd driven to her house to get her for a date.

"Check the time, cowboy," I mutter to myself. I twist and grab my phone from the nightstand, only to learn it's quarter past seven. I'm not surprised by the early time; I get up early every day. But I'm certainly not going to go knocking on Hillary's door before eight. Period. Maybe even eight-thirty.

So I freeze where there's that flutter-knock on my door. I locked it when I went to bed last night, so I'll have to get up to answer it. Maybe I imagined the sound. Maybe my mind is so frenzied over Hillary that I just *want* her to be knocking on my door.

"Liam?" reaches my ears, and it's definitely her voice. I fling the comforter aside and practically run to the door. The lock twists easily, and I open the door six inches to peer through.

Sure enough, my girlfriend stands right on the cusp of the room, and she puts one hand on my bare chest and says, "I'm coming in."

She squeezes through the intimate space, and I certainly don't back up to give her more room. She's wearing those pajamas I've seen before, and oh, that pearly pink is going to be my favorite color from now on.

"What are you doing?" I whisper to her.

"I woke up and wanted to talk to you, but I left my charger in your car, and my phone is dead." She holds it up. "Can I borrow yours for a while?"

"Yes." I indicate where my phone is plugged in next to the bed, and she goes that way. I'm wearing a pair of basketball shorts and nothing else, and I shiver in the air-conditioned house.

I slip behind her and crawl back in bed, pulling the covers up so I'm not half-naked in front of Hillary. She unplugs my device and uses the cord for hers, and then she looks up, almost surprised to see me lying in my own bed.

Shock makes me see white when she peels back the blanket and slides into the space next to me. "Mm, you're warm."

"Why is this house so cold?" I ask.

"All castles are drafty," she replies, and I grin and chuckle up to the ceiling. "Plus, my mom is always hot, so we all live by her internal temperature."

She curls into my side, her arm draped across my midsection. I like holding her like this, but it feels a little too intimate and way faster than I could've ever even fantasized.

My heartbeat beats in a circle through my chest, making my throat throb and close. "When did you want to head out today?" I ask.

"Whenever," she says, but it sounds like she's going back to sleep. After several seconds of blissful togetherness, she says, "Thank you for coming last night, Liam."

"You were right about your mama and daddy. They didn't seem to like me much." She doesn't acknowledge that I'm right, but we both know I am. "Is it really because I'm not a lawyer or a billionaire?"

"Yes," she whispers. "And you know *I* don't care about that, right?"

"Yeah," I say, but my doubts start braying, first in my stomach and then my throat, then my heart, and finally all throughout my mind.

"There's a famous producer who says he wants to talk to me," she says. "Nothing's come of it, and it's been almost two weeks."

"That's fantastic," I tell her.

Hillary lifts her head. "When you say that, I believe you."

I move my eyes to meet hers. "Why wouldn't you?"

"My job with my previous boyfriends and fiancés was to look pretty, plan parties, and find a charity I cared about and work with it. Nothing was about what *I* wanted. My goals and dreams were...irrelevant."

"You were silenced."

"You don't silence me." She lifts herself further, and I reach up with my free hand to push her hair off her shoulder. My hands brush the silk of her pajamas, and what my momma calls *irreverent thoughts* flow through my mind.

"I hear you," I say just before I strain up to meet her mouth with mine. She presses into me, and I relax back into my pillow. I can lie in bed and kiss her for a lifetime, and it won't be enough, but Hillary doesn't let me do that.

She pulls away pretty darn quick, actually. Even faster than last night. At least she doesn't roll down to the ground and under the bed when she pulls away this time.

"You're trouble for me, Liam Graff."

I only smile at her, because I think she's the one tempting me to kick down walls and barriers in my life I never thought I would.

"I'm going to go get dressed in my biking clothes." She slips out of my arms, and I watch her adjust her pajama top on the way to the door. Once there, she turns back to me. "Roderick will have breakfast whenever we want it. Requests?"

"Protein," I say. "It's hot out, Hill. We'll need lots of water and snacks."

A blip of uncertainty crosses her face. "How far are we going?"

"I chose a nice, easy path," I say. "It's about eight miles is all, and it ends in a city park with a gorgeous view of the city."

"Where I can call for lunch."

"It's like we have the same mind." I grin her out of the bedroom, and then I head into the shower. With Hillary, I'm never really sure if what she's said is going to happen—I've still never seen a little black dress, for example. But the deep purple-eggplant dress last night...

It'll be decades before I forget about Hillary in that dress.

"You're in too deep," I bubble-murmur in the shower, and when I get out, I decide to go all-in. She said she was going to get in her biking clothes, and since we're not coming back here after our bike ride—and I don't want to change at the trailhead—I put on my bright blue-almost-teal biking bodysuit, reserve a pair of socks, and pack up the rest of my clothes and toiletries.

I've told no one of this overnighter road trip, but I am going to have to confess a few things to Momma and my sisters at some point. Especially with how fast I'm falling for Hillary.

My biking shoes are in the car, and I will put those on at the trailhead. I have a backpack with my helmet, goggles, and extra water bottles in the truck too, so I pull on my socks and my cowboy boots—the only other footwear I brought and look at myself in the full-length mirror on the back of the bedroom door.

"You look like a fool." Imagine a six-foot-two man who hasn't shaved that day, his hair trimmed neatly though, wearing a neon blue body-biking-suit, his knees a little knobby compared to the muscles above and below them, all finished with a shiny pair of cowboy boots.

Everyone who sees me is going to snap pictures to put on social media for everyone to laugh at.

"Go all-in," I mutter to my reflection, and I leave the bedroom. I take the main staircase down to the first level and the kitchen, because I'm no coward. The scent of sausage and bacon combined gives me more courage than I'd otherwise have, and I take my bag and backpack into the kitchen, my boots clickety-clackety-stomping with every step.

"Morning," I say, and Hillary turns from the counter where she's putting the last bite of a toasted bagel—not protein—in her mouth.

I swear that bread and cream cheese is going to splat on the floor, because her mouth doesn't close. She blinks at me as she drinks me in, and I spread my arms wide. "Who's ready to go biking?"

I grin as I take in what she's wearing. A tight black pair of bicycle shorts. She's finally delivered on the attire she said she'd be wearing. Her tank top is a gradient of white along the thick shoulder straps to pale pink, to more pink, to bubblegum pink.

Pink in all its shades and hues is my new favorite color.

She shoves her bagel in her mouth and chews it. After she's swallowed, she says, "Well, I don't think either of us will get lost today."

"I always wear a bright color," I say. "I figure then, someone will be able to find my body."

Hillary starts sputtering. "What? This isn't a lethal activity, is it?"

I meet Roderick's eyes, and he looks one breath about from belly laughter, whether from my bodysuit and cowboy boot combo or me teasing Hillary about dying, I'm not sure.

"Hillary," I say as seriously as I can. "It's just like riding a bike." I move over to the counter and take in the magnificent spread of breakfast foods.

Roderick starts to laugh, obviously unable to contain himself any longer. I grin at him and start assembling a bagel with a sausage patty, two of the fried-hard eggs, and plenty of cream cheese into a breakfast sandwich.

"Miss Hillary said you needed water and snacks," he says, and he starts putting icy cold water bottles and little pre-portioned bags of trail mix, peanut butter crackers, granola bars, and protein bars on the counter.

Our eyes meet, and I nod at him. "Yeah, man. Thanks."

"Do try to bring Miss Hillary back in one piece," he says, and she scoffs while the two of us chuckle together.

I do want to bring Hillary to a lot of places in one piece, but I can't wait to show her a little piece of what makes me me, the way she did for me at the birthday party last night.

After I finish my sandwich, I wipe my mouth all proper-like and look at her. "Ready, sweetheart?"

She takes a deep breath and nods. "I'm ready."

CHAPTER TWENTY-TWO

HILLARY

Liam doesn't go too fast for me, which I really appreciate. He stops and goes over the next mile or so of the trail so often, and he makes sure I'm not left to my own devices.

Mountain biking is a lot harder than I expected it to be, because while it's a nice wide path, it still has rocks in it. Rivulets from where water ran down and carved out a little bit of the dirt. It's not flat either, but I knew I'd have to go up and down hills.

Liam does ride in front of me, and he's a god on a two-wheeled machine. "Almost there," he calls back to me, and my shoulders and wrists are relieved. They've absorbed a lot more weight and jarring than they normally do.

He bursts through what looks like a wall of trees, and then his bright blue suit is completely illuminated by the sun.

I follow him, and it's like going past the Pearly Gates of Heaven and basking in divine light.

Liam's slowing down, and I do too. He comes to a stop and puts one foot down on the ground as I ease to a stop besides him. His grin fills his whole face, and he says, "This is it."

I survey the park in front of me, with all the brilliant blue sky and sparkling green trees. People loiter about, doing weekend park things like lying on blankets and reading, throwing Frisbees, and tossing balls to their dogs.

"That's Columbia," I say, admiring the skyline against the nearly summer sky. I look back to him. "You were right. This is amazing."

"Eight-point-three miles," he says. "You did it, Hill."

"Thank you, Liam." I ease into his side, glad when he puts one arm around me. "I'll call for sandwiches, okay?"

"Sure," he says. "Let's find a table, and we can chill in the shade while we wait." He pushes back onto his pedals, and I let him get a couple of bike lengths in front of me before I clumsily get back on my bike.

My tush hurts, but I'm not going to breathe a word of complaint. Not on this, the most perfect Saturday in the whole world.

I wonder how much of that belongs to where I spent some of my morning today. In Liam's arms. In his bed. Kissing him. Talking about real, meaningful things.

I miss that more than I want to admit, and I want to replicate those simple ten minutes every day of the week.

I know I can't, not right now, but the thoughts linger, and I don't push them away.

My butt feels way better on the hard picnic table bench seat, and I pull out my phone and get our lunch ordered. Liam wipes his neck and face and hands with a wet wipe, and he offers me one too. I raise my eyebrows, and he explains, "Mountain biking is always dusty. This is a little trick I found I like. Helps me feel clean enough to get home."

I take a wet wipe, trying to think of something to say. Nothing comes, because Liam is practically perfect in every way. He sits beside me, facing outward, and opens his backpack. He hands me a package of peanut butter crackers and a fresh bottle of water, though he made me stop at Mile Four and eat too.

"I just ordered sandwiches," I say.

"You'll need this." He chomps into his own crackers and then wets his hands and pushes them both through his hair, moving it back out of his face. He's so sexy with his hair glistening like that, and that smile on his face, and those peanut butter cracker crumbs clinging to the corner of his mouth.

So many things swirl and storm through me. I've felt like this about a man before, and it's this soft middle part of the relationship, where things aren't so new anymore, but neither of you is anywhere near taking things to the next level.

I love the middle of relationships, and I tell myself it's okay to stay right where we are for a while.

"Ah, here it is," Liam says, and I look away from a mom tying a red balloon to her toddler son's wrist. He hands me his phone, and adds, "My momma wants to meet you."

Liam Paul Graff, that picture with you and Hillary is the most adorable thing I've ever seen. When can I meet her?

I smile at his momma's assessment of our pre-biking selfie, which apparently Liam posted somewhere his momma saw.

You look so happy, son. Admit it. Tell me when you've been this happy.

I hand the phone back and ask, "Where did you post that picture?"

"Nowhere," he says. "I only use social media for business. I have a family group text with my momma, sisters, and Stella's husband."

I eat another cracker, waiting for him to personally invite me to meet his momma. When he doesn't, and once the mom and her son have toddled past us, I lean into his bicep. He's steady and strong and so, so sweet.

"I'd meet them," I say. "Whenever you want me to."

He nods and tilts his chin down toward me. I could lean forward a couple of inches and kiss him, but I don't. "I kinda want to keep you to myself for a while." He slides his arm through mine, his fingertips along my inner forearm, which is somehow the most sensual touch I've gotten from him.

His fingers wind with mine, and I look at his tanner skin against my paler pigment. "Okay," I say. Another family walks toward us, carrying a couple of plastic sacks of groceries and towing a cooler behind them. Mom, Dad, three boys.

I've never given much thought to having children, because I've never really felt like kids would be in the cards for me. With a jolt, I realize I've never been in love, though I think I have been. No wonder I've never wanted kids—I didn't want them with the man I was with.

"Do you like kids?" I ask.

"Sure," Liam says. "I've done some construction camps with teens. They're great."

Not what I meant. "Uh, I mean, do *you* want kids?"

Liam watches the family go by us, two of the littler boys starting to argue about something. "Yeah, sure," he says. He's obviously not clued in to the seriousness of the conversation, and I back off.

We're in the gooey, soft middle of our relationship, where I can kiss him whenever I want, and there's plenty of time to get hard answers to my questions.

My phone chimes, and I check it. "Our sandwiches are here." I look up, and sure enough, a man riding a bike with a big black cooler bag on the back is heading for us. I stand and lift my hand, and he sidles up to us and puts one foot down.

"Hillary?" he asks.

"Yes, sir."

He smiles at me as he twists and lifts our sandwiches and chips and drinks from the bag. I take it all, nod-smile at him, and turn back to Liam.

"Diet Dr. Pepper," I say as I put the cold bottle of soda on the table beside his shoulder. "I guessed on the sandwich, because *someone* refused to tell me what he likes."

I give him a nasty glare and pull out his eight-inch sub sandwich. "I went with roast beef, provolone, lots of mayo and mustard, and the normal toppings. Nothing too crazy."

He grins as he takes it. "Nice job, sweetheart."

I love it when he calls me *sweetheart*, and I pull out the salt and vinegar chips and pile them on the bench seat between us. My sandwich is a BLT with turkey and cheese added, and it's salty and meaty and delicious.

"I think it's fun to see what you think I'll like," he says after a couple of bites in silence. "It wasn't me refusing to do something you wanted me to."

"Okay," I say. "Next time we go out to eat, you can order for me."

"Deal," he says without missing a beat. "Now, eat up, Hill. We have to go a mile on the regular road back to the truck." He speaks like this is the worst task ever, and I grin as I bite into my sandwich again.

Note to self: He doesn't like road biking.

I nudge him with my shoulder. "It'll still be the best Saturday ever, though, right?"

Liam's expression softens right before my eyes, and he slings one arm around me. "Best Saturday ever, yeah."

I think so too, and it'll be harder than ever to go back to my regular routine on Monday morning, even if Tanner Bridgestone happens to call and wants to whisk me away to LA.

It's what I've always wanted, but this glorious day on a mountain bike trail, in a park eating sandwiches, with Liam, is pretty impossible to even consider giving up.

He hasn't emailed back, I tell myself, and when Liam points out the Canadian geese landing on the pond, I push all thoughts of work and relocation as far away as I can get them.

I'll deal with things as they come up, the way I always have.

CHAPTER TWENTY-THREE

LIAM

Monday arrives the way it always does, but this one is especially special, because I'm starting on the roof at the Big House today. Finally.

The Summerwoods remodel took forever, and while I patched the vents enough to keep the most damage out, the Big House's whole roof still needs to be done.

And I'm here to do it.

I've arranged with Hillary and Tahlia to start at eight a.m., though not everyone is at work by then. Because she works in downtown Charleston, Hillary won't be at the Big House unless I arrive by seven-thirty. But I'm an early-riser, not suicidal.

Besides, I have to hit the hardware store this morning first. I need to pick up the tar paper and tools for the roof stripping. The shingles are all here too, but I won't need them until later in the week.

So eight-fifteen finds me swinging around the back of the hardware store and parking by one of their oversized bay doors. I could text the number on the sign and have someone bring out my supplies, but I haven't seen Aaron since Friday, when I was there to get one last thing for the Summerwoods.

Oh, and Thursday, when I needed nine-volt batteries for their smoke detectors. And Wednesday, when Mrs. Summerwood threatened to change the paint color on the walls, and I'd gone to get her some samples.

By a sheer miracle, she'd decided to stick with the original color, or I'd be picking up gallons and gallons of paint and driving across town to her house instead of whistling a tune as I enter the hardware store through the back entrance.

I find Aaron at the customer service desk, leafing through a newspaper as if he hasn't heard he can look up the headlines on his phone. "Hey, hey," I say, and my best friend looks up.

"Starting the roof today." He's not asking, and I can only smile anyway. His phone lays next to the paper, and it brightens. We both look at it, and Aaron makes a strangled sound and practically throws his whole body over it to cover it.

I laugh, because I've already seen the text notification that came up, and it's funny that he thinks he can hide something from me anyway. "You joined the singles app?"

Aaron's face flushes a deep red as he shoves his phone

in his back pocket. "We can't all meet hot redheads while mowing lawns." He gestures to the hardware store. "I'm here all the time, and do you know how many of our customers are women?"

"Five-point-seven percent," I say with a grin.

He rolls his eyes. "This is your fault, you know."

"My fault?"

"Totally. You're like this...this peacock strutting around, showing off your feathers."

I laugh again, but I ask, "What does that mean?" among the ha-ha-ha's.

Aaron rolls his head down to his chest and back up. "It's nothing. Yeah, I joined the app, and I'm talking to a few women. That's all."

"Seems like Sasha wants to meet." I raise my eyebrows at him. "Are you going to go out with her?"

"Maybe," Aaron hedges. "I'm—I was kind of hoping we could double. It would take so much pressure off me."

I watch him for a moment, because I know how hard it is for Aaron to even talk to women. Or I should've known. "Yeah, sure," I say, sobering quickly. "I don't think Hillary will care."

She's frustrated that they haven't gotten their script and storyboard put together quite yet, and thus, they haven't started pitching the documentary. She won't tell me what it's about, but I've learned Hillary has two opinions about work: either everything is going hunky dory, or she's ready to quit.

I eat ice cream with her on the roof when things aren't going well, and she shows up with pizza on my front step when she's got good news. I'm not complaining about either scenario, and our one-month anniversary was on Friday.

I didn't know I needed to plan something special for the apparent milestone, but I do now. Hillary had brought over a dart board, and I'd stood there on the front porch like a doofus. Then I'd hung it up in my garage, and we laughed as we threw darts and ate the pizza I managed to order.

She's informed me the next milestone isn't until the third month, specifically the hundred-day mark. When I asked her how she came up with these anniversaries, she'd shrugged and said, "I don't know. I just think they're fun."

At least now I know, and I've already started planning the Hundred Day Anniversary.

"I've got your tar paper in the back," Aaron says. "And if Hillary really won't care, I'd love to double with you two. You're...so fun."

"I am? Or she is?"

"The two of you together," Aaron says. "You guys are like a whole new entity as a couple."

"An entity?"

"I'm not explaining this to you, Liam." Aaron rolls his eyes and steps out from behind the customer service desk. "I'll help you with the tar paper." He does that, and before I know it, I'm on the way to the Big House.

I can't help but think about what he said about me and Hillary being an "entity" as a couple. As I strip off the crumbling shingles, pull out old nails, and strip the front side of the roof, I wish Aaron would have explained it to me.

Of course I know it takes two people to be a couple, and I bring something to the relationship that Hillary doesn't. She brings herself, and together—I suppose together, we do create a new personality. One that's a mix of the two of us.

"We're fun," I say to myself as I get down off the roof and start cleaning up the mess I've made on the lawn. The sun is brutal; I eat lunch in the shade; I text with my momma, and before I know it, I'm back on the roof, this time peeling back the capping tiles along the pinnacle of the roof.

They're thicker and more stubborn, and I have to really dig in to get them off. My fingers ache, and my back doesn't like this curve it's been in for a while now, and when I hear the crunch of tires over the gravel driveway below, I finally straighten and look down there.

"Wow," Tahlia calls up to me, her eyes shaded by her hand and a pair of sunglasses. "How's it going, Liam?"

"She looks bad right now," I call down to her. "But I'll get 'er shining like new." I grin at her, and she smiles up at me.

"I know you will." She heads inside with her backpack, and over the course of the next hour, all of the women return to the Big House, including Hillary.

When I see her car, I call down, "I'll be down in a minute."

"I'll bring you a drink." She smiles and waves and heads inside. By the time I get down to the ground, Hillary has returned with a big, frosted mug of sweet tea.

"My savior," I say as I take it from her. I gulp a couple of big swigs, and she giggles.

"You didn't bring something to drink?"

"I did. It's mostly gone," I say. "I've been working all day, Hill.

"As if the rest of us haven't." Her eyes move down my body, and I'm acutely aware that I'm not wearing a shirt.

"Some of us have harsher work environments," I say, bringing her eyes back to mine. She's wearing a black and white maxi dress and sandals, so her AC situation is completely different than mine.

I wipe one dirty hand along my forehead and smack my lips. "How was work today?"

"More of the same," she says with a sigh.

I look up into the tree tops, which are vibrant and green, bursting with life. "You wanna go out?" I'm aware I've fallen into my boyfriend skin, eager to do something now that Hillary's home.

She looks at me and shakes her head. "No, I wanna curl into the couch and have someone bring me my favorite foods."

I grin at her. "You're such a princess." I wrap her up tightly in my arms again, but she squirms the way Tabitha does. All at once, I realize she's like a cat. "You're like a black cat."

"Yeah, well, you're like a golden retriever." She finally swats me away enough that I fall back, grinning, grinning, grinning at her.

Fine, I'm like a golden retriever.

"My momma texted again today," I say. "She says she's going to make her specialty on Sunday, and she'd love to know if she can plan for two more."

I've put off asking Hillary to meet Momma, because we simply needed more time to figure out if *we* were a *we*.

"You can say no," I say.

"No," she says. "I want to meet your momma. We can go this weekend." She wears a brave face, but I know that this mask hides her insecurities and fears. She steps into me and puts her hands on my chest. "You're dirty, Liam. You need a shower."

I grin at her and grab onto her waist, pulling her flush against me. She shrieks as I lean down and brush my dirty beard along her cheek. "You like how dirty I am, Hillary."

"I absolutely do not." She pushes against me, but it's a fairly futile effort. I release her, chuckling, and she stumbles backward.

"Whoa, whoa," I say, lunging after her. I grab her hand, but she's going down. And I'm going with her.

She yelps, and I don't know what to do with my hands.

The iced tea goes flying, some of the amber liquid raining down on me and Hillary. She lands on her butt on the grass, and in some miraculous gymnastic move I've never completed before, I twist and land on her thigh, then my outer hip as I hit the grass beside her.

Laughter fills my ears, though I'm still reeling from what just happened. Hillary lays on her back, her eyes closed and her laughter painting the sky.

I grin up into the blue and green too, basking in the joy that pours from her.

"Are you okay?" she asks as she rolls toward me, and I gather her into my side.

"Yeah," I say with a chuckle. "I'm okay."

She stays in my arms for a moment, and then she pushes away. "You really do stink, Liam." She gets to her feet as I start to laugh, and she collects the big glass mug before she throws me a flirty look at heads back into the Big House.

"I'll bring you some bacon-and-cheese tater tots in a bit," I call after her.

"Promises, promises," she yells back, but it's one I'll keep. If my little black cat wants cheese, and bacon, and potatoes while she curls into the couch, I'm going to get it for her.

———

"MOMMA," I yell as I enter her house. "We're here."

"Oh, my," I hear her say from somewhere, but she's not in the main living room. She bustles through the door from the kitchen a few seconds later, one of her full-body aprons snapped around her neck. She claps her hands together once as Hillary enters the house behind me and comes to my side.

I don't stink today, thank you very much. I've showered and shaved, in fact, and I'm wearing my best pair of dark khaki shorts, a polo the color of Granny Smith apples, and my biggest smile.

"Liam," Momma says as she opens her arms to me. I chuckle as I move through the living room to hug her.

"Howdy, Momma."

"My boy." She's grinning more than I've seen before when I put her back on her feet. She looks from me to Hillary. "And his Hillary."

"Momma," I say quickly. "This is Hillary Mays. Hill, this is my momma." I beam down at her. "Dawn Graff."

"Oh, you're just lovely, aren't you?" Momma takes Hillary's face in both of her hands, and I smile though I don't mean to.

"Momma," I say. "She's not a stuffed animal."

Momma pulls her hands back quickly, a hint of redness coloring her cheeks and then steps into Hillary the way I expect my Southern momma to do.

"It's so great to meet you," Hillary says, her eyes meeting mine. "I see where Liam gets his charm from."

"Oh, that was all his daddy," Momma says. "My Paul

was a gentle giant." She steps back and looks at me. "Just like Liam."

"A gentle giant," Hillary repeats. "I've heard Liam called a few things, but never that."

"Let's not start that now," I say with a smile, though I don't particularly like it when Momma calls me a gentle giant. At the very best, it makes me sound fat, and at the worst, I'm fat *and* soft. Sensitive.

Weak.

"So." I clap my hands together to get that playful smile off Hillary's face. Momma jumps, and I almost feel bad about it. "I've been bragging about your shrimp and grits, and how good they are, Momma. Don't make a liar out of me now."

CHAPTER TWENTY-FOUR

HILLARY

"Delicious," I gush for at least the sixth time since Liam's momma put a delicious bowl of shrimp and grits in front of me. I'm looking at Liam as I speak, and he raises his eyebrows.

Me? he's asking. *Are you saying I'm delicious?*

I give him a playful smile and barely move my head up and down. Of course he's delicious, from that gorgeous beard to the glint in those dark eyes. His playful smile, which I know can be full of happiness and houses a pair of lips that sure know how to kiss a woman too.

He can work hard in one moment, but be playful in the next. He's fallen on the roof, lost at darts, and nearly bulldozed me into the ground once. But he kisses me like he could love me, and I've been steadily falling for him in the past six weeks.

I keep all of that to myself, of course. I've been the one

to blurt the three-word-sentiment first, and it's so not going to happen this time. Besides, I'm still trying to figure out if I know what love is.

And after six weeks?

No one can, can they?

"Liam tells me you're a producer," his momma says, and I pull my attention back to her.

"No," I say, though I wish her words are true. "I work for a research firm that puts together facts and interviews for documentaries." I take another bite of the perfectly cooked shrimp—totally hard to do, by the way—and the buttery, salty grits. "I haven't produced anything."

Liam doesn't jump in and correct me, nor defend himself.

"Maybe one day," I add as I give her a smile. "Tell me how you and your husband met."

"Oh, here we go," Liam says, and he's finished his dinner, so he leans back in his chair and folds his arms. Those impressive biceps—I've named them Bazookas—muscles so big they could be explosive—come out, and I grin at him.

"Paulie was on his way to report to Fort Bragg." Dawn has come alive, and I push my bowl forward and lean my face against my palm. "He and some buddies stopped at this dance I'd gone to with my sisters."

"One look," Liam booms into the story. "The stars were shining and so aligned." He leans forward, his bazookas put away for now, his face lit as if internally by the moon. "It was love at first sight."

"Oh, you." His momma swats at him, but he simply grins and leans away from her.

"You don't believe in love at first sight?" I ask him, and oh, that sobers the mood in the dining room. Dawn's house is a bit chopped up, with the living room separated from the kitchen and the eat-in dining area by a wall with an arched doorway. It's old, but comfortable, and it seems to breathe the same life she does.

"I—no." Liam lifts his chin. "I don't."

"It's literally your parents' love story," I say, surprised at him.

"Daddy had to report to the Army," he says. "He was deployed for a couple of years before they met again."

My eyebrows go up as I look at Dawn. "Wow, a love-at-first-sight long distance relationship. You two had it all going on."

"They had plenty of time to get to know each other," Liam says. "That's all I'm sayin'." He picks up a cheddar biscuit and tears off a piece. "And Momma, they renamed Fort Bragg to Fort Liberty, remember?"

"But when Daddy was passing through Santaquin, it was Fort Bragg." She glares at him, and I see now how he can handle my fiery looks.

"So you wrote Paul for a couple of years?" I ask her. Her expression softens as she looks at me. "Yes, and when he got back, he came straight to my little Alabama town and swept me off my feet."

"They kissed on the first date," Liam says in a mock whisper. "Very scandalous for the time."

Dawn simply glows, and I wonder if I'll ever feel like that about someone. I meet Liam's eyes, and something starts to rise within me. I'm not sure it's a glow, but it feels warm and shining, and I think, *Maybe.*

———

MAY IS ALMOST June as Michelle walks down the long, twelve-foot conference table. Our storyboard has been sitting here for nearly two months, and we've moved pieces, cards, notes, and pictures around incessantly.

We've scrapped it twice, and I've gone over Catarina's interview at least a dozen times. I've sent her follow-up texts, which she's answered. She's signed the proper forms for us to release the interview to a third party, and she knows they might contact her in the future.

Honestly, I'm not sure how much more future she'll have. She didn't seem too sick when I met with her, but she's living in a memory care facility, and that's probably because she needs some of the services there.

"So?" I ask impatiently. Michelle has been up and down the table twice now, and she's currently going over it in chronological order for the second time.

She holds up her hand and keeps going. She is so very

much like me and so completely my opposite at the same time. For example, she wears her blonde hair in a bob that suits her face and makes her glasses become a fashion accessory. I could never get away with that, because my face is far too round.

I wear a pair of black slacks, flat sandals, and a sleeveless blouse, while she's got on sandstorm-colored skirt suit and heels. Yes, matching heels. I don't even know where she'd get something like that, and I muse that maybe they came with the hideous skirt suit.

Then I start to wonder about what kind of store would even sell something so matchy-matchy and ugly, only snapping to attention when Michelle lifts her head and says, "This is it."

I blink a couple of times. "Is it?"

Michelle lets her hands hang limply at her sides as she gazes at the opening card laid on the table. "Yes," she finally says. "We're ready to pitch this."

"Praise the heavens," I say. "Because I'm so ready to work on something else."

My boss smiles at me, but I haven't spoken untrue. "Yes, by the time we see a product aired, it's almost like we don't want to watch it." She laughs, which is a real accomplishment for Michelle. If Liam thinks I'm a sourpuss, he should meet my boss.

"Let's go send some emails and make some calls." Michelle leads the way out of the conference room, and I follow her. My heart ba-bumps at me, because I want to ask her about Tanner Bridgestone. At the same time, I'm getting closer and closer to my hundred-day anniversary with Liam, and I'm not sure I want to leave Cider Cove to chase a dream that might never get off the ground.

"Uh, Michelle?" I ask once we enter her office. She glances up from a sheet of paper she's picked up. "Have you heard anything from Tanner?"

A frown pulls down her eyebrows. "Not for a while, but he's at the top of the list for this project." She practically flops into her desk chair. "Let me get his info, and you should send him the pitch."

My eyebrows nearly fly off my face. I need a chair stat, too. "I should?"

"Yes." She bends and opens one of the filing drawer in her desk and starts rummaging around. "You know this project inside and out," she says. "You should do all the pitching."

"But you have the contacts." I don't even want to think about the rejections that will come in. I'm not sure I'm strong enough to handle them, though Michelle has told me I need to develop a thick skin in this business.

I've seen the pile of rejections, of course, because I've been here long enough to have seen Michelle pitch several projects. Only one of them didn't get picked up, and I know she's worked hard to have the reputation she does.

"I have the Mulvaney project to vet," she says. "Yep, I've just decided." She's found a folder and she extends it toward me. "You're pitching everyone. Use my email.

Explain who you are. Tell them you're the contact point on this, as well as the lead researcher, and that you work with me in this office."

I somehow get my fingers to clasp around the folder, but I can't do much more than that. She's serious, and I realize what a huge opportunity this is. "Wow, Michelle," I gush-say in a soft voice. "Thank you so much."

"Send me a draft of the email before you actually send it to anyone."

And there it is. I tell myself that I'd do the same if my reputation and name were on the line. I nod, tuck the folder under my arm, and head toward my desk. There, I simply stare. "Come on, Hill," I mutter to myself, but I feel like Nellie Bly, one of the first female investigative journalists in the US.

The musical *Newsies* used her life as a basis for the character role of Katherine, who sings a song about having to get this one story exactly right. So much depended on it —labor rights for underprivileged workers, women, and children.

So maybe I'm being a touch dramatic, but I feel like my entire future as a journalist and a documentary researcher depends on this one email...that I'm going to have my boss go over with me. That I've sat down to write with her before.

"Some help here, Nellie," I whisper-pray as I wake my computer and open a draft email. I proceed to stare at the blank screen, feeling more and more unsure of myself with every passing moment.

My phone chimes, and I practically dive on it. It's Liam's texting notification, and I expect to see him grinning from ear to ear. The longer we've dated, the happier he gets. We still throw words back and forth sometimes, but they're always in good flirtation, teasing, and fun.

He's fun. I feel fun when I'm with him, because he likes to do fun things. I've never gone out so much in my life, and sometimes I have to text him and tell him that I just want a quiet night to myself, or with my roommates, or at his place.

He always accommodates me, and for that, I appreciate him. I've been planning a big Hundred-Day Anniversary Celebration, where I bring him a hundred of his favorite things over the course of that day.

I've already booked us a pool table and time at a dart board at the bowling alley, though we still have about another month until our actual Hundred-Day Anniversary. I know he's working on something for me too, because I pretty much laid down the law when we hit one month, and he stood there in his doorway like he'd never seen or heard of a calendar before.

His text right now says:

> Guess who just signed a huge contract with the Freedom Marina?

As I'm comprehending, a selfie of him comes in, and

my breath catches. He's so handsome, and so happy, and a smile curves my lips too.

> You're amazing.

>> It's for the next six months, too. No more pounding the pavement for the next job, at least for a little while.

> Yay!

>> Can we celebrate tonight?

> Sure. I have some good news too.

My phone rings, and I'm not one bit surprised. I answer it with a "Hey, cowboy. Ridin' high, huh?"

"So high," he says with a laugh. "The Marina wants all new docks and ramps and parking lots. It's a huge job, Hillary." Something scuffs on his end of the line, and then he adds, "And I bid them so high, because it's not easy work, and asphalt and cement are so hard to get right now."

"And expensive," I say. Liam had passed on the condo unit, claiming it wasn't the type of work he did. I didn't know there were "types" of general contractors, but apparently, there are.

"Yeah. And they didn't even blink," he says. "Taylor said he'd print the contract, and we shook hands, and ten minutes later, I'm in my truck, wondering what just happened."

"You just rocked it," I say. "That's what happened."

He's quiet for a moment, and then he asks, "What's your good news? Did that producer finally call you?"

I swallow, because I'm not so sure if Tanner calling now would be good news or not. *Definitely not*, a little voice in my head says. *Liam just signed a contract for six months of work here in Charleston.*

Not LA.

"No," I say. "But Michelle finally approved the documentary timeline and outline. And." I really hit the D hard. "She wants me to pitch it to everyone."

He doesn't burst into applause instantly, but after a moment, he says, "Wow, Hill, that's awesome."

"You don't even know what that means, do you?" I lean back in my chair and grin up to the ceiling.

"No," he says with a laugh. "But you really sold it."

I giggle with him, glad he's happy for me even when he has no idea why. My roommates would be too, and another pang of...something sings through me when I think of them. We've been through a lot together, and I don't want to leave the Big House.

Not even for LA?

Not even for Liam?

Both are valid questions, and both have an unknown outcome. I hate that more than almost anything, and the controlling side of me really wants to rage as she swipes the board clean and starts over.

"It means I get to pitch all the production companies,"

I say. "The producers, the showrunners, the streaming services. Michelle is one of the best in the business, and by having me do this, I'll get my name out there too."

"Oh, I see," he says. "You're going to be a big shot."

"Yeah," I say. "I've got to keep up with you."

We laugh together again, and something about talking to Liam always calms me down. He is a go-go-go type of guy, and sometimes I just want to sit home. But he's sweet, and attentive, and had I known such an ooey gooey middle existed behind all his hard muscles and his poisoned tongue, I may have gotten to know him a lot sooner.

Or maybe not. It's so hard to look in a rearview mirror and know what I would've done.

"Anyway," I say. "I'd love to go to dinner tonight. Somewhere quiet?"

"I'm gonna call Coy right now."

"I'm not sure who that is, but okay."

"You do too know Coy," he says. "He and his wife own the coffee shop you like. Legacy? They have a friend who caters, and I think she's the one who does those Underground Dinners. Very quiet."

"You tried to take me to one of those on our first date," I say.

"Your memory is sublime," he says. "Or maybe that's because our first date was so amazing."

"Don't flatter yourself." Though he should. Liam's always planned great dates, and I wish I could take the rest of the afternoon off and just go be with him.

He laughs and says, "I'm headed home to shower. I'll see you at the Big House."

"Congrats, Liam," I finally say, and he says, "Knock 'em dead with your pitch."

The call ends, and I'm left staring at my computer screen again. I take a deep breath, put my fingers on the keyboard, and just start typing.

CHAPTER TWENTY-FIVE

LIAM

"I HAD NO IDEA IT TOOK SO LONG FOR A PRODUCER TO decide what he wants to produce." I look over to Hillary, who's moving the baked potato soup in her bowl around like she wants to drown herself in it. Literally.

The fact that she's not eating it speaks volumes, as does the fact that I can't get her to look up at me. I lift my hand to the waiter, and he comes on over. "Everything okay?"

"We want to order dessert," I say. That gets Hillary to look up, but I keep going. "Can we get those before the main dish?"

He glances over to Hillary, like she'll be the one to say yes or no. "Sure," he says, though he sounds a bit uncertain.

"Great. I want the mousse sampler, and we want the chocolate tuxedo brownie."

"With ice cream," Hillary adds.

"Butter pecan or vanilla?"

"Butter pecan."

"Give me a minute." The waiter walks away, and Hillary finally takes the first bite of her soup.

"You've still got it out with six places," I say.

"With six rejections." She gives me the diva-cat look like I'm the dumb one for thinking six to six is still a fifty-fifty chance of getting the documentary picked up. Not only that, but it only takes one yes.

I refrain from saying that, and instead, I ask, "Are you going to start pitching to round two?"

"Maybe," she says. "I'm going to talk to Michelle about it tomorrow."

I nod and finish off the onion rings and try to judge Hillary's mood. "So I thought for the Hundred-Day Celebration, we'd go to Centennial's. You know, because it's a hundred celebration."

Hillary pulls her spoon out of her mouth slowly, her eyes searching mine. "It takes months to get into Centennial's."

"I called when you chewed me out about missing the one-month milestone." I lean back in my chair and watch her. "But it'll require certain...attire."

Hillary carefully puts her spoon down and meets my eyes. "I suppose you want me to pull out the little black dress."

"You said you'd make it up to me, and I have yet to see said dress."

"I showed you the purple one."

"True," I muse as I reach across the table to take her hands into mine. There are so many words in my mouth, and I tell myself not to say any of them. I swallow them down again and again, and when I look into her hazel-green eyes, I feel like going to vomit up the *I-love-you*.

"Centennial's sounds amazing," Hillary says. "Thank you, Liam." She smiles and squeezes my hands. "You'll be at the marina all day still?"

"Yes." I know she has something planned for me, because she's asked me about where I'll be on Friday several times.

She nods, and we both look up as two waiters arrive with a beautiful black-and-white brownie in a cast-iron skillet, an enormous melting scoop of ice cream on top. Hillary lifts her hand, and the brownie gets placed in front of her.

"And the mousse sampler," the other man says, and I get five beautiful glasses of flavored mousse placed in front of me.

Hillary smiles at me as she takes the first bite of ice cream, and she says, "You're a genius when it comes to eating out."

"It's ordering from a menu."

"It's dessert before I'm too full." She nudges the skillet brownie and ice cream toward me. "Have some."

I take a bite of her dessert, and it's literally the best thing I've ever put in my mouth. I moan, and then offer her the white raspberry mousse. I know she likes it, because she's ordered the same flavor of Bundt cake in the past.

We share desserts, and the conversation turns to lighter, easier things. "Tabby's gonna come live with me again next week," I say.

Hillary finishes her bite of brownie. "Are you two going to survive?"

"She loves me," I say. "We'll be fine."

"Are you going to put in the cat door?"

"Saturday," I say. "You want to come hang out with me while I do it?"

"What time are you doing it?"

"Very funny." I finish the caramel mousse and observe my options for the next flavor.

"Probably later in the day, because it's an inside job," she muses.

"If you knew, why'd you ask?"

She simply puts another bite of ice cream in her mouth, her smile barely able to close around it.

I can't wrap my head around the fact that this goddess of a woman has been with me for almost a hundred days, but I follow her lead and just take another bite of mousse—this one a delectable pistachio.

———

A FEW DAYS LATER, my alarm vibrates, and I roll over to silence it. It can't be time to get up yet, and I flop back onto my pillow. In the next moment, my doorbell rings, and that makes me sit straight up. I grab my phone and tap to get to my doorbell camera, and I find Hillary standing there...in a little black dress.

Adrenaline shoots through me, especially as Hillary leans toward the camera and tucks her dark red hair behind her ear. "Good morning, Liam," she says with a smile, and oh, she's exactly like my Tabby cat. She knows how to butter me up and get me to do anything she wants.

I pull a T-shirt over my head as I head for the door, and I'm glad she hasn't left before I get there. I gape at her, drinking in the swells and dips, the way her calves look in those heels...

"Do you *know* what time it is?" I ask, echoing something she's asked me before. I grin at her. "Do we have to go to work today?"

"I do," she says. "I've got that call at ten-thirty." She cocks one hip. "Thus, the dress."

I step out onto the porch, my hand moving toward her hip like they're opposite poles, and I can't help the attraction. "You're wearing this for work?" I pull her closer, and then closer, and I know I haven't brushed my teeth yet, but I kiss her.

She doesn't seem to mind the morning breath, because she kisses me back like we've been together for one hundred days—because we have.

"Or are you wearing this for me?"

"You," she whisper-admits, and then she kisses me again.

I give in to my vampiric urges and slid my mouth down to her neck. Her hands perch on my shoulders as she says, "Happy Anniversary, Liam."

"A hundred days." I smile at her as the first rays of sunshine start to turn the gray morning light gold.

She ducks her head and steps back, and I'm pretty sure I finish falling in love with her right then and there. I start smiling, and I don't care if she teases me about being the happy-go-lucky guy who wants to take her mountain biking, and have afternoon tea in the orchard, and find the Underground Dinners and attend those.

"Your first gift," she says. "Is the little black dress." She smiles like she's the overeager one. "The dawn wake-up-call-kiss."

"Number two," I count for her.

She brandishes a cookies 'n cream candy bar. I grab it from her, surprise widening my smile. "You did not get me this."

"I had to have Emma go to four different stores to find that." She nods to it. "Those aren't easy to find, you know."

"Thank you." I wrap my arms around her and hug her. Holding her is my favorite thing, even if it takes her an extra moment to melt into my arms. That's just her stubborn red-headedness or her grumpy cat attitude—or both. I know—I can *feel* that—she's falling for me too.

I'm still not going to say anything that might scare her off, but I let myself fall and fall and fall as I hold her in the pre-morning light on my front porch while she's wearing that little black dress.

———

BY THE TIME I stand on the front porch of the Big House that night, I've gotten ninety-two little gifts from Hillary. They range from a text of the picture of two of us from when we went mountain biking in Columbia, to my anniversary lunch delivered from Cayenne's, one of my favorite places, to a basket of candy sitting on my kitchen island when I got home from work.

I ring the doorbell, and the front door opens almost immediately. All five of Hillary's roommates stand there, crowded into one another. "Evening, Liam," Emma says.

"Thank you for that cookies 'n cream candy bar," I say.

She smiles and nods. "Sure. I found it at the hardware store, believe it or not." Her flower shop sits right next to it, and I'll have to have Aaron save me the white chocolate with all those miniature Oreo cookies in it.

Tahlia lifts a miniature loaf of bread that looks suspiciously like the lemon-glazed zucchini bread I love. "Ninety-three," she says.

"I don't have a hundred gifts for Hillary."

"She doesn't need a hundred gifts," Tahlia says. "She's more of an experiences gal."

"Gal." I laugh, because Tahlia's a year younger than me, and our generation doesn't really *gal* it up very often.

"Ladies," Hillary says, and my gaze goes past the other women to her. She's entered the living room, and she's wearing a different little black dress. This one has wide straps over her shoulders instead of sleeves, and the skirt goes all the way to the ground.

It's elegant and sophisticated, and I wonder why this sleek, beautiful black-cat-woman likes me. But the way her eyes meet mine and won't let go tells me she does. Her roommates part like the Red Sea, and she walks through, her steps slow and glided.

"Another black dress," I say, my voice a little throaty.

"I told you I'd make it up to you."

"Is this gift number ninety-four?"

"If you want it to be." She laces her arm through mine, and we leave the Big House. Somehow, in my SUV, there's an envelope taped to the steering wheel, and since I've already helped Hillary into the passenger seat, she sees my surprise when I get in the driver's seat.

"What's this?" I untape the envelope and give Hillary a look. "You know, it would've been nice to have a heads-up about the gifts."

"They're little things."

"But there are a hundred of them." I open the envelope to find a certificate for a massage. "And this isn't little."

"You work so hard," she says. "I swear, that's the biggest one."

I don't want to be ungrateful, but I've planned dinner and dancing. We've been texting all day, and I don't doubt that Hillary knows I'm thrilled to have reached this milestone in our relationship. But I feel...insignificant compared to her.

"You don't feel bad about the gifts, do you?"

"They're okay," I say. "I just feel a little bit like I should've done more."

"You got a reservation at one of the nicest restaurants in the city," she says. "Liam." She takes my hand and looks at me from under her lashes. "Don't be upset."

"I'm not upset." I pull out of the driveway and head down the lane. It takes me a couple more minutes to simmer all the way down, and she lets me have my time. "Sorry I'm being a little...something about the gifts."

"One of them was a link to a mountain bike trail I think you'll like."

"It takes thought."

"I know you think about me," she says.

"I feel like it's all I do," I mutter to my side window.

"What?"

"Nothing," I say. My bad mood completely lifts by the time we get to Centennial's, and I let the valet take the SUV while I take Hillary's hand. Suddenly, the night feels made of magic. With such a pretty woman on my arm, I'm sure everyone in the restaurant will be looking at us.

They aren't, because the place is full of beautiful people. And beautiful food, and as I lead her onto the elevator to go up to the rooftop for dancing, I press a kiss to her forehead.

"What do we need to talk about?" I ask.

Hillary gives me a wary glance. "Nothing. Why?"

I shift my feet as another couple of couples get on the car with us. We ride up in silence, and we're the last couple to step outside. "The rooftop is kind of our thing," I say once we're alone again.

She smiles at me and says, "It seems to be."

"Will you dance with me?"

"I thought you'd never ask." She grins and steps easily into my arms. We fit so well together, and I wonder how I can tell her that.

"Hill," I start, and she tilts her head back to see me. She's curled and swooped and pinned her hair up tonight, and there's so much about her I like. My feelings race through me, and I marvel at their authenticity.

"Liam," she says, prompting me.

I clear my throat. "I'm...I'm falling for you. Hard."

Hillary's eyes flit between both of mine, and she takes my face in her hands and kisses me right there on the dance floor. She doesn't use her voice to say she's falling for me too, but her mouth still says it loud and clear.

CHAPTER TWENTY-SIX

HILLARY

LIAM MAY NOT HAVE GOTTEN ME ONE HUNDRED little things I like. He may not have penned out one hundred things about me he likes. But he's planned the perfect date, and he looks the perfect part, and he kisses me perfectly.

I know I'm falling—hard—for him too, but I don't dare say it. I think he gets the message from the way I can't stop kissing him. He kneads me closer and closer, though we're chest-to-chest.

In that moment, I realize we're actually in public, and I break the kiss.

He clears his throat again, and I love that about him. He's so strong and confident on the outside, but he's just so dang...good on the inside. Sweet and sensitive, loyal and hardworking, true and funny and smart.

"Okay," he growl-says. "So I think there's something we need to talk about."

"And you want to do it tonight?" I look up at him as he gently sways me around the dance floor. The other couples up here are all dressed beautifully as well, and there's real trees, shrubs, and flowers lining the floor.

The air is clear and while still a bit muggy, because darkness has fallen, it's starting to turn cooler and crisper.

"Yeah." He gazes at me with all of the Liam-intensity I've seen before. Perhaps a new edge in those dark eyes, but it's hard to tell in the mood lighting on the roof. "It's about kids."

"Kids?"

"Yeah." He doesn't elaborate, and my mind blitzes back to our very first bike ride together.

"I've asked you about having kids," I say slowly.

He blinks, and it's obvious from his hard, almost blank expression that he's thinking hard. Going back in time to get those memories out. "At the park," he finally says.

I nod. "You said, if I recall correctly, 'yeah, sure' when I asked you if you wanted kids."

"Yeah, sure," he parrots again, a smile touching that gorgeous mouth. "I do want kids. I want to know if you do. You're an only child. I'm not sure if that was by choice, or because your parents couldn't have more kids, or...what."

"I don't know either." I look past him toward a lamp-post that's been put on the corner of the dance floor. It throws out soft yellow light, really creating a romantic atmosphere. As if rooftop dancing with fancy hors d'oeu-vres and champagne isn't fancy enough.

"You don't know?"

"My mama doesn't talk about things like that with me," I say, finally drawing myself back to the present, back to him. "But I'd like kids." I frown. "I think."

"More than one?"

"I don't know." I look up at him. "Is this something couples decide on their Hundred-Day Anniversary?"

He softens and smiles at me. "No," he says. "I just wanted to talk to you about it."

"Since you're falling in love with me." I can admit my stomach turns soft and gooey at the thought of being loved by him. I've been engaged twice, but I didn't love those men, and faced with Liam, I don't think they loved me either.

He does—or if he doesn't, he's dang close.

That does send a spiral of panic through me, because I'm not sure I'm quite ready to reciprocate his feelings all the way. A lot of them, yes. Some of them—the crucial ones—I need more time to iron flat and examine.

"Yeah." He kicks a smile at me. "Since *we're* falling in love with *each other*."

I don't confirm or deny his statement. I simply fold myself into his embrace and let him dance with me until he says it's time to go home.

He drives, and I doze.

He pulls up to the Big House, and we get out.

He walks me to the door, and I wait for him to kiss me good-night. He doesn't say I love you with words, but that kiss...

Oh, that kiss. The way he holds me close, and runs one hand along the back of my neck, and strokes his mouth against mine again and again...

Yeah, I'm falling for him, and I think he might already have parachuted down to the bottom of the canyon and is all the way in love with me already.

Now, I just have to pray I survive the landing.

———

THE FOLLOWING WEEK, my phone rings at work. I rarely get phone calls, but since I've been pitching the Prime Bank documentary, it feels like my phone rings while it's off the hook. This morning, I've already fielded two calls, both from producers who've shown more interest in my pitch.

They're the first two who have, and I've just returned to my desk after a mega-planning session with Michelle. My stomach growls, because it's lunchtime, and I just want to eat and think through things.

The next phase of pitching these two producers. Following up with the others I haven't heard from yet. Prepping another round of potential people to pitch. It all makes my head hurt, and I consider letting the call go to voicemail.

Michelle would be mortified though, so I pick up the receiver and say, "This is Hillary Mays," in what Liam calls my sexy-no-nonsense librarian voice. One that would chastise little boys for being too loud in the library and chase out teen couples making out in remote aisle of non-fiction books.

I sit down and lean back as a man says, "Ah, yes. Just the woman I want to talk to."

In person, I'd roll my eyes at this guy and turn my back on him. On the phone, at work, I allow a small smile to come to my face. "You do? Who do I have the great pleasure of speaking with?"

I'm not flirting; I'm telling this guy his phone etiquette could use some serious work.

"This is Tanner Bridgestone," he says, and the rest of the world goes white. I blink, but my eyes have gone blind. Thankfully, my ears still work, so I can hear what Mr. Bridgestone says next.

"My assistant forwarded on your pitch about Prime National Bank, and—" He sighs mightily. "Tell me you haven't sold it yet. The fate of my assistant's job depends on it." He bites out the last sentence, and my vision comes back to me.

"I was going to reach out again today," I say smoothly. No need to tell him that there's only been mild interest so far. I remind myself that I can't control what else is being pitched, and there have been quite a few financial scandal documentaries out in the wild recently.

"To see if you had any interest before I sign anything with..." I pause there, because I've heard Michelle do the same thing. She never says who else is in the game, because she's counting on Tanner Bridgestone imagining his biggest competitor in that pause.

"Hillary," he says smoothly, without the Southern accent I'm used to hearing. "I should've followed up with my inquiry to speak with you months ago. It's been insane here, as I'm sure you can imagine."

"I can," I say, though I really can't. "Hollywood in the summer?" I lean back in my chair, a genuine smile on my face now. "So the rumors that y'all take off in the hotter months isn't true?"

He laughs, and I'm glad to hear the heartiness of it. "You're a cheeky one, aren't you?"

I laugh too but keep it short. "Not at all. I'm just glad you finally called back. For a few weeks here, I thought I'd been stood up without even having gone on a date."

Chuckles come through the line, and he asks, "Do you have a storyboard?"

"Yes, sir," I say. "I'm forwarding it along to several others today, and I can include you."

"Miss Mays," he says, all evidence of laughter gone now. "I need you to promise me something."

"I'll do my best," I say, parroting another phrase I've heard my boss use.

"You can't sell this to anyone without at least giving me a chance at it." He states it so plainly that I want him to be the one to get the rights to produce, direct, and distribute this documentary.

"I'll do my best," I repeat. "You do understand that I'm the assistant in this case, correct, sir?"

"I will call Michelle the moment we hang up, then. I want this, and I just need to call a meeting to get the board's approval."

"Oh, don't waste the call," I say. "Her office is right next to mine. I'll talk to her."

"Wonderful," he says. "And Hillary? When can we talk?"

"About?" I ask, though I'm fairly certain I know what he wants to speak with me about.

"About you coming on as the producer of this project. I have far too much on my plate to take on EP on this. But I've seen your research, and I believe in fostering up and coming talent, especially on projects they know inside and out."

I can't stop smiling, but I don't answer right away. So many things swim through my head that it takes a while for the words, "Yes, sir," to come out of my mouth. It's not exactly the right answer, but Mr. Bridgestone doesn't poke fun at me over it.

"If you'll send along your schedule, I'll have my assistant set up a longer time when we can talk. I like to do these things via video, if possible."

"Yes, sir," I say again. "Storyboard for the Prime documentary, and a schedule of my available times for us to talk."

"Thank you, Miss Mays."

"Thank *you*, Mister Bridgestone." The call ends, and I once again find myself staring at my computer screen, no thoughts in my head and no action taking place. I'm not sure how long I sit there.

My stomach growls, and I remember it's lunchtime.

My phone rings, and I remember I'm at work.

My boss comes striding out of her office, her heels really pushing the limits of her burgundy pencil skirt, and says, "Hill, I just got off the phone with Tanner Bridgestone." Her eyes are wide and round as excitement pours from her. "He wants Prime...and you."

I somehow manage to nod as the image of my hot, handsome, smart, sexy boyfriend comes into my mind's eyes. "Yes," I say. "I just spoke with him too."

Michelle throws her arms up—well as far as her matching burgundy jacket will allow—and laughs. Michelle, who I've barely seen smile. Michelle, who doesn't even get excited on birthdays and Christmas.

She laughs, and then she does a little tippy-toe dance over to me and engulfs me in a hug. "I knew you were special, Hillary," she says among all the joy. I'm about at my limit for happy-happy things, but I hug her back, because she's right.

This is huge.

Not that I'm special, but that Tanner Bridgestone

thinks I am. Now, I just have to figure out how to tell Liam.

———

THAT NIGHT, I order pizza. I'm waiting on the front porch when the delivery driver arrives, and I don't go back into the Big House with the pie. I start the walk to Liam's, and every step is like me committing myself to the lion's den.

Still, I keep on because 1. I promised him I'd bring dinner, and 2. I'm telling him about the documentary and Tanner Bridgestone tonight.

Before I'd left the office that day, I'd already set up a time to talk to Tanner—and it's tomorrow. I can't go into that with Liam weighing on my mind. He's been there all day as it is, and while that's not super abnormal, the clenched stomach and worry over how he'll react to my good news definitely is.

Because it's only *my* good news. It means bad news for him. "If he really likes you," I mutter to myself, and it's a defense mechanism, I know. Of course Liam really likes me. I don't believe a man alive could fake the way he kisses me, and he wouldn't tell me he was falling for me, and he wouldn't be talking about marriage and family and life after being single.

I knock on the door, ring the doorbell, and then go

inside. The front door isn't locked, and Liam calls to me from the back of the house. I find him in the kitchen, sudsy up to his elbows as he scrubs his hands. He golden-retriever-grins at me—another sign he likes me—and says, "I just need two minutes, but I got that battery in. I prevailed!"

I smile back at him the best I can and slide the pizza box onto the island. "Good job, baby." I nod to the box, but his back is turned already as he goes back to getting cleaned up. "I got the chicken bacon ranch, with Alfredo sauce."

"Sounds amazing," he says. "I've got peaches off the trees and plenty of cream in the fridge." He twists and looks over his shoulder at me. "Do you want me to clean up some of those for you?"

"Peaches and cream?" I ask. "All day, every day." A certain measure of happiness does make my mouth tip up in the corners, but it doesn't last long. "Liam," I say.

He flips off the water and turns toward me, a tea towel in his hands as he dries them now. His joviality fades as he looks at me. I don't know what he sees, but I'm guessing the pure misery streaming from every pore and cell in my body.

"What's goin' on?" He tosses the towel on the counter and doesn't make a move toward the pizza. That's how serious this is.

I take a breath, but the words aren't ordered right. Still, when I open my mouth, I say, "I don't know how this is going to work."

"What?" Liam frowns. "How *what* is going to work?"

Frustration fills me, but not with him. With the situation. With myself, for allowing this relationship to continue to this point when I've been fantasizing of LA on the side. It almost feels like I've been cheating on Liam with such a dream.

"Us," I blurt out. "Tanner Bridgestone called today. That big producer who wants to talk to me about producing? He wants the documentary I've been working on for-freaking-ever, and if he gets it—which he will, because he's Tanner Bridgestone—he wants me to come work on the production with him."

Liam takes another couple of steps toward me and folds me into the safety of his chest. Tears prick my eyes, which is absolutely ridiculous, because I can't remember the last thing I cried about.

Maybe Liam's seven a.m. mow-wake-up-call.

"This is good news, Hill," he says. "I mean, it sounds good to me." He rocks with me, but we don't turn and sway and dance. I think of our Hundred Day Anniversary, when everything was so carefree and perfect, and I yearn for that night.

"If that happens," I say. "I'll have to move to LA."

That causes him to suck in a breath and pull away. "LA? Like Los Angeles?"

I nod and swipe miserably at my face. "I mean, that's the dream, you know? That's where the big producers live and work. Right now, I'm just a wanna-be investigative journalist, doing research for documentaries, in the off-hand hope that I might get to produce something someday."

I look up at him. "And that someday seems to be coming. I'm meeting with him tomorrow."

Liam blinks, his shock moving plainly and swiftly across his face. "Wait, wait," he says, dropping his chin as he steps back, creating more distance between us. "That's the dream? That's *always* been the dream? Moving to LA?"

I don't know what to say to him, because yes. "Not forever," I whisper in defense. "I don't want to live there forever."

"How long?"

"As long as the project takes." I wipe my nose and flip open the pizza box, but Liam doesn't make a move toward it. "This one? It's a documentary with very few players that need to be vetted and interviewed. I bet it takes six months. Maybe eight."

His breath scoffs out of his lungs, and then he joins me at the counter. I hand him a piece of pizza and pick up one of my own. His eyes search mine, and he asks, "When will you be moving?"

"I don't know," I say. "It might not happen at all."

He turns away, but not before I see him start to roll his eyes. His voice also gives away how he really feels, because he says, "Come on, Hill. We both know this is happening," with plenty of disdain in his tone.

Liam paces away from me, but I feel frozen next to the pizza box. "I just wish I'd have known it was going to happen so soon."

"I couldn't know that either."

"But you knew it was *always* the dream." He turns to face me, and he's definitely back to his grumpy persona. "And you didn't tell me."

CHAPTER TWENTY-SEVEN

CLAUDIA

"Oh," I say when I walk in my bedroom and find Hillary flopped on my bed. I don't check over my shoulder, because no one's followed me upstairs, and we're the only ones who live on the third floor.

I enter the room and toe the door closed. "What are you doing here?"

Hillary doesn't even lift her head. "Why does getting what you've been working for feel so terrible?"

I'm not sure what she's talking about, but Hillary usually starts conversations in the middle, and I have to work my way forward and backward. "Did Tatum Golden Gate Bridge call?" I hurry to the edge of the bed and sit beside her hip.

"Yes," she says with a moan. "Tanner Bridgestone, and he wants the documentary and me to produce it."

I gasp and try to study her face, but her eyes are

closed. If she wasn't speaking and breathing, I'd think she'd died. "Hillary." I reach for her and push her gorgeous red hair off her forehead. I've always wanted hair her color, since the moment I met her.

We lived across the hall from one another in a student apartment. Ryanne and Emma lived there too, but Tahlia had already graduated and moved out. She was still on the lease, so I'd met her plenty of times, and I'd taken over her room the following year.

I know how to talk to Hillary, and while she's not a super dramatic person, she loves the dramatic reactions. "This is everything you've wanted," I say. "You've worked your whole life for this. All through college. For the past eight years."

My fingers linger on her shoulder, and her eyes flutter open. "You're not going to let it pass you by, are you?"

Pure indecision rages in her expression, along with plenty of unhappiness. "What about Liam? Who gives up a god of a man like him for a job?"

I don't know how to answer that, and Hillary doesn't really want an explanation anyway. "When did you see him?"

"Yesterday." She sighs and her eyes roll back in her head a little. "Last night. I talked to Tanner today, and the offer should hit Michelle's desk tomorrow before we close."

I shelve that amazing news for a moment. "Did Liam say it was over?"

"No," she admits.

"Did you ask him to go with you?"

Her eyes close again. "No."

"Did you break-up with him?"

She shakes her head no.

My heartbeat races, as does my mind. "So...where did you two leave things?"

"Nowhere," she says. "Or, I mean, I don't know. We ate pizza, and he turned on some rerun of rodeo or something." She sighs, and I feel like it comes from a true place of regret and indecision. "I didn't know it would only take one hundred and nine days for us to..."

I wait for her to finish, but she doesn't. She doesn't need to. I know a heart-broken and love-distraught Hillary when I see one. She's in love with Liam Graff, whether she knows it or not.

"I don't love him," she whispers as if she's reading my mind. "But I could, and Claudia." She sits straight up, her eyes blinking rapidly. "I need more time with him, and how can I have more time with him if I'm going to leave Cider Cove?"

My heart suddenly shrinks. "You're going to leave Cider Cove," I whisper. I don't need to ask who will live on the third floor with me. We both know Tahlia needs the rent money to keep this enormous house, and if Hillary moves out, we'll definitely be getting a new roommate.

Oops. *I'll* be getting a new roommate, one who I'll

have to share a bathroom with and one who'll live mere feet down the hall from me.

"The project is projected to take six months," she says. "Up to twelve. If longer than that, I'll have to sign a new contract."

I nod, and swallow back the several questions I have. One manages to squeak out as I ask, "Will it take that long?"

"Impossible to know," she says. "And I'll have to come back here and interview Catarina at least twice." She scoots to the edge of the bed and stands up. "Tell me I haven't ruined everything with Liam."

A deep breath clears my mind and my lungs. "Of course you haven't," I say quickly. "Tell him you want him to come with you. Tell him it only took you one hundred and nine days to fall in love with him."

She shakes her head again, and I know Hillary will hold onto her feelings for another one hundred and nine days, and probably that amount of time again. She's slow to trust after her failed engagements, that's for sure. She hasn't dated in years, and now that I've broken up with Greg, I understand more about why.

One thing I've learned: Online dating apps aren't really the best places to meet a One True Love. At least not for me. There's so much that can be hidden in a profile, and plenty that gets glossed over until later, when over lattes, you learn the man you've been out with a handful of times and think you know actually has another girlfriend in Atlanta.

But hey, me and Estella exchanged numbers, and we're actually friends now. *Maybe she can come live here...*

I pull my attention back to Hillary as she crosses the room to my bedroom door. I lunge after her. "Where are you going? Over to Liam's?"

She shakes her head. "He said he'd be busy tonight, because they're doing some sort of testing something-or-other at the marina, and then it's his sister's birthday."

"Hill."

She turns back to me just as I reach her, and I pull her into a hug. "When will you have to leave?"

"I'm not super sure," she whispers. "We'll work all of that in the contract phase."

"You've said contracts take forever," I say. "Maybe you'll be here for a while still."

"I think Tanner wants to strike on this while the financial scandals are hot. His offer is going to—and I quote, 'knock our socks off,' and my guess? I'll move really soon, Claude."

She holds me tighter, and I can't let go of her either. "You'll always have a place to stay here."

She nods against my shoulder, then she ducks away from me, opens my door, and high-tails it to her bedroom. I can let her go without saying anything, and then I'll spend an hour online, obsessively searching for any hints that

Mike Bowing is going to be retiring from the City Planner position any time soon.

Her bedroom door closes, and I do the same with mine. Instead of getting online, I pick up my phone, and I start texting. The other girls in the house should know the situation, and I know Hillary won't tell them.

———

FRIDAY MARKS A NEW MONTH, and that means I'm updating the scheduling app at work, pulling up our events for September and making sure they get over to the Public Relations department, which will spend August putting together promotional materials for the parks and rec happenings around town.

The first couple of days of the month are chaotic at best, and this first day of August falls on a Friday, which means Monday will be insane too.

I've just finished that when my phone starts a flurry of notification sounds. I don't even have time to pick it up before Beckett Fletcher next door bellows as if he's just won the lottery, the World Series, and the Superbowl all in the same moment.

I look toward his wall, my upper lip already curling up in distaste, and then the man himself bursts into my office. "Mike Bowing is retiring!"

Great. Now he's bellowing in my office. But the things

he's shouting about make my pulse jig around in my chest, and I drop my eyes to my phone again.

Sure enough, all of those notifications represented texts from others in the Public Works Department, and all of them say I should apply for the City Planner position, opening up on January 1.

Well, that's the hire date, actually.

I don't respond to Beckett and instead tap to get over to my Internet browser. The insufferable man plops down in the chair in front of my desk. "Did you see the internal memo?"

"Not yet," I say, but I click on my email, and there's the email from Winslow himself. I tap on it to open it, and it's definitely like a job notice.

He says he's announcing his retirement, and that the position of City Planner will be vacated on December thirty-first. "They're looking to hire from within city government," I read aloud, and Beckett ruins the excitement growing in my chest by chuckling.

"That job is as good as mine," he says.

I look away from the computer, everything in my body that can beat hammering away loudly. "You wish," I say. "I'm going to apply for this job, and I'm in a higher position than you."

He scoffs, though some of his joviality fades. "I'm the *Deputy* Director," he says, as if I don't know what he does in that smelly office next door to mine.

"Of what?" I challenge. "Monkeys?" I scoff. "*I'm* the Public Works *Director*."

"I deal with way more money than you do."

"I manage three times the employees you do."

We stare at one another, and one of my superpowers is picking the perfect paint color for any room. If our back-and-forth had delved that far, I'd have said it. It's not really going to help me win any arguments with Beckett Fletcher, and it won't help me get the City Planner position.

Beckett has some skills too, because he does have a dual major in accounting, and I narrow my eyes at him. Then I turn back to the computer and keep reading. The list of qualifications for the job goes on and on, and I realize that if I want the City Planner position, I'm going to need every single piece of my application in place in the next four months.

"Interviews in December," I say mostly to myself.

"Don't bother, Claudia," Beckett says as he stands up. Thankfully, he's leaving already, and I manage to glare over to him as he retreats. He spins back at the doorway. "That job is mine."

He leaves a definite wake as he leaves, and my fingers tremble slightly as I promise myself, "Over my dead body, Beckett."

CHAPTER TWENTY-EIGHT

LIAM

I HAVE WAY TOO MANY PEACHES, BUT I CAN'T STAND the thought of letting them drop to the ground. I've always used the orchards as a way to make a little extra money during harvest time, and this year is no different just because I've fallen in love with the redheaded beauty next door.

I spend Saturday morning letting people come pick their own peaches for a fee, and then all day Sunday helping Momma with her yardwork, canning peaches for the winter, and then refusing to go home—all so I won't find Hillary waiting for me.

Not that she is. I have a doorbell camera, and it doesn't buzz at me once all day on Saturday or Sunday. Hillary doesn't come over, and I suppose I can't fault her for that. I did ask her to give me a couple of days to...something.

"Think," I tell myself as I climb back up the ladder early on Monday morning. "You need time to think."

About what, I'm not sure. Hillary has texted me several times, and I'm texting her back. That's how I know she got an offer—a big one—on her documentary from White Sands Studios. I looked them up, and yeah, they're legit with a capital L.

While I'd been looking at the website, I couldn't stop myself from clicking over to the STAFF page, where I saw Tanner Bridgestone. The man is much older than I'd pictured him, and funnily enough he didn't have horns or a serpentine tongue.

He's not really the one taking Hillary from me.

"She *wants* to go," I mutter-grumble to myself and the basket of peaches that's getting heavier and heavier by the moment. I can't stay out here all morning, picking peaches, so I head back to the house. I'll set up another you-pick time for Wednesday afternoon and evening, and if I post in the neighborhood groups, I'll have mommas forcing their tween and teen sons to come pick peaches.

After all, everyone in the south loves peach pie, peach preserves, peach jam, and my personal favorite—peaches and cream. That makes me think of Hillary—what doesn't, honestly?—and my chest vibrates in a strange way.

I push against the thoughts of her, knowing I'm hopelessly in love with her. She could lock me in this house and only slip raw potatoes through a slot in the door, and when she finally came back and opened the door all the way, I'd be panting and tail-waggingly glad to see her.

Love does the strangest things to a person, and there is no amount of peaches and no amount of work I can immerse myself into that can drive her away.

I don't want to drive her away. I can't say the words out loud, but they ring in my head on the way back to the house. I put the peaches in the fridge and get in the shower, wondering if I can just text Hillary and tell her I don't want her to go.

Of course I want her to go. This is the opportunity of a lifetime for her, and there's no way I'm going to be the one standing in her way of producing this documentary. I have some seedlings of a thought, but I refuse to let them grow too much.

I laugh-chat with the marina manager, and I finish up the boathouse I've been working on. I have a hard time driving past the Big House without looking longingly at it, so I don't drive back to Cider Cove. I head for Cherry Heights, and my momma's. She's going to know something is up, and I'm surprised I pulled the wool over her eyes yesterday.

Still, she'll have dinner, and maybe once night starts to fall, I can sneak home with my tail tucked between my legs.

When I get to Momma's, I simply sit in my truck for a few minutes. I'm not exactly praying, and not exactly meditating, but I do like the quiet time to think. I know what I want, but I don't know how to get it. I feel like Hillary is this enigma, a woman I still haven't figured out but that I'd really like to. She's slippery, and I can't grasp her with my bare hands, and I feel like I'm going to lose her before we've really had a chance to know if we can be two halves of one whole.

I eventually unbuckle and go inside, but Momma's not in the house. There's no evidence that she's cooked anything that day, and my stomach roars at me for leading it astray and bringing it here. "Momma?"

Nothing, and I head out the back door. She's got quite the flower garden out here, and the only reason her garden plot is empty is because I told her I don't have time to come plant it, take care of it, and harvest it for her. She finally lamented when I pointed out to her that her neighbors are always trying to give away their excess produce, and she doesn't need to grow her own.

"Momma?" I call into the yard, and she comes bustling out of the shed. My concern for her fades, but her face remains hard and surprised.

"What are you doing here?" she calls as she claps something from her hands. I'm used to being sweaty and dirty, but I'm not too used to seeing Momma with soiled hands.

"I was in the neighborhood," I say casually.

She comes toward me, and I'm not surprised to find her in a housedress and a pair of sneakers. "I didn't make dinner."

"I can order Chinese?"

Momma pauses at the bottom of the steps and plants her hands on her hips. "You're going to order Chinese?"

"Yeah, and your game shows are almost on." I wipe the sweat from along the base of my ballcap, hoping I can play off the increased heat in my face as simply the hot August evening. "So come on in out of the heat."

She grips the railing and climbs the steps, laboring toward me until I take her into a hug. She says nothing, but this is Momma, and her silence simply means she's biding her time. Inside the blessed air conditioning, I pull out my phone and call in an order for Chinese food.

"Twenty minutes," I tell Momma, and I take her place at the sink to get cleaned up. I think of this same action I was doing almost a week ago when Hillary walked in with pizza and the worst news ever.

I face Momma and say, "I think Hillary and I are... we're—" I clear my throat. "I don't think we're gonna make it."

Momma goes, "Pish," and then adds another scoff. "Of course you are. I've seen you with her."

"It doesn't matter how I am with her," I say. "It's how she is with me." I give Momma a slight glare, because it's not her fault Hillary didn't tell me completely about her dreams. I knew about the opportunity to speak to a big producer. I didn't know he'd want her to move to LA for up to a year.

"What did you do?" Momma asks, following me into the living room.

"I didn't do anything." I sigh as I sink down onto the couch. "Besides live here and own my own business here." I cast a look over to Momma and decide to tell her the whole story.

"So, she left," I say. "It was an awkward night, and we didn't really reach a resolution."

Momma keeps toeing herself back and forth, her eyes glued to the TV. I don't need to push her to lecture me, so I close my eyes, my mind too tired to keep thinking all the time.

The contestant solves the puzzle and a commercial starts. "I know your resolution, Liam-baby."

She hasn't called me Liam-baby for a long, long time. I open my eyes and look over to her. "Yeah? What's that?"

She tears her eyes from the blaring TV, her gaze clear and even. "When I met your daddy and fell in love with him, I packed up everything I owned and I moved to where he was."

"Momma, it's not that easy," I say.

"Why isn't it?" she asks.

"Well, for one thing," I fire back at her. "Daddy loved you too." I tell myself to calm down. It's not Momma I'm upset with, and it's not even Hillary. It's just...life. It feels like I've finally let down my defenses, broken down my walls, and found someone I want to spend my life with—and now I can't have her.

"You don't think she loves you?"

"No, Momma," I say. "I don't think she loves me."

"But you love her."

I press my lips together, annoyed there isn't even a question mark on that sentence. I'm also not about to admit it out loud to my mother, even if it is true.

"So what do you need?" Momma asks.

"I need her here," I say. "I need to see her every day, and talk to her, and somehow buy myself some more time until she *does* fall in love with me."

Momma smiles like she's the cat who ate the canary. "Do they do construction in LA?"

The doorbell rings, and I've never been happier for a food delivery. Momma doesn't press the issue, and I stay and watch two more game shows with her before I take my teriyaki chicken and head home.

It's not quite dark enough to obscure the amazingly strong and sexy roof on the Big House, and I keep my eyes on it as I drive by. It just so happens that Hillary's room is up near it. Of course, I don't see her or anyone else, because no one spends much time in direct sunlight in the evening in Charleston if they're not on the beach.

I make it home, and I eat a peach while standing in front of the sink, letting the juice drip down my chin. I feel like I've reached a new low, and I get in the shower for the second time that day. This routine isn't that unusual for me, but the loneliness that follows me everywhere is.

I finally go out onto the back deck and settle into one

of the chairs at the table I have there. It's shady and there's a slight breeze whispering through the trees tonight, and I'm settled enough, full enough, and clean enough to text Hillary.

> When are you moving to LA?

Maybe it'll be months from now, and she'll be madly in love with me and ask me to come with her. Or we'll be engaged, and of course that means I'll go with her.

"I can't believe you're even thinking about going with her." I shake my head and curse my mother, though I love her so.

> I was going to call you. Or come over, because Liam…it's so much faster than I thought.

> How much faster?

> End of the month.

It's amazing to me how only a few words can change lives so completely.

> The end of this month?

> They want me on-set at the beginning of September. I'm trying to figure out how long it'll take me to drive, and if I can fit everything I need in my sedan or if I should upgrade to an SUV like yours.
> It's all overwhelming.

I can just picture Hillary trying to do all of this. She'll have one of her notebooks out, and little boxes made that she can *tick, tick, tick* off as she completes tasks.

I don't use much paper; I even have a digital app to measure things for my projects. So I navigate over to my Notes app and type in the one thing I need to figure out before I can take another step in any direction.

I read over the words again and again, even though Hillary texts me again.

Can I move to California with my girlfriend?

CHAPTER TWENTY-NINE

HILLARY

"Can you make up one of those medium boxes?" I glance over my shoulder to Tahlia, who's helping me pack today. All of my roommates have helped at some point in the past couple of weeks. None of them are happy about me moving, but they love me, and they've helped me.

As she stretches the tape over the bottom of the box, Tahlia says, "Liam was here this morning. Dropped off some more bins."

I nod, my tongue suddenly too thick for my mouth. Liam hasn't abandoned me either, and I truly don't understand it. I fold another sweater—which I probably won't even need in sunny LA, though it is short-sleeved—and lay it on top of the stack of tops I've been working through.

Thoughts of Liam overwhelm me the moment they start, and a fresh round of tears seethes behind my eyes.

The fabrics in front of me blur, but I don't let the moisture out.

I do sniffle, and that gets Tahlia to quit making the box and come over to me. She says nothing as she puts her hand on my shoulder, and I look at her.

The tears slip down my face then, and we both sit on my bed. "What am I doing?" I ask.

"You're taking an amazing opportunity," Tahlia tells me. She's used to working with teens who have attitude, so she knows how to talk to me.

"I don't mean to be so standoffish." I wipe my eyes and my nose with a tissue I've plucked from the box on my desk. "I want this. I know I do."

"You just want Liam too."

I nod, because I do. At the same time, I haven't done anything to find out if I can keep him. "We barely talk about this," I whisper-admit. "I see him, and sometimes we just sit together." I study the crumpled tissue in my hands. "It's nice, but I don't know. I want him to—to—come up with a solution."

"Oh, honey." Tahlia wraps me in a hug and holds me tight. "I know you don't see it, and I know you've had a rough time with men in the past, but baby." She pulls away and looks at me the way a caring mother would. "He's waiting for *you* to offer the solution."

Pure helplessness fills me. "I can't ask him to come with me."

"Why not?" she challenges as she settles back on the bed.

I shrug one shoulder and go back to studying the tissue. "He owns a business here, Tahlia. He has a contract with the marina that lasts three more months."

"Then he'll come then," she says. "You haven't talked about long-distance anything?" I shake my head, and she scoffs. "Hill. Come on."

"Come on what?" I get up and pick up another shirt, this one purple with butterflies all over it. Do people wear butterfly blouses in California? What if all of my clothes are stupid and need to be replaced with something fresher, hipper, more...West Coast?

"You have never held your tongue with this man." Tahlia stands too. "With anyone, about anything." She pushes my hair off my shoulder and then turns me toward her. I let her, because I need to be bossed around right now. "Go over there and ask him to come. At least go over some options with him."

I nod and say, "I will, once we get these clothes packed." We both know I probably won't, but I toy with the idea. The scene between us plays out in my head, and I have all the perfect things to say to mend everything that has bent and broken between us.

If only reality was as easy as the fantasy I can concoct.

Tahlia and I finish with today's packing list—yes, I've broken it down into bitesized, manageable chunks from now until the day I move—and she heads downstairs. I step over to the window and look out. I see Liam's orchards to my right, past the waves of green grass on our side of the property line, as well as some on his.

I can't see his house from here, and I can't imagine he would ever, ever leave that farmhouse. Not for LA. Not for a tiny apartment.

Not for me.

———

A COUPLE OF DAYS LATER, I make the drive to Columbia alone. I haven't told my parents the good news about my fantastic job opportunity, nor the fact that I'm moving across the country in literally thirteen days.

It's time.

I wanted Liam to come—I even got brave enough to ask him—but he said he had a prior engagement, and he'd meet me back at the Big House tomorrow. I can't believe I'm staying overnight in the mansion-castle again, but I figure I won't be seeing my parents in person for a while after this.

"It's a really amazing job," I say, testing out the strength in my voice. I sound decently happy to my own ears. "I'll be producing, Mama. It's a documentary I've put together from scratch, and I've been working on it for almost two years."

When I say all of that, it becomes clear to me why I'm doing this. Why I'm giving up my room in the Big House.

Why I've spent literally every last penny I have to rent a truck that will tow my sedan across seven full states and an entire country—heck, the width of a whole continent. Why I haven't been able to ask Liam to uproot himself and do the same.

My heart feels like it belongs in South Carolina, but I can survive somewhere else for a while.

"I get to work with one of the biggest, brightest, and best producers in the country," I continue. "He loves the concept, and I got the exclusive interview." I need to make sure I fit in all the pieces of the degree my daddy paid for. Investigative journalism. Film. Check, check.

What about Liam? I hear my mama ask. In fact, she asked if he'd be accompanying me for tonight's dinner. I'd told her about his "previous engagement," and she hadn't said another word about it.

I sigh at the Columbia city skyline, remembering my first mountain biking expedition with Liam. We've gone a few times since, but he's stuck to the trails surrounding Charleston instead of making the almost two-hour drive up here. That's given us more time to ride, talk, and then go get something to eat.

Liam really gets how eating out is important to me, and he always checks the menu before we go somewhere new, just to make sure there's something potatoey that I'll like. He packs up all of the gear I need to go with him. He drives us, and he lets me pick the music in the car, and he takes care of everything.

He takes care of me.

As I make the turn onto my parents' estate, I realize I'm in love with Liam Graff.

And not only that, he's in love with me.

He hasn't said those three words in that exact order, but he has admitted he was falling for me. "I don't need the words," I whisper to the live oaks lining the lane.

But of course I do. I just also happen to be able to *see* how he loves me, the way Tahlia said.

"I'm in love with him," I say out loud, and my voice sounds awed now. "And he loves me." I have to whisper the last part, because Liam is the first man to be in love with me.

My heart seems to grow to twice its size, then three times, then four. I don't feel like crying now. I feel like laughing.

I come to a stop in front of the mansion, and today, there's no butler or valet rushing to help me. I get out and retrieve my own bag, then climb the wide, tall staircase to the porch. Everything sits in its rightful place, because Mama says first impressions are the most important impressions.

She's not wrong, and in my softened-heart state, I realize how much my parents love me too. They maybe show it in a different way than my roommates or Liam, but they still love me.

I push into the house and call, "Mama?" It's Friday afternoon, and Daddy will probably still be on the golf course. He doesn't really change his plans for anyone, and I don't expect him to be home.

Mama doesn't immediately appear either, and I take the stairs up to the second floor and my room there. I leave my bag there and take the back staircase down to the kitchen. Roderick is there, and he somehow has a plate of sliced green apples and homemade caramel sauce ready for me.

"Thank you," I say as I sink into a chair at the table that's been placed in front of the windows that look out over the deck and then the backyard beyond. "Where's Mama?"

"She had a nail appointment," Roderick says. "But I'm making surf and turf for dinner." He smiles and goes back into the main part of the kitchen to keep cooking.

I dip an apple and take a bite, the peacefulness of the expansive yard and garden beyond the glass settling into my mind. I've just finished my second apple slice when I hear voices coming from the foyer.

They're not loud or explosive, but one definitely belongs to my mother. The other is low—a man's voice— and it's probably Daddy. I get up and go through the doorway that leads into the foyer behind the staircase.

I know instantly that the male voice is not Daddy's. I also recognize it as one I know—and don't want to engage with. My steps slow as I approach the edge of the staircase. A couple more steps, and I'll be able to see the front of the foyer. Mama has an ornate table there that I've never seen without a big vase of fresh flowers. I've already walked by them once, and I pause against the corner, still unable to see anyone.

"She's here," Mama says. "Her car is out front."

"Perhaps she's upstairs." The way he forms that first word tells me my mother has brought Charles Vaughn the Third to this house.

I press my eyes closed even as anger simmers in my veins. I don't want to deal with Charlie, and I can't believe my mother would do this to me. I'd rather be home, alone in my room, than here, and I push against the wall and walk around the corner.

"Mama," I say, my voice a bark more than anything else. Liam's called me a black cat, and it's time for me to be aloof and all-knowing. I glare at my mother as she turns toward me. She's wearing a pink and beige jacket with a white pair of shorts, and she looks like a million bucks. She always does.

"What's going on?" I ask, looking from her to Charlie. "Did Charlie's car break down somewhere?"

"No," she says smoothly. "Hello, darling." She swoops toward me, her clear-as-glass heels clicking on the tile in the foyer. "How long have you been here?"

"Ten minutes," I say. She hugs me, and I allow it, but every muscle in my body is still. In my practice sessions where I tell Mama and Daddy about my cross-country move, Charlie was nowhere in the picture.

She steps back, and I ask, "We're still having dinner

tonight, right?" I refuse to look over to Charlie, who's wisely stayed closer to the table with the vase of flowers.

"Yes, of course." Mama smiles at me and turns halfway toward Charlie. "I ran into Charlie at the grocer, and he said he doesn't have dinner plans." Her face beams light at him, but I can't make myself meet his eyes.

"I don't think so," I say. "I wanted to talk to you and Daddy alone."

Mama looks at me blankly, her deep black eyelashes fluttering as she blinks. "Your father is in a meeting."

I sigh, the diva-ness of felines moving through me. "Okay." I step past my mother and face Charlie head-on. I've been here before, and he's not that hard to talk to. "Charlie, you're uninvited to dinner, okay? I don't want you here, and I have something to talk to my parents about that's private. Not for you to hear."

He too blinks like he's never had someone talk to him like that. Maybe he hasn't—besides me. I ended things with him a few years ago, and I'm going to handle this too.

"I'll get the door for you." I give him a wide berth, which is easy to do in the expansive foyer, and open the front door. Mama won't like that being open for long, as she hates the heat, and I face the two of them.

"Hillary," Mama chastises. "You're being rude."

I say nothing, and Charlie doesn't move. There's a moment of time where everything hovers on a pinpoint. Charlie isn't leaving. Mama isn't standing up for me.

They're both looking at me as if I'm the one with neon green horns growing from my forehead.

I leave the door open and head for the stairs. "Okay," I say loudly. "I'll go then."

"Hillary," Mama calls after me, but I don't slow down. I hear her click-steps behind me, but I don't care. The hallway upstairs is carpeted, and I'm able to move much faster. I have my bag over my shoulder before Mama reaches the door, but she blocks my exit.

"Hillary." She huffs and pulls on the end of her jacket. "You're being rude."

"You're impossible," I say, but I don't want to get into this with her. "I am not getting back together with Charlie. Ever. How *dare* you bring him here?" I shake my head, because this isn't the conversation I want to have with her.

"I'm moving," I say as I lift my chin. "I got an incredible job in LA, and I'm leaving in two weeks. I wanted to tell you and Daddy, but you'll have to pass along the message."

Mama's mouth drops open, and I take advantage of her stunned surprise by pushing past her. I hear her sputtering behind me, but she doesn't say anything else. It wouldn't matter if she did. My feet move me down the steps at lightning speed, and I don't even acknowledge Charlie still standing in the foyer.

I don't have to wait for my car, and I toss my bag in the back seat and get behind the wheel. I drive away, and I don't look back to the mansion once.

The drive back to Cider Cove and the Big House feels like it takes forever. My stomach wishes for some of Roderick's surf and turf, but I drive through a fast-food joint and order a huge container of cheese fries. They come in an aluminum bowl, so they'll be nice and hot when I get home.

I bet I can even take them upstairs and avoid having to explain to anyone why I'm back already. I scoff at the very idea of that, because my roommates will have a myriad of questions.

As I near the house, I see an unknown car parked in one of the spots. The back of the SUV is open, and it appears as though someone is loading something into it. Ryanne sometimes sells things online, and maybe she's got a buyer here for something.

Then Liam comes around the back of the SUV, and he's carrying a packed box. Claudia and Lizzie are with him, and they too carry boxes and bins.

"Those are *my* boxes," I say as I finally reach the driveway and pull in. All three of them look at me, and it's clear I've caught them doing something they didn't want me to catch them doing.

I've seriously had enough for one afternoon. I jam the car in park, and I don't waste a moment before I get out. "What's going on?" I ask as I stride toward them.

Claudia looks like she's seen a ghost, and Lizzie actually slinks around the side of the SUV and out of sight.

Liam gazes straight at me, and steps forward. "Hey,

sweetheart," he says, and he sounds like the boyfriend I had three weeks ago before I got the job offer.

He reaches me, and he wraps me up into a hug. I didn't know I needed that until he does it, and I cling to him as he says, "You're back early."

Yeah, I am, and I want to know why he's here and what he's doing. But for right now, I also just want him to hold me and love me, so I don't say anything as he does exactly that.

CHAPTER THIRTY

LIAM

Holding Hillary is the single best thing in the world. I can't give this up. I can't let her leave me here.

"I can't do it," I whisper into her hair. "I can't let you go to LA without me." I pull away and look into her pretty eyes. She only shows confusion, and I get that. "I want to go with you. In fact, I *am* going with you. I came over to see what I could fit in the back of my SUV and what I can have driven out later."

I indicate the SUV behind me, noting that both Claudia and Lizzie have vacated the area. "I ordered the same bins and boxes as you, but I can't pick them up until tomorrow, and I wanted to see what would fit."

"But..."

"I can't," I say, focusing on her again. "I'm in love with you, Hillary, and I can't let you walk away without a fight."

"A fight?"

I grin at her. "We like a little back-and-forth argument, don't we? I've been silent for weeks now, and I'm ready to fight."

She searches my face. "Your business is here."

"There are construction jobs in California."

"What about your contract with the marina?"

"I've already spoken to them about it. I'm getting them set up with a buddy of mine." I take her by the shoulders, because she seems a little shell-shocked, and she's worried about all the wrong things.

"We just have to adjust how we've thought about our future, Hill. Yeah, I've been thinking of you in that farmhouse with me, and we'll have teatime in the afternoons in the orchard, and we'll have the most beautiful babies in the world."

I grin at her, but she only blinks back at me. "But my future has to shift," I say. "Because I don't care about the farmhouse if you're not there. I don't care about Blue Ladder Builders if you're not at my side. So I've been shifting my vision for the future, and I'm starting to see me and you on the beaches of LA, and basking in the glorious West Coast sunshine, and me taking cellphone pictures of you on the red carpet when that documentary premieres."

She finally smiles a little bit. "There aren't red carpets at documentary premieres."

"Then I'll get you one, and we'll pose ourselves." I move my hands from her shoulders to her hands, where I squeeze. "My future has you in it, plain and simple."

I step back, because she gets to make her own choice. "The only way I'm not going with you is if you tell me you don't want me to. That you don't want me. That you don't love me too."

That fire I love so much enters her eyes, and she says, "I can't ask you to give up your whole life and come with me."

"You're not asking me to do that," I say. "I'm *offering* it to you." I reach up and adjust my ballcap. "Do you want it or not?"

"Yes," she whisper-says, and while it's a quiet sound, it's the best word in the world.

I start to move toward her again, but she holds up one hand. I'm grinning, and I can't stop, but Hillary is dead serious. "Are you really going to do this?"

"Why wouldn't I?" I ask. "Seriously, Hill, tell me one reason why I can't do this."

She simply looks at me, and I have no idea what's going on in her head. I hadn't anticipated her being here right now, and that means something happened at her mama's. Something not-good.

My beautiful redheaded black cat looks lost, and I simply can't stand that. I pull her into my chest and say, "I've been looking at apartments. Nothing you're doing has to change; I'm just going to tag along."

"I love you," she smash-whispers against my shoulder, and a zinging shock moves through me. It's so strong and so electric that I step back from her quickly. She stumbles forward slightly, and I don't have a lot of brain cells to help steady her.

"You—what?"

She finally starts to morph into the woman I know, and she gives me that diva-cat grin. "You heard me."

"Say it again," I challenge her.

She lifts her chin slightly, and oh, I've seen this defiance before. "I love you, Liam Graff."

More happiness than I've ever known fills me soul. I whoop, and I grab onto her and swing her around. She yelps as I laugh, and when I set her on her feet, we're both grinning like overeager dogs, ready to please our masters.

"You love me," I say.

"I love you." She reaches up and runs her hands through my hair, as my ballcap has fallen off somewhere. "And you love me."

"I love you so much," I say, and my gaze drops to her mouth. "I'm going to kiss you now, and then we're going to go talk about why you're here when you should be at your mama's, and then you're going to help me find an apartment where I won't get shanked my first night in LA."

"Okay," she murmurs, and I match my mouth to hers.

Kissing Hillary has always been full of magic, unicorn horns, and passion, but there's nothing like kissing a woman when she loves you, and you love her, and the two of you are going to be making a cross-country move together.

I kiss her until it feels like we've said everything we

need to say, and then she tucks herself against my chest. "I don't want to live in LA forever," she murmurs.

"Okay."

"We'll come back here." She lifts her head and looks at me, all that earnestness I've come to expect from her swimming in her eyes. "You're not to sell the farmhouse, okay? We'll come back here."

"I wasn't planning to sell the farmhouse," I say. "I own it outright. No mortgage."

"Who's going to take care of it for you?"

"I asked Aaron," I say. "He said he'll take care of the property until he can move in."

She nods, her eyes so soft as she gazes at me. "I'm sorry I couldn't have this conversation a few weeks ago."

"I needed time to re-visualize my future anyway," I say. "I wasn't ready for this talk until now." I sling my arm around her, and we face the Big House together. "Did you eat, baby? Want me to take you to Potatopia? I read online that they have smoked brisket this week that you can put on top of your au gratin."

Hillary does the most surprising thing in the world— she starts to cry.

"Hey, hey." I fold her back into my embrace. "I didn't mean to upset you."

"You didn't." She sniffles as she holds me tight. "You just...take such good care of me, and I love that about you."

"All right." I take her hand and deliberately don't look at her. "Let's go to dinner then. I sense a story about your parents that will require a *lot* of potatoey goodness."

I know I'm right by the hardening of her jaw, but it's okay. I'm going to be right there at her side, and I hope at some point I can tell her that she doesn't need anyone but me. That I'll never let her down, and never let her go, and never walk away without a fight.

It almost sounds like song lyrics, and I smile to myself as I close the back of my SUV and then open the passenger door for the woman I love.

CHAPTER THIRTY-ONE

HILLARY

I CARRY MY OVERSIZED PURSE, MY TUMBLER, AND TOW along my carryon bag behind me as I approach my new apartment in LA. It's hot here, just like in Cider Cove, but it's a different kind of heat. Not as muggy, and definitely dirtier, but still incredibly hot.

I arrive in front of the appointed number, Liam's steps behind me coming closer fast. "This is it." There's a keypad on the door, and I fumble for my phone to get the code. Tanner found the apartment for me, and he says it's in a good building, with plenty of good people, and one I can afford.

Right now, my bank account screams at every single thing around me, so I've taken to using my credit cards instead. They only groan silently, and then I have what I need and I'm walking out of the store.

"Six, seven, four, two, one, nine." I mutter the code again as I touch on each number, and the lock makes a grinding disengagement noise that's somehow one of the most satisfying things I've ever heard.

The knob twists; the door opens; I'm facing my new apartment for at least the next six months.

It's not much bigger than the bedroom I had in the Big House, but I have my own kitchen, living room, and bathroom, which I didn't have there. The single bedroom sits down the hall, and I can't see it. Doesn't matter.

"This is perfect," I say, though it's hotter than Hades inside—no AC running yet—and there are some very obvious wear spots on the carpet in the tiny patch of living room. Some sort of cheap linoleum runs through the rest of the place, and as Liam crowds in behind-beside me, he says, "I can fix this floor, Hill."

"It's a rental, baby."

"Still." He looks at it with disgust, which only makes me smile.

"Come on," I say. "Let's get things unloaded." We do that for me, and then we trundle a half-mile away to the apartment Liam found. He's also been interviewing for jobs here, and he's expecting a call from one of the foremen today.

In the end, we decided to share the truck rental—which saved me a lot of money—and somehow make everything fit for both of us into the truck, his SUV, or my sedan. By some miracle, it worked out, and I can't wait to simply relax on my own couch.

Except I don't have a couch yet. It's getting delivered tomorrow, and as I follow Liam this time and wait for him to fit his key into the lock and open the door, I decide I can't wait to relax on *his* couch.

See, his apartment comes partially furnished—and that includes a couch, love seat, and dining room table and chairs. As the door swings open and we both peer in, I even see a TV stand—sans TV.

"It's not bad," I say, drinking in the plush, dark brown couches. "Those look like they're made out of velvet."

"They'll be hot," he says as he steps inside first.

"I don't care," I say. "I'm sick of having only a bed to sit on." Or driving. That's what we've been doing for four days now. Driving, interspersed with staying in some cheap motel for a night.

His kitchen is a little bigger than mine, but as we explore the space, everything else seems very similar. "This is great," he says, ever the optimist. Sure, he can pull out a grumpy card here and there, but the fact is, Liam is a fairly agreeable man. "I mean, I don't want to live here forever, but it's nice enough."

"Six months," I say.

"Maybe." He shoots me a look. "I read your script, Hill. It's going to be closer to eight or ten months."

"Maybe," I say, because I don't want to concede to

him. I also don't want to think about staying here for much longer than six months. "I've never produced anything before. It could be forever."

"It's not going to be forever." He sets down the box he carried in with him and turns back to me. "Okay?"

"What if I love it?" I ask. "What if I want to stay?"

"What did you tell me about what-ifs once?"

"Nothing," I say, confused.

"Maybe it's my momma who says this." He smiles as he takes me into his arms. "There's no sense in getting all foamed up about what-ifs, Liam." He speaks in a higher-pitched voice. "They're just bridges you'll have to cross later."

I smile too, but it's harder than I imagined it would be. "What are you going to do about your momma?" I whisper-ask.

His countenance falls for a moment too, but he quickly puts his smile back on. "Well, she'll be here in a month, so I think this is just another one of those bridges, baby." He kisses me quickly, pulls away, and adds, "Now come on. We're not ready to flop onto the couch just yet."

I groan at him, but in his usual golden retriever way, he bounces out of the apartment and back down the hall, the steps, and the parking lot to the moving truck. I follow at a much slower pace, and I look at the two dozen boxes still inside. And his bed. A nightstand, a couple of end tables, a dresser, and a TV.

I remind myself that we've come all this way. He

helped me with all of my stuff. I can help him with his, because that's what you do when you're part of something bigger than yourself.

So back and forth, forth and back, we go, and in the very moment when he kicks the door closed behind him and then stutter-steps over to the TV stand with his enormous TV, his phone rings.

He's sweaty, but oh-so-delicious, as he pulls his device out of his back pocket and answers it with, "Liam Graff here."

I go adjust his thermostat, surprised we haven't done that yet, and turn back to him when he says, "Well, that's just great news, Mister Yardley." Pause, while he grins like a fool. "I can start on Monday, sure."

I grin at him, and he gestures me over to him. He pulls me into his side and plants a kiss on my temple right before he says, "No problem. Happy to do it."

And with Liam, I know that's one-hundred percent true.

The call ends, and he whoops. "I got the job!"

"Yardley is the good one, right?"

"Yep." He leans down and kisses me again. "Now, let's talk for a second."

"Oh, boy." I grin at him as he leads me over to the velvet couch. We both sit on it, and Liam sighs.

"I know you won't want to get married here," he says. "But we haven't talked about marriage much at all."

I'm not sure why my heartbeat stutters the way it does. Or maybe I am. "I don't want a long engagement," I say.

"How long is long? Or how short is short?"

"A few months," I say. "I can plan something without having a diamond on my finger."

He tilts his head at me, and I say, "The engagement was really hard for me. Both times."

"Maybe because it was with the wrong guy."

"Yeah, but...can it just be short?"

"Yeah, sure," he says in that easy, Southern way he has. "Short engagement. When do you want to get married? Spring? Summer? Fall?"

I like that he doesn't even mention winter, though in both LA and Charleston, there's hardly a winter to be spoken of. It definitely gets cooler, and there's more rain. But people can obviously still get married outside in the winter months.

"I want to get married outside," I say, just now realizing it. "I feel like spring is too soon, Liam." I look at him, really watch him. "Is that okay? I mean, I'm doing the documentary, and it might be crazy, and there's so much I don't know about how life will be."

"I'm hearing an autumnal wedding," he says good-naturedly. "Because summer is way too hot."

"We might even be back in Charleston by then."

"Yes, ma'am." He pauses, but he doesn't press me on the next question.

I already have my answer ready, though, so I just go ahead and say, "I want to get married in your backyard. Our backyard. With all the trees, and maybe some of those twinkle lights that you'll hate, but you'll put them up because I love them."

I grin at him and lean closer. "What do you think?"

"You want to get married in the orchard," he says. "Next fall, after a short, few-month engagement." His eyebrows go up. "Can I surprise you with the diamond?"

"You better," I say, and then I lean in to kiss him, this handsome-hot, sweet-sexy-smart, golden-retriever-god of a man. "I love you," I murmur-kiss, and he covers anything else I might've been able to say.

As he moves his lips along my earlobe, he whispers, "I love you too."

———

Oh boy! I love Hillary and Liam separately, in all their black cat-dog and golden retriever-ness. And the two of them together? Unstoppable!

Read on for a couple of sneak peak chapters at the next book in the Cider Cove series - **A VERY BAD BET** - and meet Claudia and Beckett.

Get new free stuff every month, access to live events,

special members-only deals, and more when you join the Feel-Good Fiction newsletter. You'll get instant access to the Member's Only area on my new site, where all the goodies are located, so join by scanning the QR code below.

SNEAK PEEK! A VERY BAD BET
CHAPTER ONE: CLAUDIA

I PAUSE TO WAIT FOR GENIE TO SNIFF THE TRUNK OF A tree, which is a huge mistake. The other two dogs I'm walking this morning think it's okay to turn our morning walk into a sniff-fest. I'm really off my game this morning, and it's all because of the announcement about the City Planner position with the city of Cider Cove.

The application packet is *in*-tense, and I need letters of recommendation, a portfolio, the experience, and it's at least a three-interview process. Application packets are due November fifteenth, and that gives the current City Planner and his team of people six weeks to find his replacement before his retirement begins.

"Come on," I say to Genie as I tug on her leash. "Walk. Let's walk." With dogs, you need to use short, easy commands. I take these three dogs on their morning walks every weekend, and Genie—a miniature poodle—looks up at me with her happy little smile on her face.

Yes, she's cute and she knows it.

"Walk," I say, tugging on the goldendoodle's leash, as well as the black, full-sized schnauzer who needs way more exercise than I can give him in an hour on Saturday and Sunday mornings.

Part of me wishes I could start and run a full-time doggy walking business, but that's only on pure, clear, somewhat cool Saturday mornings like today. I definitely love my job, what with all the cute skirts and slacks and blouses I get to wear.

I'm not like Lizzie or anything, who's started doing some plus-size modeling, but she's good with fashion, and she gives me plenty of items that I actually really like.

Right now, it's my job causing me to lose focus on the dog-walking. And it's *walking*. It's not hard.

The path we're on is one I've walked many times, the emerald green-grass on my right side opening up to a large field where several people have come to throw balls and Frisbees to their canines.

I'm not paid to do that, and it would make me a little nervous anyway. I have good control of my dogs, but Willie, the schnauzer, tends to bolt when he sees someone or something he likes. Even now, he's tugging on the leash a little too hard for my liking.

"Don't pull me," I say as I give his leash a hard tug. It pulls him back to me, and he looks over his shoulder as if

I've done him a horrible wrong. But he slows down and keeps pace with the other two dogs. If anything, Genie's the one working the hardest, her little tawny legs moving at twice the speed of the other dogs.

I make plans to work on my portfolio when I get back to the Big House, because I have plenty of experience in terms of events from my last several years as the Public Works Director.

The desperation to make sure every single thing is exactly right with my application claws at me, and I round the bend in the path, now turning into the sun. Some people complain about the heat in South Carolina, but I personally love it.

It's not as bad as South Texas, where I grew up, and it's got the beach instead of the border of Mexico. I love the beach, and sometimes, if I'm feeling particularly peppy, I walk the doggos on the beach.

It's a harder walk for all of us, as the sand shifts in mysterious ways beneath our feet, and Lucy, the golden-doodle, is a little bit psycho around water. But I determine that tomorrow, I'll take the dogs to the beach to do our morning walk.

"I'm going to get this job," I tell the trio of canines. "I managed the clean-up of Discovery Park, and that place was a mess." Now, it's one of the most-reserved pavilions and the pickleball courts there are impossible to get on.

I've been working on that layout in my portfolio for a week, and I think I've about got it done. Right.

As they often do when I'm stewing over work, my thoughts move to the only person I think could get this job over me.

Beckett Fletcher.

He's the Deputy Director in the Public Works Department for the city, and he does a lot of work with private investors and businesses, using their donations to improve public lands. He's done some incredible projects too—including a riverwalk improvement that I sometimes take the dogs to—and I know his portfolio will be as flawless as mine.

I scoff under my breath, because there's no way he can put together a double-page display that shows the before-and-after the way I can. For once, my scrapbooking skills have come in handy, and I never thought I'd say that.

My phone rings, thankfully distracting me from the downward spiral of my thoughts. Ry's name sits there, and I swipe on the call with my thumb while maintaining control over the three dogs with my left hand. They trot along on my left side like the good puppers they are, and I say, "Hey, Ry," as I lift my phone to my ear.

"Hey, are you out walking the dogs?"

"Yep."

"Emma says she could use some help at the shop today, and I got the task of calling everyone." Her voice slows on the last few words, almost turning into a question without becoming one.

I suppress my sigh, because I don't mind helping Emma at her florist shop. "What's she got going on?"

"She has a wedding tonight," Ry said. "And someone just came in, begging and crying for flowers for their company party."

"A company party?" My eyebrows go up toward the sun.

"You know how Emma is," Ry says with the sigh I wanted to make a few moments ago. "She can't say no."

I've been walking at a brisk pace for half an hour, and my breath scoffs out of my mouth. "It's a company party. Not a last-minute funeral."

"Is that a no?" Ry asks.

"No, of course not." I spot a man jogging toward me with two dogs on my side of the path, and I need the use of both hands for this. "I'll be there, but I won't be home for another hour or so."

"We're going to go over at ten," Ry said. "I'll have Tahlia make you a breakfast sandwich. Emma said she'd order us pizza."

"All right," I say. "I have to jet." I slide the phone in the side pocket of my stretchy pants, and I tug all three dogs closer to my side as Shirtless Jogger continues toward me. He's wearing a visor and a pair of sunglasses and the shortest shorts I've seen on a man—and I've seen plenty jogging around the city, the beaches, and on this very path.

He's got muscles from here to the West Coast, and I'm

glad my own eyes are shaded behind a pair of sunglasses, so he can't tell how I'm ogling him.

His dogs—both brown canines that look like mutts—are on leashes, which are connected to a belt around his waist. He's got earbuds in, and I see the slightest movement of his head toward me as he gets closer and closer.

His dogs' tongues hang out of their mouths, and it sure looks like they're going to trot right past us. I'm not sure who moves first. It could've been Willie, who definitely crosses in front of me. Genie follows him, and in the next moment, I'm trying to high-step over their leashes while the guy slows and pulls on his dogs' leashes.

Both of them are tail-waggingly sniffing Willie already, and all five dogs have decided their greeting chain is happening right in front of me.

How they stop so fast, I don't know, because I feel like my forward momentum is still propelling me forward—right of top of them.

"Move," I bark at the same time I'm trying to find a place to put my feet that isn't dog flesh. They move like snakes, and just when I see a spot of open cement, it disappears under a bushy, brown tail.

I'm going to fall, and I know it. I look up into a face I recognize, and it's not until I'm descending backward that I realize the muscular, two-dog owner behind the shades is Beckett Fletcher.

Then I'm down, pain smarting through my tailbone and up into my spine. I only hold one dog leash, which means my other two are loose, and I'm not sure if my pulse is panicked because of that or because Beckett has A Body.

And two dogs. And jogs in this park where I walk my canines.

"Whoa, whoa, whoa," Beckett says, and he's instantly on his knees in front of me. "Are you okay?"

If he knew it's me on the ground, he wouldn't be so nice. I feel put together wrong, like everything that's usually straight is all askew, from my sunglasses, to my ponytail, to every stitch of clothing on my body.

"I've got the dogs," someone says, and I look to my left, where the dog pile was. The dog pile I'm now part of. Only Genie sits there, and I don't see a stitch of black anywhere. Great. Willie's gone.

"I have—" I try to say, but my voice feels stuck behind my lungs. Until I can get a proper breath, I won't be able to speak. I have to try. "A schnauzer," I manage to say.

"I've got him," that someone says again, and Beckett looks over to them.

Then back to me. "The dogs are right here," he says. "Can you get up? Did you twist or sprain something?" Beckett puts his hand on my shoulder, and the touch burns partly against my bare skin and partly through my tank top strap.

In this moment, with him looking at me with concern, and touching me, I realize—he has no idea who I am.

I never wear my hair up at work. I don't wear athleisure attire. I don't have dogs, or wear sunglasses, and

Beckett and I never talk about personal things. I don't know where he lives, or that he had dogs, or anything about him really.

Now, I see the little bit of scruff on his face that indicates he hasn't shaved today. It's the color of the rich brown floors in the living room at the Big House, and he's got a mouth full of white teeth as he flashes me a smile.

My heartbeat clangs strangely in my chest, and I know this feeling inside myself. If he was anyone but the annoying, obnoxious, arrogant, grumpy Deputy Director who works next door to me, I'd been interested in him.

I'd get to my feet and try to flirt with him enough for him to ask for my number. The thing is, Beckett already has my number, and he would never, ever use it to ask me out on a date.

"I'm okay," I say, my voice lodged down in my throat. I'm relieved I don't sound like myself, and with Beckett's hand in mine, I get back to my feet.

I straighten my tank top and take the leashes back from the second man who'd stopped to help. I recognize him too, because he comes to this park all the time. My heart drops to the soles of my feet as Landon smiles at me. He's asked me out before, but there's no fizz between us.

Not like there just was when Beckett put his hand on my shoulder.

"Thank you," I say to him, adjusting the leashes in my hand so I'm holding them the way I like.

"Sure thing, Claudia," he says, and I press my eyes closed.

So close.

"Claudia?" Beckett asks, his voice pitching up into a near-screech.

Oh, so close.

I can't believe who's standing in front of me. Claudia Brown.

I can't believe I didn't recognize her, but she's wearing clothes I've never imagined her to even own. Her dark-as-midnight hair is pulled up into a ponytail, and she doesn't have her bangs. Her forehead is more like a fivehead, but I think it's kind of cute.

I can't believe I think my nemesis is *cute*.

But she'd sprawled on the ground because of Duke, because the silly dog can't stay in his own lane, and that was stinking cute too.

Silly Duke—he thinks all other canines come to the park just to see him. He's sitting right at my side, panting like I've run him ten miles today when we've only gone four.

In front of me, Claudia pushes her sunglasses up onto her head, and yep, there are the deep pools of beauty. They've never looked at me with anything like softness or attraction or even tolerance.

I always get the defiance and disgust she currently wears in her expression, and I've never felt my blood running so hotly through my veins. It's from all the running, I'm sure. I'm out later than normal today, as I'd normally be done with my Saturday morning workout by now.

The sun has fried my retinas, that's all.

I mean, any man with even one working eye can see how gorgeous Claudia is. I've never entertained those thoughts for long, because it's clear the woman dislikes me greatly. I can admit I've never made it easy for her—for anyone—to like me, but the know-it-all, arrogant grump has kept my heart safe for a long time now.

It's a persona I'm comfortable with, though even I can admit I'm growing tired of putting up such a strong façade for everyone.

"Sorry about my dogs," Claudia says, and I jerk back to attention. I can't just stand here in the park, staring at the midnight beauty.

I clear my throat and nod at her. "I didn't know you had dogs."

"I don't."

I raise my eyebrows, and even behind my mirrored

sunglasses, I'm clearly asking her about the three very real dogs whose leashes Claudia holds.

She startles and looks down at the dogs. The littlest one has laid right on down, taking shade from the shadow of the huge black schnauzer. "I mean, yes, I walk these dogs. They're not mine. It's a...side gig."

I can't help the way my mouth curls up. "A side gig."

"We're not at work." She brings the leashes closer to her. "I don't have to talk to you. Come on, guys." She looks down at her dogs, and adds, "Walk. Let's walk." She practically barks at them, and they go right with her.

She strides away in those skin-tight leggings, her high ponytail bobbing with the movement, all three dogs falling right into line at her side. So she's a good dog trainer. That doesn't mean we're going to become friends.

"Or frenemies. Or anything at all." I look down at my dogs, and Duke and Rocky look back at me. "Let's go." I don't have the sexy dogwalker bark down, but my dogs get going again without an issue.

We finish our run after I cut it short by a couple of miles and open the back of my king-cab pickup truck for the dogs to get in. They do, and the annoying sound of panting accompanies me all the way home.

As a city employee, I decided I have to live in the community I serve, so I've got a quick drive from this park that was built on the border of Cider Cove and Charleston to my place on the border of Cider Cove and Sugar Creek.

Everything about my life feels stale, from the way I run every morning, to how I clip my grass on Saturdays, to how neat everything is in my house. I do my dishes after every meal, because I hate the smell of leftover food. I'm obsessive about taking my trash out, and I do it every morning before I go to work. That way, my house won't smell when I walk in after work.

Somehow, I manage to allow the dogs to live in the house, and their scent doesn't bother me.

"You need therapy," I mutter to myself as I hang the leashes on their appointed hooks in my garage. The dogs trot off to drink out of their fountainous water bowl, and I go back into the garage to fire up the lawn mower.

I have a square little house, in a common little neighborhood, for my fits-inside-a-box life. By the time my grass is exactly the right height and I'm scrubbing the sweat from my skin in the shower, I can't hold back the sigh anymore.

I don't need therapy. I need some color in my life. Some spice. Some...something. The talk of the town is Matchmakers, and I get out of the shower, pull on a pair of gym shorts, and go join the dogs on the couch.

The three of us fill it up, and I commit to filling out my profile all the way. I put in my name; I use a real picture from my gallery; when it comes to the two hundred characters I can use for my description, I pause.

This is where I'd make up something totally

outlandish that somehow sounds real. Like, that my favorite food is chicken gumbo, and I love holidays with my family, and there isn't a mountain I don't want to climb.

I like gumbo just fine, and my family knows me better than anyone, and I do like spending time outdoors. So it's not entirely untrue, but it's definitely not true either.

City government. Dog lover. Outdoor enthusiast.

That's what I put down, because those three things do sum up my life. They're generic and vague, but honestly, so am I.

With all the pieces in place, I submit my profile for approval, and I get a notification that it could take up to twenty-four hours for it to be live. I look over to Rocky, who only moves his eyes toward me. His eyebrows are so expressive that it looks like his whole face moves.

"What do you think, boy?" I reach over and scrub his face. His eyes close in bliss as I ask the second half of my question. "Should I start dating again?"

My phone makes a noise I've never heard before, and I look down at my lap. A heart icon sits in the top notification bar, and I swipe down to see what that's all about. It's Matchmakers, and it says my profile is approved and live.

Another heart pops up, and then another. "Husky pups." I'm too old for this, and I can't believe I let my insecurities get the best of me.

I'm getting matches already, and my profile is only five minutes old. The women in this town and surrounding suburbs of Charleston must smell fresh meat, because wow. Some of them simply tap on the heart-match, but a couple of them do that and then message me too.

I don't know how to do this type of dating. I failed at the in-person kind too, and I feel like I need to take a George-Constanza approach.

"Opposite George," I whisper. In one of my favorite episodes of *Seinfeld*, one of the characters—George—does everything the exact opposite of what his natural instincts are.

I need to do the same.

So no, I normally wouldn't even be on this app. I wouldn't message women who probably have fake profile pictures and probably have these half-truths on their personal descriptions too.

"Maybe I should start tomorrow," I tell myself. After all, I've gone jogging this morning, and I've mown my lawn. Those are Normal Me things, not Opposite Me things.

I sag back into the couch and close my eyes. When it's just me and the dogs, the ceiling fan moving air around my house, I can be the Real Me. And at this moment, I ask him what he wants.

An image of Claudia Brown enters my mind, and she waltzes in real slow, like she wants me to see all of her before she gets too close. I have the woman's number, because we work together. Closely.

My office is right next door to hers, and no, I haven't been the picture of Prince Charming or anything like that. I hate it when she closes her office door, because it makes the air conditioning in the ancient building where we work malfunction. My office grows hot within a minute, though that might be because I get irritated that she's talking to someone about something I'd like to know about.

I lift my phone up in front of me and start sliding and tapping. I start a new text and type in the first few letters of her name. It comes up, and all I have to do is tap it. My pulse starts to race, and I'm sweating as if I'm still outside pushing the mower back and forth in neat, trim lines.

I tap on Claudia's name, and the text has begun. I leap to my feet, because I don't even know what I'd say to her. "Complete opposite," I mutter to myself, and the next thing I know my thumbs are flying.

Hey, Claudia. Just checking to make sure you're all right and made it home okay. Duke sometimes just gets excited around other dogs, especially those smaller than him. They're like dognip to him.

I don't even read over it again, and I always, always read over my texts before I send them.

This time, Opposite Me simply hits send. I smile as the message pops up and I see I used the word dognip. I know it's not a real word, and I fully expect Claudia to correct me on it.

But while I have hearts flying into my phone and

messages popping up on the Matchmakers app, Claudia doesn't answer right away.

I let my eyes drift closed again, and Duke snuggles his part-golden-retriever self into my side. I cuddle him close and stroke down his side. My dogs are my best friends, and I do talk to them throughout the weekends and evenings when I'm home.

But I need more than a couple of dogs to chatter at.

My phone makes a normal noise, and I yank my eyes open to see who I've gotten a text from.

"Claudia." I sit up straight, my dog suddenly too hot against my side. She's said: *I made it home fine, thank you.*

Hardly an invitation for me to text her again. I opened the door, but she's practically kicked it closed again.

Still, I start texting again, abandoning all reason and praying I can face her on Monday morning.

———

READ **or preorder A VERY BAD BET now! Scan the QR code below.**

Sometimes a wager only makes things more fun...

BOOKS IN THE SOUTHERN ROOTS SWEET ROMCOM SERIES

Just His Secretary, Book 1: She's just his secretary...until he needs someone on his arm to convince his mother that he can take over the family business. Then Callie becomes Dawson's girlfriend—but just in his text messages...but maybe she'll start to worm her way into his shriveled heart too.

Just His Boss, Book 2: She's just his boss, especially since Tara just barely hired Alec. But when things heat up in the kitchen, Tara will have to decide where Alec is needed more —on her arm or behind the stove.

Just His Assistant, Book 3: She's just his assistant, which is exactly how this Southern belle wants it. No spotlight. Not anymore. But as she struggles to learn her new role in his office—especially because Lance is the surliest boss imaginable—Jessie might just have to open her heart to show him everyone has a past they're running from.

Just His Partner, Book 4: She's just his partner, because she's seen the number of women he parades through his life. No amount of charm and good looks is worth being played...until Sabra witnesses Jason take the blame for someone else at the law office where they both work.

———

Just His Barista, Book 5: She's just his barista...until she buys into Legacy Brew as a co-owner. Then she's Coy's business partner *and* the source of his five-year-long crush. But after they share a kiss one night, Macie's seriously considering mixing business and pleasure.

———

Bonus for newsletter subscribers! Just His Neighbor, Prequel: She's just his neighbor...until his dog—oops, his brother's dog—adopts her.

Get this book by joining my newsletter here: https://readerlinks. com/l/3887964 **or scan the QR code below.**

BOOKS IN THE CIDER COVE SWEET
SOUTHERN ROMCOM SERIES

**A Very Terrible Text, Book 1:
Sometimes the thumbs slip...**
She's finally joined the dating app everyone in Cider Cove is raving about...when she accidentally sends a message about wanting to meet up for a first date to her enemy.

A Very Bad Bet, Book 2: *Sometimes a wager only makes things more fun...*

She's got seniority over the obnoxious grump next door, and she's determined to beat him out for the top job in their charming hometown. But a bold bet spins their rivalry into a flirty attraction that could change everything.

———

A Very Merry Mess, Book 3: *Sometimes the holidays are messy...*

Christmas is the season of joy, mistletoe, and, unfortunately for Ryanne, the pressure of bringing home a date. When she vents to Elliott, her best friend and co-manager at the small-town office supply store, he impulsively grabs her phone and texts her mother that they're dating.

Date. Ing.

ABOUT ELANA

Elana Johnson is a USA Today bestselling and Kindle All-Star author of dozens of clean and wholesome contemporary romance novels. She lives in Utah, where she mothers two fur babies, works with her husband full-time, and eats a lot of veggies while writing. Find her on her website at feelgoodfictionbooks.com.

Printed in Great Britain
by Amazon

45458657R00202